SAI-KO

and other stories

Gabriela Harding

TSL Publications

First published in Great Britain in 2017
By TSL Publications, Rickmansworth

ISBN / 978-1-911070-81-8

Image courtesy of https://pixabay.com/en/woman-lake-sky-clouds-water-swim-645705/
Photo by Paula John-Jules

To all those who didn't believe in me.

You gave me a reason to fight and the strength to win

very few of us are what we seem

Agatha Christie

Contents

6

Sai-Ko

First I heard Mother's scream.

Then the thump, a horrible splat like a watermelon bursting. Alex and I race each other to the front of the building, but it's too late: the sheet, a flutter of white in the still summer air, has already landed on the object of our curiosity.

A dead body. People surround it: curious, rat-like, armed with fans and sunhats. *Think with Alex's brain, Carmen. Think*: broken back, *check*; broken neck, *check*; open skull fracture, *check*; *check*; *check*.

Daddy bought a giant watermelon for the midsummer feast. He carried it all the way to the car, and there, when he relaxed his hold for just a second, searching for his keys, it slipped from his hands and burst open.

Daddy: *Puta madre!*

After two years in Spain, Daddy still swears in Spanish.

Alex: What does *puta madre* mean?

Me: It means your mother is a whore.

The lady has dark hair and the crack on her head is like the crack on a burst watermelon: lightning shaped and full of juice. The juice sizzles on the hot pavement like eggs in a pan.

Me: Do you get vertigo when you throw yourself off a building?

Alex: I don't know, why?

I point out the mushy puddle spread across the faded chalk lines of a hopscotch.

Alex: That's her brains.

Me: Would you like to cut her open? Find the cause of death?

Alex: I'm not as sick as you.

Me: Who says I'm sick?

Alex: Everyone.

Me: Everyone who?

Alex: No one loves you.

I get it, I'm weird. This is a dead person I'm looking at and I think it's beautiful. All the mess, the way the body has broken, at an odd angle, almost as if she's posing. I can only imagine what's under the sheet. The open eyes, the parted lips. Kissing someone invisible. *Death.*

I hate geeks. I'd never date one, not even for a million dollars like in *Pretty Woman*. Yesterday the chief inspector's son offered me a hundred German marks to suck his cock. He showed me the money: a wad of greasy notes in his jeans pocket. I punched him square in the face. It was meant to be a joke, a mock warning, but the next thing I knew he was on the floor, covered in blood, screaming. I ran to the toilet to wash: I didn't want Giuliano's DNA anywhere near my skin, in case it made me pregnant.

Mother's sunbathing on the balcony when she gets the call. We have a cordless phone: you can move around when you talk. Pointless during *siesta*-time, when the entire neighbourhood is anaesthetised by the heat.

Mother: Hello?

Mother has a high, girly, hotline voice. I called the hotline myself to see what the fuss was all about. A lady answered who talked just like Mother. She asked me if I was naked. I hung up.

Across the road, the Colonel's puffing his pipe. Watching Mother, I bet. He reminds me of a dog with his little dog thing sticking from his hairy crotch like a bright red lollipop. In the loft of his decrepit mansion live about a hundred breeding pigeons. I smell pigeon shit. I smell acacia blossom. I smell lambs from the lamb wool Mother's drying around to make cushions. Once I saw a lamb munching on acacia buds. I waited for the lamb to drop dead but it didn't.

The Colonel is Mother's type. I don't know how I know but I do. You see people who're meant to be together because they're each other's type and people who don't look right together but they're together anyway.

There's chemistry between them. Mother's skin explodes into a million goose bumps; her nipples go hard behind the *lycra* fabric of her swimming costume. The Colonel observes her through his birdwatching binoculars. They make him look like a robot. I read somewhere that in a thousand years' time robots will be as common as normal people are now. Common people may even be extinct.

Mother: I understand. I'll have to speak to my husband about this.

That's what she always says: *I need to speak to my husband.* It makes her sound like a husband-fearing Orthodox woman. In fact she only consults Daddy when it suits her.

Mother puts the phone down.

Mother: Wait until your father hears about this. Why do you always have to embarrass us?

It's always about *them. Their* friends, *their* status, *their* image. It's never about me. They didn't even ask me if I wanted to go to that swanky school. It was drilled into my brain since I was in nappies: SAI-KO, SAI-KO, SAI-KO, as if attending the National College Anna "Sai-Ko" Lambrino was a matter of life and death.

This is how things work at *Sai-Ko*: every parent has an inside person to bribe. The competition is high so your natural grade has to be high but just a high grade won't get you into a grammar school. The inside person can add up to eight-tenths to your grade. The price? 50g of Russian caviar; a bottle of French perfume, and cash. Some of the caviar tins are real and others are fake, with labels such as The Russian Ministry of Fishery on it. But the Ministry of Fishery doesn't exist.

The papers are anonymous. The inside person asks for a sample of your writing. They tell you how to mark yours so that they know it's yours. For example, on your second page you cross the very first word out and you write it again, or you write a letter twice, or other things that make you look retarded but single you out to the impostor. I wanted to leave the paper blank like the girl in front of me but I didn't have the guts to do it.

Mother: Do you have any idea what it cost us to get you into that school? All the tutors. The *intervention*.

Me: I would've gotten in without the intervention.

Mother: Not a chance.

I don't tell Mother I forgot to do the marks Daddy paid black gold for. She wouldn't believe me anyway. Worse, she'd get mad that I wasted their money.

I wonder if my *intervention* went to someone else. Maybe to Catalina Radu. She really does look retarded. That would explain how a Gipsy girl got into our class. Her mother wears a headscarf. And they believe in God. Catalina Radu's always alone at break.

People talk. They say the Colonel has something to do with the sixth-floor suicide, and I believe it, he's so feral. His wild silver beard reminds me of the bird nests Grandpa took down with a pole so we can look at the eggs. He wears a Taiwanese hat like a patchouli tray turned upside down. He's capable of anything: seduction, adultery, *murder*.

Me: The dead lady was the Colonel's mistress.

Alex is half-buried in her anatomy atlas. She doesn't answer at first. Then she says: Did you take my dollar?

Me: What dollar?

Alex: You know what dollar.

Me: No, I didn't.

Alex: I was keeping it as a souvenir. I didn't even know you could exchange a dollar.

Silence. Alex starts crying. I feel miserable. I shouldn't have taken that stupid dollar.

Me: Maybe the wife put a spell on her. And she went mad. And she just jumped.

Alex: You should be dead. *Dead.*

The headmistress' office is stuffy hot. She has a large ficus plant in a pot and even a computer. On the wall behind her desk is a large oil portrait of Anna "Sai-Ko" Lambrino, the poet-aristocrat who donated her mansion to public education. Through the white curtain, the school yard shimmers like it's not really there. Two boys in Year 12 are playing basketball.

At the other side of the desk, Giuliano's parents. Daddy, wearing one of his expensive, dry-clean-only suits. Mother, her lips bright red like the *Girl with a Pearl Earring* by Vermeer. The chief inspector goggles at her until his wife gives him a look. Giuliano's nose is bandaged. His eyes, bruised. His eyebrows, invisible on his pasty white face.

Madame Papp slams a folder shut and narrows her eyes at me over the gold rim of her glasses. She places a silver spoon on the saucer and sips her coffee in silence. *One small sip. Two. Three.*

Madame Papp: A most unfortunate situation, I daresay, Miss Manole-Martin. And not the first time you find yourself in it. Miss Manole-Martin, may I remind you that you are attending a grammar school, a prestigious college, not a high school. If you can't keep up with our standards by all means, leave. That way we can give your place to someone who really wants to be here.

I look at Daddy, thinking of the lecture he'll give me later.

Daddy: We apologise profusely.

Madame Papp: I'm afraid that's hardly enough. I feel compelled to suspend *her* until we conclude the investigation. And you will pay for Giuliano Banu's medical bill.

The headmistress' voice is like knives grinding against each other: SWISH, SWASH, SWISH, SWASH. I think of Grandpa sharpening his knives, I think of the chicken heads, I think of the bodies running blind.

Mother: *Her* name is Carmen. You can address *her,* Mrs Papp. She is here. (Mother takes a sip of water; Giuliano's father watches her lips.) Besides, hospitals are free.

Madame Papp (stiffening): Mrs Manole …

Mother: Manole-Martin.

Madame Papp: *Manole-Martin.* Do *you* go to a free hospital for a check-up? Not to mention a serious intervention? Do you want me to believe that you queue up with all of those who can't afford to pay for treatment?

Mother: We shouldn't be paying a medical bill that the Banus clearly chose to foot at one of the most expensive clinics in the country. Besides, my daughter acted in self-defense. On both occasions.

The headmistress' mouth drops open. She's not used to being spoken back to like that. You can see that she wants to eat Mother alive.

Madame Papp: Self-defense, you say.

Another folder is opened before her, a slimmer one this time. Handwritten.

Madame Papp: Fifteenth of December 1999. Perhaps you can explain how Carmen acted in self-defense when she kicked Ciprian Radu repeatedly in the face. When she then proceeded to snatch a broom from a member of staff and smacked him with it so hard, she broke the wooden handle in half!

Madame Papp removes her glasses. She's watching Mother with her bare, white-blue eyes.

Mother (sitting up straight): On that particular day, three boys dragged my daughter from the classroom, threw her outside in the snow, held her down and beat her with snowballs. An innocent tradition, you may say, just a bit of fun, only girls don't think it's funny, they just play along with it. Carmen didn't, and you know what? I'm proud of her.

Madame Papp: Mrs Manole-Martin, I really can't find my words. Well, as you say, this is a tradition, an innocent game … all the other girls accept it.

Mother: Just because all the other girls accept it, doesn't mean my daughter would or should. Tell me, Mrs Papp, what if the boys didn't take Carmen to the schoolyard? What would you have to say if my daughter lost her virginity as a result of that brutal attack?

Madame Papp: If your daughter lost her virginity, Mrs Manole-Martin, it would be entirely because of her lax morals.

Mother: If my daughter is still a virgin – as it happens, I had her tested – it's certainly not because your prestigious school offers the correct supervision suitable for the young unmarried girls that parents trust you to protect.

Daddy: Cut it out, Camelia.

The headmistress is speechless for a few seconds. She pours water from a jug into a cloudy glass. Six pairs of eyes watch as she downs it in one gulp.

Madame Papp: If you're not happy with the school, madam, then you're free to take your daughter out.

Mother: That's very convenient, isn't it? Now that we've paid the non-refundable annual fees up to Christmas.

Madame Papp: What is it that you want, madam? Are you a trained lawyer by any chance? Are you trying to excuse your child for breaking a student's nose on the school premises? Because there's no excuse for that, and she's going to suffer the consequences.

Me: He told me to suck his cock!

OH. MY. GOD. I've actually spoken. I've said the dreadful words aloud.

The chief inspector blinks. His wife's mouth curls into a contemptuous snarl. Giuliano's eyes smile.

Madame Papp slams her hand on the desk. I can smell her perfume: it escapes from every fold of her wrinkled skin.

Mother (fanning herself): Jesus, can someone open the …

Madame Papp: Miss Manole-Martin, you will not, I repeat you WILL NOT, use this language in my office!

Me: He told me to suck his cock for a hundred marks. He showed me the money. Told me his father got it as a bribe.

Giuliano (jumping from his seat): Shut up, you fucking weirdo!

The chief inspector puts a hand on his shoulder.

Madame Papp: You will both be suspended until further notice. Frankly, I'm considering handing this matter over to the police.

Mother (laughing): The police are here.

Madame Papp: Madam, please leave my office before I lose my temper. You have no elementary notion of manners. I can see where Carmen gets it from.

Mother: If you expect me to sit in silence while you lash

unfounded accusations at my daughter ... Mrs Papp, don't make me regret I sent my daughters to a mixed school. I'm a modern woman. I did so in the absolute certainty that they would receive protection.

Madame Papp: May I remind you that this is the safest school in town. Our gates are always locked. We have a security alarm. Besides, Mrs Manole-Martin, your daughter can look after herself, it seems. This young man here told me she "knows how to punch."

Mother: What's the point of the gates being locked, if the danger comes from the inside, from the so-called educated kids of the upper class?

Madame Papp: Do you mean to say that you don't consider yourself ... well, I'd better stop here, so that we can at least part on civilised terms. Patience is a virtue and I must admit, not one of mine.

Daddy (back in the car): Why do you have to be so rude?

Mother: Why do you have to be such a pussy?

Daddy: If you want to be part of this world, you have to play by their rules.

Mother (laughing): Act like them? They're just a bunch of enriched peasants, living off corruption.

Daddy: And what are we? A couple of impoverished aristocrats?

Mother: You've got your tongue back now? Why don't you fight the real tigers, in the arena?

Daddy sighs.

Mother: You can't buy blue blood.

Alex: What does that mean?

Me: It means fake bitches can't pretend.

We giggle.

Daddy: Who taught you how to punch?

Me: No one.

Mother (narrowing her eyes): You stay away from Sebastian. He's bad news even on a good day.

Daddy nods and starts the car. It's late afternoon. The town is in the midst of that mysterious metamorphosis, spring to summer, when the days are long and the air smells good enough to eat. I open the window to let the wind in my hair.

Mother: Where's that draught coming from? Carmen, are you mad? I'm shivering.

Daddy catches my eye in the mirror. The unanswered question is still in his eyes. And something else too. *Admiration. Caution. Worry.*

A girl who can knock down a man might earn a medal in another world, but in ours, it's a loss of marriage opportunities. And that, for all Daddy knows, is a disaster.

Professor Nae, our neighbour, was abandoned in the rubbish as a baby. He's so old I can't imagine how he looked like as a baby.

A couple of childless Gipsies found him. They took him home. From then on it's a fairy tale: the Gipsy woman fell pregnant, blah-blah-blah. Whether it was karma or the fact that the Gipsy Mamma had an affair, it's hard to say.

Today, the professor talks to Gipsies in their language. It's crazy because they actually listen to what he says, and the Gipsies don't listen to anyone. If he says, *Don't let your kids play naked in the street, damn it!* you see them giving the young ones clouts over the head and throw their slippers after them, yelling at them to get inside. If he tells them to cut a rooster's throat because it makes too much noise at dawn, they do it, even if they're left with a dozen horny hens.

Mother spreads plum jam on thick slices of white bread. I hate plum jam; I hate the bread because it's full of fingerprints. It comes from the bakeries where women in white throw bread loaves on racks like they're bricks. The women in the bakery have fingers that look like toes. It's because they eat too much free bread.

The plums arrive in crates from the orchards, hundreds of them. We have hundreds of plum trees, more than we need. When the Communists took power, they confiscated our land

and made us rent it from them instead. We shared the profits with the Republic. (I wonder if she knows her Colonel was a Communist. I guess that doesn't count so much when you can paint and you have a Hemingway hat.) You can make alcohol from plums. Everyone loves brandy. It's very strong, and the taste comes out the same even if the plums are bruised.

We have millions of wine-grapes, too. The vineyards grow on the hill, with the wild blackberries. Wild blackberry jam is the best thing in the whole world.

Mitzi (hacking at the brambles with a machete): Don't eat them, they'll be bitter from growing in the shade.

We eat them anyway. Our tongues are black. Our lips are black. Our hands are black.

Behind Mitzi's house is a field of ripe corn. It ripples in the wind like a gold sea. In spring the corn leaves are green.

Anne-Mirabelle: They can cut your tongue in half.

Me: We can behead the Colorado bugs with them!

Anne-Mirabelle: No. Drowning is better.

We sit in a circle around the Colorado bugs while they piss themselves with fear. We watch the earth go orange around them. The babies don't wet themselves, they're too small to know what's going on.

Me: We could chop them with a knife.

Alex: Pestle and mortar.

Anne-Mirabelle: Burn them with caustic soda.

Stamping wins. The Colorado bugs are playing dead with their pink fleshy babies. Drowning doesn't work because they always crawl out of the bucket. So we crush them instead. Their blood is yellow. Their piss smells like paint. They wet themselves because they're scared. We kill them anyway.

Mother: Eat your jam.

Me: I'd rather eat a Colorado bug.

I tried it, once. It was bitter, like Mother's head-pills, only the Colorado bug didn't make me high.

Today Alex is getting her legs waxed. About time, too. She hasn't even got her period yet, and her legs are so furry they make you sick.

Me: I shaved my legs when I was seven. You can't go around looking like a werewolf. You'll never get a boyfriend.

Mother: Oi!

Alex: I don't want a boyfriend.

Me: Everyone wants a boyfriend.

Alex: Just because you're always chasing after boys …

Mother: Who is she chasing after?

Alex rolls her eyes: She would date anyone.

It's kind of true. Only no one asked me yet, apart from Val in year 8B, but that turned out to be a bet. I wish I hadn't said yes. I didn't even like him that much anyway.

Me: Waxing hurts. You can have it cold turkey, or you can be put to sleep. Or maybe it'll hurt so much you'll faint anyway. Your call.

Alex looks at Mother.

Mother: It won't hurt.

Alex: Will I be put to sleep?

Mother: Don't be ridiculous! Stop making fun of your sister, Carmen!

Our cosmetician, Lydia, is stirring hot wax with a large wooden spoon. It looks like polenta. It smells of burnt caramel.

Lydia: You're lucky. The wax is new. Just arrived an hour ago. You're my first customer.

She winks at Alex. Wax ladies like hairy ladies. It makes them feel important.

Lydia: First time?

Alex nods, her eyes wide.

Lydia rolls the hot wax over her spoon. She blows on it, then spreads it on Alex's calf like honey on toast.

Daria P. has waist-long blonde hair and a gap between her front teeth like Vanessa Paradis. Every day at break, I kiss her in our hiding place behind the gym. Just practising for our FIRST BIG KISS. She lets me touch her breasts. They're small, soft and fuzzy, like peaches; they taste of her strawberry body lotion.

We call them Peach number 1 and Peach number 2. I wonder

if one day the Peaches will look just like Grandmother's boiled tomatoes.

Daria's mouth is wet and silky, like a vagina. I kiss her until my tongue hurts. The bell rings. The shadow of a boy vanishes around the corner and Daria giggles.

Giuliano grips my arm in the corridor.

Giuliano: So that's what it is. You're a *lesbi* girl!

Me: I'd screw men if I could find any.

Giuliano: Cunt!

He spits in my face.

The boys hate me because Daria P. is the best pull in the whole school, and she's *my* girlfriend. I've even seen her in her underwear. Under my bed, there's a shoebox full of her letters.

Mother sits in her *chaise-longue* painting her nails. A large Brigitte Bardot hat shades her from the sun.

Mother: Goodness, the heat. And it's only May.

She's taken a head-pill, I can tell by the shine in her eyes, by the way she's painted the skin around her nails. I can tell by the way she lunges at me with her arms around my neck, getting nail varnish all over my hair. Her cognac glass shatters on the marble floor. The *chaise-longue* snaps shut like a crocodile biting her arse.

Mother giggles.

Me: Get off me. Jesus.

Mother: Don't you love Mamma?

Silence.

Mother: I carried you inside my womb. The tiniest thing. I didn't even look pregnant. The smell of cucumber made me retch.

Me: Tell me something new.

Mother: You're ...

Her voice trails off. A pigeon has landed in her lap. Across the road, the Colonel tips his Hemingway hat to one side.

Mother's trying to get rid of the pigeon, but they're persistent things, pigeons.

Me: It's got a message.

Mother: Maybe it's the wrong destination.

Mother unfolds the note from the pigeon's leg.

Me: What does it say?

Mother slips the note in her bra.

Colonel Boc has an exciting life story. His first wife died from an epileptic fit. Then Carmela came along. In fact, she came along well before the wife died: this cast some shadow of doubt over the first wife's death, but rumours are rumours, and who on earth would prosecute a former security colonel?

The new wife, Carmela, raised the dead wife's children. Mother says this is a big thing, something she could never ever do.

Mother: I have enough with my own brats.

One day, Carmela received a phone call from her 'in' man at the hotel she owned with her husband. Professor Nae saw her getting in the back of the car with a loaded shotgun. (The Colonel doesn't only like to watch birds; he also likes to shoot them.)

Professor Nae: She's going to kill him!

Carmela ordered the cab to stop in the woods. She walked the last mile shaking, the gun in her hand.

Mitzi: A man should only know your lower half. Keep your thoughts to yourself.

Mother: Mamma, stop filling the girls' head with rubbish!

Mitzi: You'd better watch your mother, she's the falling-in-love type.

Professor Nae: A band was playing Gipsy songs in the beer garden.

If you really love me, don't look back
Delete my number and our photographs
I know it's hard but don't keep them please
My wife will kill me if she ever sees …

Carmela watched the lovebirds through a web of leaves. Her husband, wearing a crisp shirt – ironed by her – drinking wine with a young and beautiful Moldavian woman. *Varvara.*

Doorman: Good evening, Mrs Boc.

An impertinent smile danced on his face. When he looked down at her dress, his smile faded.

Doorman: Madame, you ...

Carmela knew her dress was wet. She'd wet herself. Her hands on her belly, she walked through the beer garden straight to her husband's table.

Professor Nae: The Colonel didn't look surprised. Varvara looked delighted.

Carmela: I've come to kill you.

In a flash of inspiration, she grabbed a glass and threw it at his face. The ruby wine glittered on his silver beard like blood.

Varvara: Mother of God. Call an ambulance.

The doorbell makes the whole house vibrate. DING-DONG, DING-DONG, DING-DONG.

I slide the golden lid of the eyehole aside. On the other side of the magnifying glass is another eye.

Zamfir Boc is standing in the doorway, in torn jeans and a leather jacket.

Zamfir Boc: The bell's buggered.

Me: No, it isn't. I could hear it on the other side of the house.

Zamfir is the baby taken out of Carmela's womb with kitchen tongs, at the restaurant in the woods. Zamfir was the name of the cook who cut his cord with a kitchen knife.

But Zamfir isn't a baby anymore. He's a proper man and drop dead gorgeous. His front teeth overlap, but that's the best thing about his smile.

Zamfir: Are you going to put something on?

Me: Oh.

Zamfir: Forget that.

His hands in fingerless gloves cup my face. His lips are soft like corn silk. Something enters my mouth: hot and cold at once, like snow.

He's blowing his soul into my body, and I receive it like the body of Christ. From now on Zamfir is part of me.

It's his body that was given up for you, or to you, what difference does it make?

Zamfir Boc has the biggest cock in the world. The size of my biceps. You can't close your fingers around it, *really*, you can't. We've tried a few times to get it in. In the end we had to give up.

Zamfir: Maybe we should use some cooking oil. Next time, can you practise first?

Me: What with?

Zamfir: Don't know. A carrot. A frankfurter. Use your imagination.

We're in his room at the top of the house, stoned out of our heads. Zamfir plays around with his set of drums. His parrot Kurt is fast asleep on his swing. I love the Colonel's house. They have an upstairs lounge and a shower cabin, a terrace and a garden with walnut and cherry trees.

Zamfir: If you sit under a walnut tree for too long you'll fall asleep and die.

Me (choking on the joint): How do you know?

The smoke burns my throat. He takes my hand, runs his tongue around my ring finger – and, as if to spoil the moment, one of his father's filthy pigeons lands on the rail. A moment later a poo splashes on the marble tiles.

Kurt: Crap! Shit! Fuck!

It's the night after the "promised" first time with Zamfir and I'm still a virgin. I'm so disappointed I could do it myself with a gherkin. I know a girl who masturbated with a frankfurter at her boyfriend's house, then put it back in the fridge. I always wondered who ate the frankfurter.

I think Mother put a spell on me. Virgin until wedding-day no matter what. That's why my magic cave didn't open. *Sesame, open! And it didn't.*

In the end I take one of Mother's head-pills. The pill is called Xanax. It makes my jaws go numb.

Alex: You're a piss head, you know!

Me: Shut up or I'll choke you with a frankfurter!

Alex: What?

Alex likes frankfurters. I should threaten her with something else.

Me: Can I borrow a syringe?

Alex secretly practises giving injections. Her dolls' bums look like they've been in the radius of a machine gun. She's lying on the bed with her prayer book, her epilated calves covered in camomile tea soaked bandages.

Alex: Don't you go nicking Daddy's whisky! I'll tell him!

Me: What's that you got there? Camomile? Traditional medicine, eh? I thought you were a scientist.

Alex: I want to be a nun!

Me: Good idea! Keep growing that moustache!

Alex is right. I know the best way to nick Daddy's whisky. First, the syringe. I push the needle inside the cork. I draw out the whisky, fill the syringe with water, inject it back in. Then – and this is the part I love most – I light a candle and drip the hot wax seal into the hole.

Me: Let's pray together.

Alex narrows her eyes. I shut mine.

Me: Our Father, please don't let Daddy see half of his whisky is water. Next time I'm in Zamfir Boc's bed, please let my cave open so that Alladin can walk inside. Lord in Heaven, please bless me with a life full of orgasms.

Alex slams her prayer book on my head.

Alex: Slut!

I'm out on the terrace, sipping my whisky. Zamfir's bedroom is dark. The curtains are blowing in the wind. I think of the first time he looked for me at school. His crooked teeth. The line of dark hair on his belly like a row of black ants. It's like the ants are queuing to get into his pants. You can't blame them.

Zamfir dumped me. It's been a week. He doesn't take my calls, either. Would he, if he knew I'm at the other end of the line?

Varvara, the Colonel's mistress, lives in a tower block in a not so nice part of town. *Why buy the cow, when you can have the milk for free?* His house is just tall enough to glimpse the moon floating over the hills. Sometimes the moon is full, and sometimes it's slim like a slice of watermelon, eaten away until a luminous smudge is all that's left on the sky. The Colonel bought Varvara a studio flat. His wife had moved away with her stepchildren, all girls. The boy stayed with the father.

Mother: Men are beasts of habit.

The Colonel thinks he'll get Mother to fall in love with him, but she's not as easy as she seems.

Mother: Stop mourning, Carmen. When you're white, young and beautiful, everything else is secondary.

Women from the Republic of Moldova are poor. They'd do anything to get a man. Here in the South the sugar daddies fatten them up with rare steaks and sweet wine.

Mother: They have no dignity.

Me: I'm not in the mood for your anti-equality sermon.

Me: You don't suppose I ought to consider myself equal to a Moldavian woman? A Gipsy? A negro? Someone who didn't go to school? A retard?

Me: Now you sound like Mrs Papp.

Mother: Cut the sarcasm, or you'll know the back of my hand.

Me: It's kindness, *Maman.*

Mother: Kindness is patronising.

Daddy met Angela and Denise's father the other day. He lost his job, like all the other workers when Daddy's factory was sold to the Russian mafia. They made Daddy fire his own brother-in-law. Daddy says they should have sold it to the Germans instead.

Daddy: The Germans are a million times better than the Russians.

Mother: They don't look it. I've seen them on the beach, with their saggy bellies and floppy old cocks. Red as lobsters.

Daddy: The Russians want to sell their own products in Europe. The labels, that's what. They rounded everyone up in the yard, ordering them to pick up scrap metal. They got a million euros for the metal.

Angela and Denise's father sells knives he made himself in the forge.

Daddy: He looked hungry.

Mother: Did you give him something?

Daddy: How do you give a man money?

Angela went mad because the boy she loved married someone else.

Mother: She was a virgin, you know.

She gives me an inquisitive look. My mind drifts to Angela. Her long braid and how I pretended to snip it with my fingers. *Snip-snip.* She showed me how to stick acacia leaves on my nails with spit.

Eight year old Me: I look like the Tree-Goddess.

My green claws glimmered in the sunset. The twin tower enemies faced each other. The kids in the other block, B, raised their sticks. They pulled back their slings with murder in their eyes.

The cold war between A and B never ended.

I might as well admit it. I'm not myself in the rich people's apartment block. I don't like their spoiled Pekinese dogs and the gold plated name-plates on the doors. Doctors, lawyers, judges. We even share a cleaner, to which Mother gives our leftover food.

Mother: Don't let her in when we're not here. Look what happened to Mitzi.

Mitzi is the only person I know apart from Professor Nae who talks to Gipsies. You're not really supposed to look at them in case they hypnotize you and suck out your baptism blessings. Without your christening angel you go to hell. Of course that's all rubbish, but Alex and I still skittered off when a Gipsy woman asked us for directions.

One night, Mitzi was robbed. The thieves got in via a secret entrance and raided the pantry. They stole smoked pancetta and brandy.

Mother: Mitzi heard some noise in the kitchen. She got up,

turned on the lights, checked the doors. All the time, the thieves were hidden behind the bathroom curtain.

Alex: Mother of God!

Me: *Mother of God, Mother of God.* It's all you can say. You're like a fucking parrot!

Mother: Watch your language.

The rich people have separate bedrooms. That's because they think it's not polite to fuck each other.

Alex: They only do it at full moon.

Ah, the ecstasy of sharing a bedroom with Zamfir.

All night long.

All life long.

For eternity.

My uncle Sebastian owns a theatre – the only one in town.

There's a red carpet. If you take your shoes off, it's like walking on a giant sponge cake. Victorian lanterns shed their spectral light over the musty brick walls. Underground it's so cool you don't even need air conditioning. It smells like Mitzi's cellar where she keeps all the wine demijohns and homemade pickle jars.

Uncle Sebastian: Welcome, welcome. Happy name day, Cami. I hope you enjoy the play.

Mother: *The Seagull* by Checkov. Love it!

Uncle Sebastian: There's a modern twist to it. I hired a new director, Mr Dhaka. A Serbian.

I look at Alex. She looks at me. Scattered all around us are dozens of scruffy shoes.

Alex: Yuck!

Me: It's meant to be *avant-garde.*

The seats are burgundy. They suck you in like giant, velveteen teddy bears.

Alex: I'm sinking!

The theatre goes pitch dark, so dark the brilliant red of the seats vanishes and the stage vanishes and even the yellow rectangle of the door fades. I imagine I'm blind. The black turns white: the swirls of a lollipop dance before my eyes. Zamfir is licking the lollipop and smiles with his crooked teeth.

The curtain lifts to reveal a grotesque spectacle: naked men climbing ladders. I study all the bottoms: big and white, small and hairy, skinny or fat. Mother gasps and covers my eyes. I still see the bottoms through her fingers.

Half an hour later. The sky bleeds like a blister that went *pop.* The BCR bank is the first thing I see as I scramble out, pulling half-conscious Alex after me. Air at last. Can't have enough of it. IN-OUT, IN-OUT, IN-OUT.

Mother's coughing her lungs out. There's a chorus of coughing and spluttering. The unnerved spectators scatter, followed by clouds of thick dust.

Bald man: My God! You go to the theatre these days to get gassed!

Lady in flowery hat: I'm sick to death of their *avant-garde*!

The fire engines are monstrous trucks with giant wheels, their sirens blaring. Heads pop up at the balconies: puppets in a puppets' theatre. The puppets are watching us, the real people. But who's to say that we are real?

Passer by: What happened here?

Middle-aged man: Special effects gone wrong! They baked us alive!

Old man: Turned us into smoked meat!

The naked actors went out a different way. I don't see them anywhere.

Daddy (shutting the car door): Well, that was a hell of a flourish.

Mother: Don't blame me for it!

Professor Nae (shouting over the fence): How was the play?

Daddy: A disaster!

The professor retreats to the shadow of his gazebo. Men know when to leave each other alone.

At night, I lie in bed thinking of all the bums I've seen. I count them in my head. I didn't think men's bums can look so different. And then I get it. They were meant to symbolise the solar system, suspended on the ladders in the darkness of the universe. I think it's a cracking idea.

The Colonel is a crocodile in a swamp, watching Mother through his half-closed eyelids.

Me: What did Varvara see in him? He's old and ugly.

Mother: Moldavian women see beyond old and ugly. They're clever like that.

Me: I thought you didn't like Moldavians.

Mother: I don't like anyone who pays rent.

Me: Don't we?

Mother: Don't be ridiculous. The apartments in this block will only go for rent the day pigs fly.

Me: So we own it?

Mother: What planet do you come from?

Kids at school: *How much does your father earn? Where do you live? What car do you have? What make are your jeans?* Grown-ups are the same.

Me: He's a monster.

Mother: When you're young you can't see the beauty in the more mature. Take a painting, for instance. It takes a few minutes of close observation to see its true face – *its meaning.*

Me: I don't see anything in paintings anyway.

Mother: You're just like your father.

Me: If you think he's good looking, why send him that note?

Mother: Cheeky. I didn't send him a note.

Me: Yes you did. I saw it.

Mother: Okay then. What did it say?

Me: You told him to fuck off.

Mother: Okay so I did. I'm a married woman.

Me: He's a communist, Maman. And a pigeon breeder!

Mother: He's an artist. He paints, you know.

Mother lied to the Colonel when she told him she wasn't interested. It was just a trick to make him give her his full attention. Mother knows lots of tricks. She learned them from dating the gangsters on the Communist estates.

When she goes to make lemonade, I find the note she's been trying to hide at page 92 in the book of Indian sonnets.

"You ask me for more than others, that is why you are quiet."

Tagore. The Colonel is changing tactics. He's figured out that poetry is the way into Mother's knickers.

Godmother's house is very central. It used to be a mansion, you can tell by the doors with lion-shaped knobs, the heavy knockers, the wide staircase. The linden tree in her patio is a thousand years old. Godmother plucks all of the leaves to make *sarmale,* rolls stuffed with rice and meat, but the leaves grow and *grow* and GROW, like the cursed woods around *Sleeping Beauty*'s castle. The princess inside is Godmother, only she's not asleep and definitely not a princess. She's awake all hours of the day scrubbing dishes; more of a *Cinderella,* really. When she's not scrubbing or cooking or ironing she smokes in the shadow of the tree, thinking that marrying a prince is a happy end only in fairy tales.

The castle is a labyrinth of snaky corridors, high ceilinged bedrooms, abandoned music rooms. The bathroom – a humid cave where cakes of homemade wormwood soap lie scattered among musty long johns. The boiling hot water tank spits fire, the Victorian tub discreetly sucks the last bath's juices into the plughole strategically placed between its curly iron feet. A tiny window opens into Godmother's back garden. The view changes: lilac trees in bloom in the spring, ripe golden apples in summer, hairy quinces in autumn. In the winter the window is always closed: a white, dead glass eye.

Godfather lives in one of the old servant rooms, the same room where his own mother committed suicide. When people get old they are moved to the servants' quarters. It's quieter there. It's dark. They need to get used to being dead.

Mother: God bless her soul.

Me: Why? You didn't like her anyway.

Mother: She's dead now.

Me: So? Just because someone is dead you've got to like them even if you never did?

Everyone in Godmother's family commits suicide. They're pathological gamblers. A family sickness.

Me: What if it rubs off in our family, too?

Mother: Impossible.

Alex (pushing her glasses up her nose): Mental illnesses are contactable by "induction." It's a phenomenon that ...

Mother (rubbing her arms): Look, you're giving me goose bumps.

Alex got my attention. This is the smartest thing she's ever said.

Me (late at night): Tell me more about induction.

Alex: No.

Me: I'll pay you. Look, I'll give you ten bucks.

Alex: You don't have ten bucks.

Me: Yes I do!

Alex: OK. Twenty then.

Me: No way.

Alex: Twenty bucks, or you get a reading list.

I pin Alex down on the bed and press a pillow on her face.

Me: Ten bucks.

Alex waves her leg in the air like a cockroach. She kicks me in the shin. The other leg is pressed down by the weight of my body. She's sweating with laughter. We wrestle some more then she tells me all about induction. It's very interesting. And scary. She draws a picture of the human brain. It looks like a nut kernel.

Alex: Schizophrenia is contagious.

Me: Get away!

Alex: You get away!

Alex tells me a story. Once upon a time there was a girl who lived with her brother, a schizophrenic. One night she found him in the bathroom, naked, covered in his own excrement.

Me: Yuck!

Alex: They're both dead now. *Suicide.*

Me: Like the dead lady!

Alex: That's something else. She had an affair with the Colonel, and her husband found out.

Me: What?

Alex: Everyone's talking about it. You're too busy messing about with that rocker boy to listen to the gossip.

Me: What rocker boy?

Alex: Don't think I don't know. Do you use condoms as pain relief?

Me: Yes. It still hurts like hell. Just to warn you.

Alex: I'm never having sex. And I'm never waxing my legs ever again.

This week is the 'outfits you haven't worn in a long time week' for Mother. Today she is wearing the stripy dress I haven't seen in donkey's years. It makes her look like a zebra.

Me: You look like a zebra.

Mother is pulling silk stockings over her smooth legs. She pins up her hair. She steps into her shoes.

Mother: Ah.

She cuts the tag off a pair of knickers with a delicate pair of nail clippers. I wonder how could she have forgotten all about them until the very last moment. Mother's pubic hair comes through the red lace net.

Mother: Stop staring at me, Carmen!

Mother has small breasts with protruding nipples like the teats on baby bottles. She taught me everything I know about love. It's very rare to like and love someone at the same time. That's because love and hate are a lot alike. So if you love someone, you could actually hate them too. You could even hate them enough to kill them.

It's kind of true. I want to kill Zamfir. I want to kill his memory and his body and his smile and I want to kill the girl I saw in his room last night.

Uncle Sebastian: Harder!

I punch the muscles of his abdomen. It's like punching a brick wall.

Uncle Sebastian: Don't be afraid of other women. It's your fear that makes them strong. Do you understand?

I nod.

Uncle Sebastian: No matter what happens in your life, you can always turn things in your favour. Remember that.

Grandpa wears a crisp shirt and tie, even on Sundays. Mitzi washes his shirts in her semi-manual washing machine that they bought in the *Talcioc* market from a pair of dodgy Russians.

The Russians: *Spasibo!*

Mitzi: *Pozhaluysta*!

Mitzi was born in time of war. She learned Russian by talking to the Russian soldiers camped in her village, while her father was at war. No one else went near them.

The machine has two parts: a "washer" and a "squeezer." The hose drains the dirty water into the sink. The large mole on Grandpa's cheek looks like a smear of the chocolate cake he's eating.

Grandpa (bending over the rail): Wow.

Mother decorated the balcony with flower pots, some comfortable straw chairs and a low coffee table. Hand woven rugs adorn the limestone floor.

Grandpa (chuckling): If you fall from here, *salud.*

Mitzi stands by the kitchen sink. She's washing her coffee cup. It's something she insists on doing even if Mother washes it again when she's gone.

Mitzi: It makes my head spin.

Mother: It's only the fourth floor.

Grandpa (sipping coffee): How's school?

Me: Fine.

Grandpa (smacking his lips): Do you know who Anna "Saiko" Lambrino was?

Me: A baroness?

Grandpa: An aristocrat. A poet. Daughter of one half-Italian baron, Emil Lambrino.

GABRIELA HARDING

Mitzi: He had her with a prostitute.

Me: What?

Mother: There was a brothel in Bucharest where he met this Japanese geisha. He suffered from priapism. That's when you have a constant erection.

Grandpa (spitting coffee all over his shirt): Hah ha hah!

Mitzi: When the daughter was born, Baron Lambrino took her home to his wife.

Mother: Stole her, you mean.

Me: But didn't she look Japanese?

Mother: No one dared say anything.

Me: What happened to the mother?

Mother: She continued to serve the Baron, for the rest of her life.

Grandpa: And when he died, they couldn't close the coffin!

Everyone: Hah ha hah!

Mitzi is in mourning. She still wears the black dress and head-scarf she put on last year, when her mother died. Godmother disapproves.

Godmother: The dead with the dead, the living with the living. A headscarf can't hide the bad thoughts in your head.

Dead people are cold like fish. Their hair feels dead, too, like the hair on a paintbrush. Last year was the second time Great-grandmother died. First time, it was in childbirth. They brought her body to the morgue in the evening. By midnight, the night guard was dead, and Great-grandmother was wandering the corridors of the Infirmary, naked. The night guard had died of fright.

Great-grandmother: My death died!

It turned out that it didn't; death can't ever, *ever* die.

Today the cleaning lady on our block was found dead. Daddy couldn't open the door because her body was blocking it.

Daddy: Bloody hell!

It's a sin to swear near the dead. Daddy crossed himself. Too late, though. Our Lady was already frowning in the gold-framed icon by the door.

Mother: What's going on?

She was coming down the spiral staircase in her satin gown. When she saw Manuela's body lying on the landing, it was just an excuse for her to take another head-pill.

It's all in the news. The cleaning lady hadn't been paid in two months. She only had one kidney: she'd given the other one to her sick daughter. She was 48 years old.

It was after the cleaning hours that the idea came to Manuela. She could've left the stairs dirty but she didn't. It wasn't even hard. She just lay down on the freshly mopped landing and died. As if it was the most natural thing in the world. Only it wasn't. She had cleaned herself inside out with bleach.

Me: I'm not coming to the wedding.

I'm on a stool and Mother's brushing my hair.

Mother: Don't be ridiculous. It's your uncle's wedding.

Me: Is the Colonel going to come? With his son?

Mother: You leave that boy alone, you hear me?

Mother turns the stool around so she can face me. Her eyes are shiny, *shiny*, SHINY like the purple ogre's eyes in a book Mitzi used to read to us. I want to put my head under a pillow but I can't. Mother's nails are digging into my skin.

Mother: I saw you spying on him. What's wrong with you? Have you got no pride?

Before I can open my mouth to speak Mother slaps me so hard I fall off the stool.

Uncle Sebastian will be thirty this summer. We share a birthday, July 30th, just one of the many things we have in common. This miraculous wedding came as a result of many prayers and a trip to the monastery on the hill by the women in my family, covered from head to toe like the Ninja turtles, their pockets full of tiny silver icons and donations. He's marrying a frigid woman, he says.

Uncle Sebastian: My other girlfriends will keep me warm.

Me (turning the tube around in my hands): How does this

work?

Uncle Sebastian: You should never go around without a pepper spray. Just aim for the eyes. Hey, I heard you defended yourself at school. Well done.

Me: They nearly expelled me.

Uncle Sebastian: Bullshit. They wouldn't do that. Your father's a big fish in this town.

Me: Is he a gangster?

Uncle Sebastian: I can't comment on that.

Me: Are *you* a gangster? Like the mafia lords in *La Piovra*?

Uncle Sebastian: I'm someone who makes easy money.

We have our self-defense lesson at Uncle Sebastian's boxing barn. Today I learn how to poke someone in the eye. Last week was the "punching in the Adam's apple" session. And the week before that he taught me the self-defense G-spot. That's when you jab your finger at a spot behind someone's ear to immobilise them. The first thing he taught me was how to punch someone with a closed fist. Uncle Sebastian is a belt-*noir* in martial arts.

Uncle Sebastian: Any idiot can use a gun.

Me: You have one. I saw it.

A real gun, too: *illegal*. Uncle Sebastian keeps it in the inside pocket of his coat. When he wants to threaten someone, he pretends to look for his wallet. He's subtle like that.

Uncle Sebastian: Focus, Carmen! What's wrong with you today?

Me (sighing): Zamfir Boc.

Uncle Sebastian (laughing): And your mother thinking you were a lesbian. I told her, maybe she's just experimenting. I did that, too.

Me: Really?

Uncle Sebastian: I was drunk. He was drunk. We gave each other a blow job. No big deal.

This makes me giggle. I can't imagine Uncle Sebastian giving another bloke a blow job, but he's as unpredictable as Mother.

I tell him what happened with Zamfir. Anyone else would just say that hey, there are other fish in the pond, but not Uncle

Sebastian. He really, *really* gets me.

Uncle Sebastian (handing me his phone): Call him.

Me: What?

Uncle Sebastian: Call him. Go on, what's his number?

Me: If I call him I lose my pride.

Uncle Sebastian: If you don't call him you lose *him*. Are you going to leave him for some Moldavian bitch? A guy with a cock as big as your arm?

He laughs.

Uncle Sebastian: Think of it this way. How do you think you'll get something you don't try to get?

Me: Christina got you, and she didn't try very hard. Is she any good in bed?

Uncle Sebastian: It's like fucking a plank of wood. But that's different. I'm marrying her for the money. She's my trophy, not the other way around.

Me (shaking): I don't know. What about the girl I saw?

Uncle Sebastian: Don't worry about that. While there is honey, there'll be flies. Just don't let it get too cold. That's the worst thing you could do.

Zamfir answers on the first go. His voice is honey and I forget all about the flies. I close my eyes to savour it. I can almost taste it on my tongue.

Me: Hi, it's me.

Zamfir: Me, who?

Me: Me, Carmen.

Zamfir: Hey! What have you been up to?

Me: Just the usual. School. Home. You?

Zamfir: Same.

Zamfir goes to a real high school. He failed his exams, even with the intervention. His school looks like a prison, but I know that my school is the *real* prison.

Zamfir: Hey, are you going out with another guy?

Me (shocked): No!

Zamfir: I saw you with a guy driving a Mercedes.

Me: That's my Uncle Sebastian!

Zamfir: I wish I had an uncle who drives a SLK.

Me: Now you do.

Uncle Sebastian (taking back his phone): See? Love is war. And Carmen ...

Me: Yes?

Uncle Sebastian: Sometimes not being together isn't the worst thing in the world. On the contrary ...

Me: What?

Uncle Sebastian: Love has an expiry date.

Me: Are you saying that promising eternal love is cheap?

Uncle Sebastian: I'm saying that believing it is cheaper.

Zamfir (holding my hand in the back of Uncle Sebastian's car): Wow!

Uncle Sebastian has a girl and his dog, Felipe, in the front seat. They're not wearing seatbelts; seatbelts are for pussies.

It's the night before the wedding. A dark road snakes through the undergrowth. The invisible lake blows its bad breath through the woods.

The girl: Are there crocodiles in the lake?

Uncle Sebastian: Don't be stupid.

The girl: How about the one in the river?

Uncle Sebastian: That's different. It escaped from the zoo.

The crickets are loud, like dozens of cats purring, *purring*, PURRING. The forest watches us with its glow-bug eyes. It smells of tree bark and summer.

When Uncle Sebastian and the girl are gone, Zamfir kisses me. The front seat is all the way down. This time his cock enters my cave: it goes all the way in, just the way it should. Uncle Sebastian lent me something called a lubricant. It works like magic.

Making love doesn't last as long as I thought. It ends almost as soon as it begins.

Zamfir: How are you feeling?

Me: Empty.

Zamfir: That's normal. So do I.

Zamfir holds me as we smoke in the dark. His muscles through his Iron Maiden T-shirt feel nice and firm. I want to freeze this moment so it lasts forever.

Me: My stomach hurts.

Zamfir: That's because it was your first time.

Me: It wasn't my first time.

Zamfir: Oh. It was my first time, you know.

Me: You're joking. This was your first time, and you're fifteen?

Zamfir shrugs.

Zamfir: Everyone I asked said no.

Me: I hate virgins.

Zamfir: Me too.

Uncle Sebastian, the girl and the dog return to the car. The girl is not one of us, I saw it even before I heard her broad District 4 accent. I wonder if I'm turning into a snob like everyone else at my school.

Casablanca megastore sells Italian fashion: shoes, stockings, office suits. Their dummies are better than real people: beautiful women with round breasts and wigs of long flowing hair.

Alex: That's what the robots will look like in fifty years.

Every week the display changes. Dresses, shoes, handbags, umbrellas.

Woman by my side: Something is different. Ah, there it is. A new dummy.

Her friend screams.

Woman (dropping her bag): Good God!

Mr Hera, the shop owner, is on display. If it wasn't for the noose around his neck, he'd look smart in his Italian suit and lacquered brown shoes pointing downwards to the floor they only just barely touch. A grotesque ballerina sticking her tongue out at the crowd.

Woman who dropped her bag: My handbag! Come back here, you thief!

But the barefoot Gipsy boy has already vanished in the crowd.

Me: Too many people are dying. Don't you want to know why?

Alex: My job is to prevent death.

Me: You don't have a job.

Alex: Don't you go nosing around. Mother won't like it.

Once, when I was eight years old and we still lived in District 9, I crossed the border to Gipsyland. It was horrible: blocks black with damp, broken windows, a sea of rubbish where rat tails twitched about like worms. A half-naked lady was stopping cars on the other side of the road. I was in mortal danger. I never ran so fast in my life.

Me: Mum and Dad are away this week-end. Alex and I are going to the country. And you can have the keys.

Uncle Sebastian: Name your price.

An hour later, he parks outside a block of flats.

Uncle Sebastian: Jesus, Carmen. This is grim.

An adolescent girl in a miniskirt appears in the chagrined entrance.

Uncle Sebastian (grinning): Or maybe not.

He honks the horn. The girl is attracted to his sleek Mercedes. He keeps his engagement band in sight.

Uncle Sebastian: It's worth showing them you're hard to get.

Me: Wait here.

Uncle Sebastian: No way. I'm coming with you. What are you up to, anyway? Changing the world?

Me: That's what Alex says.

The lift is broken; the banister rails have been stolen. The smell of stewed cabbage makes me retch. Behind the identical doors, cooking and snoring noises. TV sounds. Barking.

Uncle Sebastian is panting.

Uncle Sebastian (looking down): Jesus.

I pull out the scrap of paper where the administrator wrote Manuela's address. The door is off-white; the paint peeling, the handle hanging out of its socket. I lift my hand to ring the bell.

Uncle Sebastian: Careful.

He rings the bell with a thimble on his finger. A pin drops to the floor.

Uncle Sebastian: Told ya.

Alex: You're nuts. Who do you think you are, Robin Hood?

Me: It's philanthropy. You pray, I act.

Alex: You stole the money though. You can't do bad to do good. God always knows when to intervene. He doesn't need you to get involved.

An idea shapes up in my head.

Me: I'm his assistant. His guardian angel.

Alex: Suicides don't have guardian angels. They go to hell. That's what Father Darius says.

Me: Then Father Darius should go to hell! He's too ugly for heaven anyway!

Alex jabs her fingers in her ears and starts mumbling her chemistry formulas.

Zamfir sent me a message on mIRC with a link in it. I clicked on the link and now he has access to my computer. I was sitting on my bed in my underwear when I saw a mIRC message pop up on my screen.

Zamfir: You look bored.

Me: You pervert.

The key logger takes a photo of me every three seconds, and knows everything I've typed, including my passwords. I kind of like the idea of Zamfir watching me all the time.

Alex walks into my room in her underwear.

Alex: Where's my hair brush?

Zamfir (typing): She's pretty.

Alex is having a shower. Without her glasses, she looks different: all legs and breasts and hair. Her nipples are the colour of Mozart chocolate. A scar of childhood surgery makes a pink line on her stomach. Her narrow feet with unpainted toenails are beautiful.

Alex (slamming the shower door): Go away!

Five minutes later, Zamfir and I are in my room listening to Nirvana. His hands are under my shirt. My hand, in his trousers.

Alex (banging loudly): I'M STUCK! HELP!

I find Alex pounding on the shower cabin.

Alex: Can't open the doors!

Me: HELP!

Zamfir walks in. He just stands there, his hands on his studded belt, his neck covered in love bites.

Alex: What's he doing here?

Me: Never you mind!

Zamfir tries to split the doors apart. His muscles are bursting with the effort.

Alex: I can't breathe!

Zamfir: Get a knife.

I run downstairs. The kitchen is tidy; it smells of lemon disinfectant. The sharp knives rest, blades down, in a wooden block. I pick one made of stag horn. The *Psycho* shower scene comes to my mind. The screams. The blood-splattered curtain.

Zamfir: The knife!

I run back upstairs. Zamfir sticks the blade between the rubber bands.

Zamfir: Get back!

He stabs the shower cabin again and again. Just like the shower scene from *Psycho*.

I burst out laughing.

Alex: Shut up!

Zamfir yanks the doors open. The rubber bands are in shreds.

Alex: Mother will kill us.

Her hair drips water on the mosaic tile floor.

Alex: Get out of my house!

Zamfir (holding out a towel): Who, me?

Alex (snatching the towel): Both of you!

We go back to my bedroom. Zamfir acts distant, like he's got something on his mind. He keeps clicking his Zippo lighter. He clicks it so many times it drives me nuts. I wish we could just carry on what we started before my parents get back from their day trip to the mountains.

Mother (a few hours ago): Are you sure you don't want to join us?

Me: Absolutely!

Daddy: Alex, look after your sister.

Alex: She's out of control.

Zamfir slips his lighter in his pocket. He runs a hand through his hair, flashing his cool leather bracelets and massive silver ring. When you look close enough at the ring, you see the two entwined naked women with their heads between each other's legs.

Zamfir: It must be fun having to deal with *her* all day.

Me: Tell me about it!

Zamfir: I'd better go.

When he's gone I stand in the bathroom for a long time. I'm missing something. Something important. A clue, somewhere in this room.

And then, just as I'm about to turn off the lights, just as the front door bursts open and Mother's laughter erupts in the hallway, I know.

The shower cabin is topless. I could've thrown Alex a towel.

She could've asked for one.

The church ceremony takes forever. When we get married, Zamfir and I won't have our wedding in an Orthodox church.

Zamfir: I'll take you to Vegas. My Harley will be parked outside. We'll take our wedding photos on it.

Me: I'll wear a black dress.

Zamfir: Leather, studs, Iron Maiden T-shirt.

Christina Petru is the woman Uncle Sebastian has married. She's a lot of first things. She's the first married woman in town who kept her maiden name. She's the first person I know who was born by *in vitro* fertilisation. She's the first ever bride I see in a real crinoline dress. Not wearing a petticoat, either: every time she moves you can see her skinny legs in white stockings. She reminds me of one of Mitzi's ruffled white hens.

Mother has lots of petticoats. They're made of real satin and lace. If she wears a red dress, she'll have a pink petticoat underneath. If she wears a brown dress, her petticoat will be cream. I've seen Mother modelling all the underwear in her wardrobe around the house. She has all kinds: briefs, hipsters, bikinis. The only types she doesn't wear are thongs.

Mother: Only whores wear thongs!

Once I bought a Turbo chewing gum at the sweet shop opposite the Montblanc megastore. Every gum comes with a free sticker. My sticker was a blonde woman lying face up on a Ferrari, wearing nothing but a G-string. She had glossy skin like the vipers you see sleeping on rocks. Her breasts were big with nipples like the delicate plugs peasants cut out of watermelons.

Try this one, boss? See how ripe it is. Customers take a bite of the red juicy watermelon flesh from the tip of the knife: a secret taste from deep inside, warm, soaked through by the sun.

See how ripe it is. My mouth waters.

Alex: Girls don't look at photos of naked girls!

Maybe if I wished hard enough for the girl on the sticker to come alive and take off her G-string, it would happen.

Christina Petru (handing me a flute of champagne): Good morning!

Me: Good morning!

It's actually evening, but the greeting is meant to symbolise a new beginning. The bridesmaid pins a large fake rose on my dress. Her perfume flits over to me. Her eyelids are gold, her lashes stiff with mascara. Her breath minty.

The scent of creepers in bloom and tuberose floats around the beer garden. June is an unusual month for a wedding, but *Garden of Eden* gets booked years in advance. Uncle Sebastian never planned to have a June wedding; he was just eager to get his hands on Christina's inheritance.

Uncle Sebastian: Love can wait. Business can't.

The orchestra are playing a traditional folk song. The guests pour in, relatives on a catwalk. Every time a couple walks in, someone somewhere whispers their name, their connection to either the groom or the bride, followed by a commentary on their outfit.

Mitzi: Leonora has new dentures. When was the last time we

saw her with such handsome teeth?

Grandpa: A woman borrowed a friend's dentures to go to a wedding. When the dentures were returned, the woman stuck them in her mouth and knew exactly what the menu was.

Mitzi (roaring with laughter): Eeew!

The guests scrutinize everything: the tables set with pristine tablecloths and sparkling silverware, the chairs adorned with silk and satin. Warm light pours over the pots of exotic plants: fig trees, lemon trees, wild aloe from suspended lanterns.

Woman in black fur cape (rubbing her arms): Brrr! It's freezing!

Woman in white fur cape: Why are we in the garden?

Woman in black fur cape: There's another wedding inside. What's the rush, is the bride pregnant?

Weddings are like that: if you're from the groom's family, the groom's guests are the ally; the bride's guests are the enemy. And vice-versa. The groom's family have more weight than the bride's family: Mitzi and Grandpa Vasile are the Big-In-Laws. Christina Petru's parents are the Small-In-Laws. My position as the niece of the groom is a privileged one.

Aunt Nelly: Carmen, and this dress? You look like a priest.

Me: It's a gothic dress.

Mother: She'd be wearing her boots too if she could get away with it.

The worst thing about weddings is that you have to wear normal clothes: dresses, church shoes, bras. I was sneaking out of the house when Mother pulled my arm to examine me in the hall light.

Mother: Carmen!

Me: I hate bras!

Mother: We've had this conversation before. Your tutor says everyone's talking about it at school. You can't go around with your nipples showing.

Me: No one should be looking at my nipples.

Mother: Why is everything a problem with you? First, you refuse to wear underwear. And now this?

Me: No one knows if you have your knickers on. Unless you decide to tell them.

Mother was already tying me up with the bra.

Me: Stop harnessing me!

Alex (sniggering): NEIGH! NEEEIIIIGH!!

Me: Shut up, you breastless beast!

Eighteen minutes past eight. Nineteen minutes past eight. Eight twenty. When you're bored, time crawls. When you're doing something you enjoy, it just slips through your fingers like sand.

The plan is this. Sometime tonight, the bride is going to be stolen. A wedding is not a wedding if the bride doesn't get taken. In the commotion, I escape. Everyone will think I'm in with the kidnappers. That'll give me a couple of hours, at least.

I've brought a change of clothes with me: ripped jeans, my Kiss T-shirt, proper walking boots. Uncle Sebastian drives past and I throw the bundle from my window.

I've been staring at the Colonel all night. He shouldn't be here, but Wallachia is a small town, and you can't always avoid everybody.

Me: Look at that gorilla. He's ugly like the devil!

Uncle Sebastian: Clever like the devil, too.

Mother and the Colonel are dancing. His hands are two hairy tarantulas on Mother's naked back. Mother's breasts are flattened against his beer belly. The Colonel's red-rimmed eyes are hungry even if he's just finished a large plate of *appetizer:* cold pancetta, Boeuf salad, Prosciutto crudo. He looks at Mother as if she's just another sausage on his plate.

Mitzi's wearing a high-necked blouse and bright red lipstick. Her hair is frizzy like she's just been plugged into a socket. Her hands, black from the farm work she loves: ripping wormwood with her bare hands, chopping boiled nettles for the spring ducklings, digging up weeds.

Mother: Mamma, your hair is awful. And look at your hands. Why are you paying those men to sit around on their arses all day?

Mitzi: You can't find reliable farm work anymore. The men won't even start work without a full meal in their bellies, and half a litre of brandy in their hands.

Mother: Outrageous!

Mitzi: Maria, she helped me in the kitchen. I gave her food, things for the babies. That excuse of a husband beats her when there's no food to eat.

Grandpa (his fork in the air): As if it's a woman's job to put food on the table!

Mother: Not so loud, Papa.

Mitzi: Last summer I offered her a three-day job, plum picking. We have so many plum trees, you know, an entire orchard, and not enough hands. Last year the plums rotted, unpicked, we lost so much brandy. So I accepted we need help, we're not thick, we move on with the times ...

Mother: Good!

Mitzi: Maria didn't show up. On Sunday, a neighbour saw her begging at church.

Grandpa: Sure, sitting around on your arse begging is easier than picking plums!

Mother: Why don't you sell the farm?

Mitzi: You'd better kill me before you bring me to the city.

Grandpa: Do you want us to live up high like storks?

Mitzi: Promise us you won't sell the orchards when we die.

Mother: This is not the time, Mamma.

Grandpa (taking a mouthful of caviar from his plate): Mamma Mia!

Woman from the enemy camp: May I steal the Big-Father-In-Law for a dance?

Grandpa (mopping his mouth with a tissue): You sure can!

Mother: And your knee?

Mitzi: His knee only hurts when it's work time. The rabbits, their hutches are in pieces. I keep telling him, the skunks will get them. The skunks dug a tunnel to the chicken coop, remember? I found all my chickens lined up with their blood sucked dry.

Mother: Mamma, I'm eating.

Grandpa and a lady with permed hair are jumping up and down on the dance floor. His smile is so wide you can see the gold fillings at the back of his mouth.

Mother: And that top? Can you breathe?

Mitzi: I love a *décolletage*, but old age gave me the chicken neck.

She laughs and jabs her fork into an olive. The olive disappears in the pink cave of her mouth. Her eyes are black and beady like the olive. It's very rare for someone to have deep black eyes like Mitzi.

Zamfir has blue eyes. Alex's eyes are boring brown, like mine.

Me: I don't like her. She's stuck up.

Mitzi (chewing): She's what he needs.

Me: When are they going to steal the bride?

The appetizer plates are collected. The waiters bring the next course. I'm surprised that Uncle Sebastian has allowed something as uncool as stuffed cabbage leaves on the menu.

Mitzi: You can't have a wedding without *sarmale* and polenta.

Me: Yes you can, it's called a civilised wedding.

Uncle Sebastian: Don't get too stuffed with appetizers, Mamma.

His groom suit is light grey with a crisp white shirt and a *lavaliere*. On his little finger he wears his grandfather's gold ring, on his left hand he wears his brand new wedding ring.

Uncle Sebastian: May I?

I put my hand in Uncle Sebastian's, and he closes his fingers around it, gently, the way you catch butterflies. We're on the dance floor: me in my ridiculous velvet dress, him in his white Fred Astair shoes. If I wasn't in love with Zamfir, I'd want a man just like Uncle Sebastian.

The bride's family follow us: spiteful eyes, feathers and ties and bows and hats, not a friendly face anywhere in the enemy camp. They think Christina could've done better. Screw them, even if they're right.

The orchestra start playing a waltz. Pairs mingle. We dance.

I don't know how I know the steps but I do. We dance like pros.

Me (giggling): I can't dance. Shall I follow you?

Uncle Sebastian: I was following you.

Me: I'm dizzy.

Uncle Sebastian: I'm holding you.

The dance floor spins. The ground spins. The garden with the white tables and the black and white waiters spins. The guests' faces spin like a grotesque carousel.

Uncle Sebastian's arms are around me. His smile bright. His tobacco and Coca Cola breath in my face.

Me: Would you ever marry me?

Uncle Sebastian: If you were the last girl on earth, I'd think about it.

Me: No, seriously.

Uncle Sebastian (laughing): Cut it out.

Me: So, do you feel "married"?

Uncle Sebastian: Not yet. I'm sure it'll kick in in the morning. Waking up in a woman's bed and having no excuse to get away. It'll be a hell of a shock.

We laugh.

Me: Zamfir and I are getting married.

Uncle Sebastian: Nice.

He swirls me around to a ripple of applause.

Lady's voice: They've always been close. Like brother and sister.

Man's voice: What a fine pair!

Me: You can do better than her.

Uncle Sebastian (smiling): Where did this come from?

Me: Did you see the way she looked at Mitzi?

Uncle Sebastian: She's a heiress. Would I be going through this marriage charade if I thought I could do any better? This isn't love, Carmen. This is life.

Me (whispering): I need to see Zamfir tonight. When's *she* going to be stolen? I could disappear in the commotion.

I can't say Christina Petru's name aloud – not yet. It's a dirty word, a secret. Though I'd rather say a dirty word than the name of the woman who stole Uncle Sebastian forever.

Uncle Sebastian (checking his watch): I imagine they'll wait for the steak. Don't worry, I'll hold up paying the ransom. Take as long as you like.

He stuffs a wad of notes in my hand. It's more money than I've ever seen. Uncle Sebastian is the only person in the world who really gets me.

The mountain road is deserted, apart from the occasional call-girl on duty. The bridge looms in the distance, bright in the lights from the petrol station. Behind the petrol station is the woods, quiet and dark.

The woods are full of whores. I saw them close up when Daddy stopped at a roadside restaurant to use the restroom. I waited in the car. A man was walking through the trees doing up his belt. He was the kind of sleazy man you don't even want near you. Behind him, a girl trickled water from a bottle on her private parts.

Uncle Sebastian: They punch holes in the lid. Fuck, you have to be pretty retarded to take a girl from the woods. They're all sick and dying. I know someone who got Aids from one of those sluts. He infected his wife and unborn baby.

Me: Shit!

Uncle Sebastian: The guy went back to the woods with a sword. Before the whore could even open her mouth, he cut off her head.

Me (gasping): What happened to the body?

Uncle Sebastian: If anyone cared about her, would she be sucking cock in the woods?

You can only see the call-girls in the glow of the cars driving past. They shine and dim, shine and dim, like Christmas trees when it's no longer Christmas. If a car stops the girls surround it. You can't drive off without picking up one of them. They hold on to you like leeches, giving themselves almost for free. Maybe all they want is someone to talk to.

I check the time. I must have slipped out around eleven, just as Christina was being ambushed by a group of tipsy men. They carried her through the cheering crowd to the parking where an Audi was waiting with the boot wide open. Her dress made a sound like popped bubble wrap when they squeezed her inside: POP-POP-POP; her dress was ruined, but who cares, she's not going to wear it again, no one else will.

The fake kidnappers would've taken her to a club, drinking on the groom's account. In about an hour or so they'll phone up to negotiate a ransom. It'll be too high in the beginning. The groom will say no. Then they'll send someone over with her shoe. The groom will make a speech with the shoe in his hand. I read a story about a groom who didn't pay the ransom so the kidnappers raped the bride. But that would never happen to someone like my Uncle Sebastian.

I don't know why we can't have weddings like those in Beverly Hills, with brides being walked down the aisle and saying *I do*. You never say *I do* in our churches. You never say anything.

The gate is open. Rock music blasts from the speakers. A stone path snakes through the garden to a flight of ancient stairs. Tufts of grass sprout from the cracks. Through the open window I see the bar lady picking up ashtrays, wiping tables with a cloth bloated with dirt water. We have a cloth like that at home; I've never *ever* touched it. I can't even look at it: a wet dead rat on the edge of the sink.

Terassa reminds me of Godmother's house: arched doorways, crumbling rooftops, decadence. A mansion, a Communist office, a bar: the house's reincarnations are multiple. Mother says that Hindus turn into animals when they die. I wish people could turn into animals while they are still alive. The Colonel would be a Colorado bug. Alex would be a ringworm. Christina Petru would be one of those skinny neck chickens that Mitzi calls *"throaty."* *Here, here, throaty,* she sings, and the skinny neck chickens follow her like creatures from a nightmare.

The pub is a collection of rooms with high ceilings and wide open doors. The smoke is so thick you can cut it with a knife. Men in leathers, girls with pierced noses, bandanas, American music. Smelly is asleep, curled up on someone's lap. I've never met her, but I know three things about her: she has a sister in America, she takes cocaine, and her father's a judge.

Bar lady: Can I help you?

Me: Vodka, please.

Bar lady: 100?

Me (blinking): Times 20.

I nod towards the table where the empty vodka glasses are stacked in towers. Eagle and Ribbit are there. Daria P. and I went to Ribbit's house once. Daria P. was the speaker.

Daria P.: It's about Eagle.

Ribbit: I'll pass it on.

Eagle (on the phone): They're too young, mate. I like girls with boobs.

Daria P. (walking through the hedge tunnel): I told you he was gay.

Me (holding her hand): Maybe we should've offered money. I'd pay him to take my virginity. I really would.

Daria P.: Me too.

The bar lady understands. She pockets my notes and starts pouring out the vodkas.

The clock on the wall fills with time. Smelly stumbles past me several times to be sick in the back. Her lips, nose, eyebrows, and ears are heavy with piercings. There's no one like her in the whole town.

The ground slips from under my feet. Everything is too bright. Smelly's sitting astride Eagle. His hands on her bum, his fingers tracing the line between her buttocks. They're kissing. I don't fancy Eagle anymore. Zamfir is a million times better.

But where is he?

The garden smells of Mitzi's marmalade roses. The breeze is cool like freshly laundered sheets.

Mitzi: You're not hiding a cat in there, are you?

Me: No.

Pisa purrs. Grandpa smacks the duvet with the poker.

Grandpa: Zsatt!

It's midnight. The taxi station is empty. There are no buses on this route and, even if I saw one, I don't have a ticket.

Daddy: What do you need a travelcard for? I drive you everywhere!

Mother: If you go out with your friends, Daddy can pick you up.

The park is dark, *dark*, DARK. I walk faster, *faster*, FASTER. I'm almost running when I hear something behind me. An echo.

Footsteps. Think, Carmen, think. My pepper spray. My knife. *My boots.* Jacob Pilsner wears his granddad's old boots all day long. They look fabulous, like nothing you've ever seen. The granddad took them off a dead Russian soldier. They smell of war, he says.

Clench your fist, with the thumb inside, so the blow doesn't break your fingers. Lift up your arm. Punch from slightly above your height.

I'm running. The fear in my stomach is a bomb ready to go off. The silence is deafening. Light from the lampposts pours on the dark street like honey from a jar. A dog appears in the headlights of a car. It bares its teeth in a growl.

Dog: Grrrrr! Woof-WOOF!

HALT. I turn around slowly, then step back, until I'm almost against the wall. The trainers close around me: *Nike, Puma, Adidas.*

Daddy: I'm not paying a month of minimum wage for a pair of designer trainers.

Me: You earn more than the minimum wage!

Daddy: Still.

The boys grin. They look at me like I'm a Colorado bug crawling out of a bucket. We used to wait for the Colorado bugs to crawl all the way up the bucket wall only to blow them back in when they reached the top.

Damian and Robert's bodies move aside to let a third boy step ahead of them.

Giuliano: Well, well, well, if it isn't the town cunt.

Damian: Look at the state she's in. Maybe she sucks cock at the bridge every night.

Laughter.

Me: What are *you* doing here? Looking to bribe someone to suck *your* cock? Bribe for a bribe, is it?

Giuliano steps closer. Anger makes me bolder.

Me: You want to see what it's like with a girl, is that it? I heard you like it in the arse.

Damian and Robert howl with laughter. Giuliano throws me against the stone wall.

Giuliano: Are you saying your old man doesn't take bribes? He's a saint, is he? Let me tell you something, if he was a saint, you would *really* be sucking cock.

Robert: Does Zamfir Boc's bedroom smell of pigeon shit?

Me: It smells better than your friend!

Giuliano's repulsive breath floats between us: a flavour of his infected molars. He pushes himself into me. The front of his jeans hard against my thigh. One hand on my mouth. The other rips my zip: his fingers in my trousers, fast and urgent, but it's not just the fingers he forces in: it's his entire fist.

Giuliano: You like punching, eh, slut?

His lips curl back from his black, rotten teeth. Then his mouth opens and the darkness inside it takes over the world.

Alex: Carmen!

I snap awake, taking in the room around me. A desk, a window, chairs and an old carpet curling at the corners.

I blink. And then I remember. We're at Isleworth Crown Court, the Probation Office. The old man next to me takes off his glasses. I blink again, and the reality falls into place, only just.

Alex: Jesus, Carmen. You're not doing Daddy any favours by falling asleep during his interview.

Alex is glancing at her Armani watch. We're sitting on either side of Daddy, opposite a black woman with glasses.

Probation Officer: I was asking whether you've noticed your father abusing alcohol during the time that he lived with you.

Me (surprised): My father? No, I mean, he doesn't drink.

Alex: He went through a drinking episode back home, years ago.

Probation Officer: I see. When you say *episode*, how long did it last?

Alex: A year, maybe two.

Probation Officer: That's a long episode.

Daddy: I was lonely. I made bad friends.

Probation Officer: Were you drunk at the time of the offence?

Daddy: No.

Probation Officer (her pen in the air): Now tell me what happened on 22nd September 2017.

Daddy's eyes mist over. When he talks, it's in a voice I barely recognise: an old man's voice.

Daddy: It began like any other day. I woke up, made my bed, went downstairs. I drink Turkish coffee – so I made a big pot ...

Probation Officer: You were living with your daughter, Alexandra.

Alex: That's correct.

Probation Officer: Please, your father needs to answer my questions himself.

Alex narrows her eyes. I look away to the window that offers a view of Ridgeway Road snaking to the left.

Daddy: Yes, Ma'am.

Probation Officer: How long had you been living with her?

Daddy: About six months.

Probation Officer: I can see from your police interview that you were there mainly to help with the children, is that also correct?

Daddy: Yes. I'm better than a childminder. I do all the housework, and I only require room and board.

Alex: Dad!

Probation Officer (scribbling): Now, I want you to carry on telling me what happened on that particular day, in as much detail as possible.

Daddy rubs his eyes. That's when I see how red they are – and the black circles around them.

Daddy: I had my coffee, and I remembered a job I'd forgotten to do. The gardener, I've seen her hacking at the roots with a machete. From the window I saw the machete. It was raining. That gardener doesn't care about the children's tools, when her time is up, she just drops them anywhere. Why leave a brand new machete out when you know it's going to rain?

Probation Officer: Go on.

Her lips mouth the word "machete" while she scribbles energetically in her A4 notebook.

Daddy: I went out and got the machete. The blade was blunt, so I wiped it with a towel and proceeded to ...

Daddy hesitates, then sighs.

Probation Officer (pen in hand): To?

Daddy (blowing out a sob): Sharpen it.

Everything I hear is blurred. All I feel is weightlessness. I'm floating through water, beyond life and death. *Beyond pain.* Did they kill me and dump my body in the river? Am I still alive?

The smells are familiar. Wormwood soap, hot bathwater, vinegar.

Mitzi: Hurry up, sunshine, your bath is getting cold.

I'm naked. I step into the bathwater holding Mitzi's hand. I search for the bottom with my foot, but there is no bottom.

There's no bottom, and Mitzi's hand on my head gets heavier, pushing me to the bottom that doesn't exist. Through the soapy water I see her face contorting, her features sharpening, until Giuliano Banu emerges from her body.

Giuliano: What is it, slut? Can't you breathe?

Sharp arrows of moonlight filter through the tree branches. My eyes sting. I must have woken up before; I remember shadows, feeling sick with the stench of my own blood. I'd dreamed that I was devoured by wolves: the monstrous shapes loomed over me, *wolves*, all ears and tails and teeth. One of them blows in my face, a swarm of wasps that chokes me.

My pepper spray.

Giuliano: What is it, slut? Can't you breathe?

The sounds take on meaning: the shuffle of trousers being pulled up, the tinkle of belts, laughter, footsteps. I fall back into blackness.

Zamfir's voice: Carmen?

I open my eyes. The moon is still shining. Uncle Sebastian's Mercedes is parked illegally on the promenade.

Zamfir: This way, Sebastian.

A torchlight dances over the trees.

I'm in the back of the Mercedes. The dashboard clock reads three a.m. Felipe, Uncle Sebastian's wolf-dog, is in the front seat.

Uncle Sebastian: They can't be far.

Zamfir: Over there.

The three boys appear in the headlights. Uncle Sebastian's hands shake hard on the wheel. He looks bitter and old, not the Uncle Sebastian I know.

Uncle Sebastian: Hold on.

The engine screams. The Mercedes reverses. The boys see the car. They're blinded by the lights.

Uncle Sebastian: Felipe, boy, get them!

Felipe springs. The boys vanish in the darkness of the trees, the dog on their trail. Giuliano is still running. Uncle Sebastian waits. He knows, as well as me, that the Puma trainers he's so proud of won't get him very far.

Uncle Sebastian's hands have stopped shaking. The ruins are quiet. The park is quiet. The hand flapping against the side of the car has gone limp. Only a dripping sound, like petrol leaking, disturbs the silence.

Uncle Sebastian: Felipe, here, boy.

The dog jumps back in his seat. His muzzle is wet. A story Mitzi used to tell me unfolds in my mind.

Mitzi: Once upon a time, a woman and her husband were stacking hay. It was around sunset. The man went to relieve himself. While he was away, the woman was attacked by a dog. She fought it off, but the animal ripped her apron. When her husband returned, she saw threads the colour of her clothes on his mouth ...

Me: What did she do?

Mitzi: What do you think? She put the pitchfork through him and killed the werewolf once and for all.

Uncle Sebastian types something on his phone.

BLEEP-BLEEP-BLEEP-BLEEP-BLEEP-BLEEP-BLEEP.

When he's finished, he steps out of the car and takes out his packet of Davidoff Lights (most expensive brand on the market). For a while we stand smoking, trying to ignore the human shape at our feet. A disturbing thought: Giuliano Banu's dead, but his sperm might survive for three days in my womb.

The familiar sound of a van disturbs our thoughts. It stops at a distance from us with the lights off.

Uncle Sebastian: They're here.

And then I know that what's dripping down on the promenade isn't petrol, but Giuliano's brains. His head got stuck in the mysterious underside of Uncle Sebastian's Mercedes, like a nut in a nutcracker.

Eleven. Daddy's still telling the officer how he made his dumpling soup.

Daddy: If you don't watch them, the dumplings are going to get hard, rock hard.

Alex: Dad! Stick to the facts. I haven't got all day.

Probation Officer: Take your time, Mr Martin.

Daddy (nodding): Then he came in.

Probation Officer: Who?

Alex: My father-in-law.

Probation Officer: Madam, please.

Daddy: My in-law.

Probation Officer (looking through her papers): I take it, this was your son-in-law's dad.

Daddy: Correct.

Probation Officer: How long had *he* been living there?

Daddy: About two weeks. He'd come to see the grandchildren.

Probation Officer: So, in total, how many people were living in the house?

Daddy: The kids, the twins, and ...

Alex: I have a six bedroom house.

Probation Officer: So your daughter and her husband, their two children ...

Alex: Young children.

Probation Officer: ... your father-in-law, and yourself.

Daddy nods.

Probation Officer: Tell me what happened next.

Daddy: I heard him come in. It was nine o'clock. I was in the kitchen, my back to the door. He just stood in the doorway watching me.

Probation Officer: So he just stood in the doorway watching you. Nothing else.

Daddy: That's correct.

Alex's foot is twitching. She flicks her hair. Her skin is perfect, even if she's just turned thirty and should be showing the first signs of middle age.

Probation Officer: Tell me what happened next.

Daddy: He walked through the kitchen to the utility room: one of his chores is the washing. Sorting it, hanging it out to dry, ironing.

Probation Officer (her eyebrow raised): *Chores?*

Alex: I didn't ask them to do anything ... but Dad sacked my housekeeper, so ...

Daddy: I didn't sack her. This paper slipped from her bag, a note from her psychiatrist, something about a missed appointment. Can't have someone like that around the twins.

Probation Officer: So since the housekeeper ... *left,* you did all the chores? How did that affect you?

Daddy: It made me feel useful. Until he came along, and everything changed.

Probation Officer: How?

Daddy: The washing was my job. So was the washing up. How would you feel if you came to work one day and found someone in your office, doing your work, telling you to have a coffee and relax?

Probation Officer (smiling): I see.

Daddy: I waited for him to get close enough, and I grabbed him by the collar of his shirt.

Daddy makes a gesture with his hand to imitate the grabbing movement.

Probation Officer: Stop there. Why did you grab him?

Daddy: I told the police it was an impulse. You see, the truth is, I'd been fantasizing about this moment for a very long time.

Alex: Dad!

Probation Officer: Go on.

Daddy: Our history goes back a long time.

Probation Officer: I have time. My job is to write this report for the judge to assist with your sentencing, and I need to make sure it's as accurate as possible. (To Alex) Ma'am, your father doesn't need your assistance. He speaks English. And your sister is here in case we need interpreting. You're not expected anywhere, are you?

I shake my head, *no.*

Alex: I have a little time.

Daddy: It all started in 1995, when we moved house. My wife wanted to live somewhere nice, with the "right" people. She had big aspirations, you see. I worked hard and bought a duplex apartment in a residential block, very central, just as she wanted-ed.

The probation officer stops writing. Daddy rubs his eyes. She hands him a tissue.

Probation Officer: Take your time.

Daddy: Would I change anything if I could turn back time? The answer is yes. I'd change everything. I'd stay in District 9 in my small flat living my small life, getting up every day to go to my small job.

Probation Officer: What happened in that apartment?

Daddy's answer is a loud, desperate sob.

"Here comes the groom! Who stole the groom?"

Drunken laughter erupts from the dinner tables. The orchestra livens up, violins screeching a welcome song for Uncle Sebastian. His bride is sitting on a chair, pretending to fend off the women trying to cover her head with a traditional headscarf.

Mother (looking flushed): Was Carmen with you all along?

Uncle Sebastian: Yes.

Daddy: Honey, you look like death. We should be going soon.

Mother: Don't be ridiculous, the night is young.

Daddy (checking his watch): It's four in the morning. And you've had enough to drink.

Mitzi: You're not going anywhere, they're playing the *hora*.

Everyone's clapping. Uncle Sebastian and the Godfather dance the *hora* together. The clapping is loud. I want to cover my ears. I want to look away from the blood on Uncle Sebastian's shoes but I can't.

Uncle Sebastian: *Shit. Fuck, at least it's not on my trousers.*

Man in balaclava: There's a patrol at the roundabout. Something happened. We have to go back that way.

Uncle Sebastian: If any of it gets on my Merz ...

Man in balaclava (to his partner): Let's try again. *One, two, three ...*

I shut my eyes. When I open them again, the blood isn't there anymore.

Ten minutes earlier, Uncle Sebastian's Mercedes had slipped soundlessly between a BMW and an Audi in the hotel's guest parking lot.

The terror in Zamfir's eyes mirrored mine. Giuliano's body was in the boot.

Uncle Sebastian: This never happened.

Me: How about the other two?

Uncle Sebastian: Witness protection is none of your business.

Zamfir: Am I missing something here? There's a fucking body in the back of the car. And we saw you kill him.

Uncle Sebastian opened the window to spit outside. Then he

turned around and punched Zamfir in the eye.

Uncle Sebastian (flexing his wrist): You have a big mouth, my friend. If this wasn't my wedding day, if you weren't Carmen's toy boy, I'd show you what I think of mouthy motherfuckers.

Zamfir (groaning in pain): I was only trying to help.

Uncle Sebastian: I said I'll deal with it. Now get the fuck out of my car.

A damp smell of rain wafts around the room from the cracked window. It's the end of lunch break; the school down the road quietens suddenly, as if magicked into silence. The houses, rising like gingerbread shapes from the luxuriant vegetation, hint at an unspoken order that nothing can ever break. A Polish nanny crosses the road with a Sikh boy on a scooter.

Alex: That's it, then. He'll be lucky not to get a prison sentence.

Me: He was lucky with the probation lady.

Alex: You're joking. She was trying to make it look like we're the typical filthy Romanians, living in overcrowded shared houses, off social welfare. She must be congratulating herself for having a cushy office job dealing with offenders. Gawd, she'd need a brain transplant to even dream of getting a degree like mine, and yet she's patronising me.

Me: Offenders like Daddy, shared houses like mine?

Alex: Mother was right, the poor deserve their fate. Really, I never appreciated the Gipsies until now. Repulsive they might be, but at least they know their place. Nobody in England knows their fucking place. I'm really glad Mother didn't live to see the day when a black cunt treats her daughter like she's better than her!

Me: This isn't the English we learned at the Mill Hill School for Girls.

Alex: How would you know? You left with no qualifications. I remember you going around like Mother Theresa, stealing money to pay for that cleaner's funeral, and don't think I don't know you never had any money because you just gave it to everyone. You used to dream about being a human rights lawyer, ha hah ha! Where did that get you? You're a loser, just like those losers you've been defending all your life!

Me: Can I get a lift?

Alex takes her car keys from her purse. The sound grinds against my brain: the first sign of a headache. I shouldn't have had that last drink.

Alex: Can't you drive?

Me: No.

Alex: Of course you can't. You're always drunk.

Me: I can't afford the lessons.

Alex: I gave you £500 three years ago to pay for twenty lessons.

Me: Maybe twenty lessons weren't enough.

Alex: Well, I learned from ten. Carmen, I'm not a bank. Why don't you get a job? Oh, forgive me. You have no qualifications from your pre-paid independent school because you moved in with your boyfriend at seventeen.

Me: Where's Daddy?

Alex: Shit. Good point.

She drives around for a few minutes, swearing under her breath.

Alex: I hate these fucking narrow streets, and all the arse-holes who block me!

She honks her horn, loud and rude.

Me: There he is.

Daddy's wearing the shirt and jumper we got him for Christmas, and the pair of Adidas trainers he claimed to have found brand new in a charity shop. Alex buzzes her window open.

Alex: Get in the car!

Daddy: I need some fresh air.

Alex: Fine. I'll see you at home. Remember. Six o'clock.

Daddy smiles and rolls up his sleeve to show he is aware of his curfew tag. A few months ago, a specialised team arrived at Alex's address, measured the house and garden, and left a big black box in his bedroom. Daddy is only allowed to leave the house between six in the morning and six in the evening.

The drive takes twenty minutes; we're lucky, the midday

traffic is light. Alex drops me at Boston Manor station.

Me: Go on. What's wrong?

Alex's hands clasp the wheel, tight.

Alex: Don't know what you're talking about.

Me: Do you remember what you told me when Zamfir left me? You said there were plenty of fish in the sea. Now, I'm giving you the same advice.

Alex: Time to get over that, don't you think?

Me: When were you going to tell me?

Alex: Tell you what?

My eyes are fixed on Alex's stomach, swollen under her pristine white shirt.

Alex (her voice shaking): Okay, I'm pregnant. But I'm not keeping it. Another baby would ruin my career. I work 60-70 hours a week. I travel all the time. It wouldn't be fair.

Me: That's not why you're crying though, is it?

Alex's head drops down on the wheel. I gently touch her shoulder: the first gesture of tenderness in what feels like forever.

Alex: Just go.

The commotion in the house wakes me up. The red numbers on the digital clock change to 00. It's midnight. What are Mitzi and Grandpa doing here?

Alex has fallen asleep with her glasses on and the *Anatomy Atlas* next to her on the bed.

Me: Wake up.

The apartment smells of cigarette smoke, coffee and Mitzi's flowery perfume she only wears on very special occasions. Alex and I peek through the rails. Grandpa's voice fills the living room, BOOM, BOOM, BOOM. He's always loud when he's drunk, but now he's stone sober. Mother's curled up in an armchair with a glass of brandy in one hand, a cigarette in the other.

Daddy: Go on, tell them what you told me.

Mother: For God's sake, darling. I'm a grown woman.

Daddy: When I married you, I married all of you. And this is how you repay me.

Mother (sitting up): Don't you understand? It's over. It's been over for many years. I fell in love with another man. I'm moving in with him and I'm taking the children.

Grandpa slaps Mother so hard she drops her brandy all over our hand-embroidered armchair, but she doesn't seem to care. She bursts into a fit of mad laughter.

Daddy: I don't deserve this.

Mother: Me neither. Have you ever wondered what it's like for me, having to sleep with someone I don't love?

This time, it's Daddy who slaps her.

Mother: Clowns, all of you. Nothing of what you do or don't do will change what's written in the stars.

Daddy looks at his hand like it's a bloody dagger.

Daddy: Fine. If that's what you want, leave tonight. Alone. You can keep the moth eaten coat you wore when I first met you. Everything else stays here.

Mother: Keep your rags, you dirty son of a bitch. But the kids are coming with me. The girls need their mother.

Daddy: Now you remember you're a mother.

He removes a box from a cupboard and opens it. Lots of smaller boxes spill out of it. Pills of all colours, shapes and sizes roll all over the floor.

Daddy: Thorazine, Prolixin, Xanax. How would you look after the girls when you're drugged most of the time?

Grandpa: What are those for, Camelia?

Daddy: Your daughter is addicted to medication, Vasile.

Mother: I'm taking the girls. Mamma, help me pack. I don't need a cab.

The mad laugh again. Mitzi doesn't move. Nothing moves but the smoke of my parents' cigarettes drifting to the open window. Then Grandpa's voice booms again, loud, authoritative: It's out of the question, Camelia. The girls can't live with you and another man. We won't allow it!

Mitzi: Aren't you forgetting something? The apartment belongs to my daughter too, Stelian.

Daddy: What are you suggesting? That he moves in here with us? The plaque on the door reads Stelian Martin.

Mitzi: That may be so, but Camelia works, and she's been working since the girls were in nappies. I know because I looked after the children. You can't throw her out from her own house, not without some kind of compensation.

Grandpa: Don't take her side!

Mitzi: He called us here, didn't he? Now he needs to hear us.

Daddy: I'm listening.

Mitzi: The girls can't live with you and the new man, Camelia. I'm sorry, but I agree with your father.

Mother: You too, Mamma? What do you suggest, that they stay here? He's never home. Who would look after them?

Mitzi: They can live with us.

Mother: In the country?

Uncle Sebastian: I have a better idea.

It's drizzling when I arrive at Bellmarsh. James Hunter's white-blond hair is covered in raindrops.

James Hunter: Did you get here all right?

I nod. The lawyer has kind, blue eyes. He must be in his fifties, a strongly built man with a wide chest and powerful jaws. On one of our rushed meetings he let slip that he played rugby in his youth; I have to giggle every time I picture him chasing a ball.

Me: My sister gave me a lift to the train station.

James Hunter (checking his watch): This won't take long. The defendant has applied for his trial to be transferred to Romania, and I don't see any reason why his application shouldn't be granted – as far as I'm aware, he committed the offense in Romania, and was seized in Manchester – my home town, by the way – on a European arrest warrant. Deportation is, of course, unavoidable in convictions of over twelve months.

Me: Of course.

James Hunter (pressing the buzzer): May I ask you something?

Me: Yes.

James Hunter: The defendant seems to have a morbid prefer-
ence for you. I mean, he sits in silence every time we bring him
an interpreter, unless it's you – but of course you're not even an
interpreter. What are you to him, exactly?

Me: I speak English. He's someone I know, that's all.

James Hunter: And he has a crush on you. Is that what it is?

Me (smiling): You're flattering me.

James Hunter: Flattering never does any harm.

Me: I suppose not.

James Hunter: You want my advice? Stay away from Orlando
Batista. If that's even his real name.

Me: That's what my mother used to say.

James Hunter: Your mother knew him?

Me: You could say that. Although I don't think anyone really
knows him.

James Hunter: You could say that, too.

Mitzi: Ready?

Me: I think I have everything.

Mitzi: Your sister's downstairs. And your Godmother's here,
too, she wants to say goodbye.

Me: Where's Uncle Sebastian?

Mitzi: Couldn't make it. Christina fell ill again. She's at the
hospital.

Me: Not again?

Mitzi shakes her head. I don't know how she's not hot, wearing a black headscarf in midsummer.

Mitzi: It's her fifth miscarriage. She's not only frigid, but also
barren. (whispering) Sebastian has mentioned divorce.

Me: That's brutal.

Mitzi: Yes, but what can he do? Put her on a shelf and watch
her all day? She can't cook. She can't clean. She can't breed.

In the hall the mirrors are all covered. It smells of Mother's
Nivea hand lotion. I take one last look at the apartment.

The lift doors are closing when Mr Iacob, the veterinarian, enters with his sausage dog. The dog has sad eyes and ears like meat steaks from the *Tom and Jerry* cartoons.

Mr Iacob: This dog heat is killing us, Mr Martin.

Daddy takes us to the airport in his Espero. The heat is scorching. One time Mother's kitten heel got stuck in the hot pavement.

Mother: *Get me out of here!*

Daddy: Have you got everything?

He watches us nod in the mirror. We're travelling light. A few days ago, Uncle Sebastian took seven bags of my clothes to an orphanage.

Uncle Sebastian: Look after yourself.

Me: What about Zamfir?

Uncle Sebastian: Forget him, Carmen. You'll find someone else. A bigger fish. An English count.

We laugh.

Me: As if a count would ever notice someone like me.

Uncle Sebastian: You're going to a thirty-thousand pound a year school. What kind of people do you think go there?

He pats my knee.

Uncle Sebastian: When you feel intimidated, or small, remember, no matter how outrageous a man gets, or what a hotshot he thinks he is … well, we all have a cock, that's all.

Me (laughing): Not one like Zamfir's!

Uncle Sebastian: For as long as the cock is hard, the heart is soft. I'm not telling you to use this to your advantage … actually, yes I am.

Me: You never really liked him, did you?

Uncle Sebastian: I always knew you and him won't last.

Daddy drives past the scorched corn fields. A man cycles down the side of the road. I open the window. The rusty bicycle makes a creepy screeching sound in the torrid silence.

Mother: *Shut that window, Carmen, the draught will give me a toothache.*

When I glance behind me, Mother's seat is empty. Actually,

my seat is empty, because I'm sitting in Mother's seat, at the front.

A few summers ago, on our way to the seaside, we had a picnic. Fresh bread, sheep's cheese, tomatoes. Ice-cold water from the well.

Daddy: Fancy some watermelon?

The car halts. The dust sticks to our skin. We sweat, *sweat*, SWEAT, like beer bottles in Grandpa's summer fridge.

Grandpa: *Only two things are allowed in my summer fridge – beer and watermelons!*

A triangle of ripe watermelon balances on the tip of a knife.

Peasant: Sweet as honey, boss.

Daddy buys the watermelon. The peasant chops it up for us, and we have it in the car.

Mitzi: *Run the peel over your face, it's called a watermelon face-mask.*

I run the peel over my face. It's sticky and wet and it smells sweet, *sweet*, SWEET.

Mother: *Mamma, stop filling the girls' heads with rubbish.*

The airport is cool. Alex and I remove our sweaty clothes in the bathroom. In summer, we don't travel anywhere without a set of spare clothes.

Alex: I'm scared of flying.

Me: Me too.

Daddy: Coffee?

Daddy feeds a coffee machine a handful of coins. Hot chocolate, black Americano, cappuccino. If Mother was here, she'd have herbal tea and we'd all laugh at her.

Daddy: It's time.

We check in our bags and follow the line of passengers. On the other side of the glass, the airplanes are like iron creatures out of a science fiction movie. Delicious fear bubbles in my belly. *We could crash. We could get hijacked. We might arrive to a different destination: the Bahamas, Mauritius, Morocco.* When I look back, Daddy's still waving.

James Hunter: *Carmen?* Can you ask the defendant if he understands everything I said?

Carmen. Always surprises me. My own name. It's been with me for more than three decades, deceitful, soothing, a mask concealing ... Concealing what? ... Sometimes I wonder if Carmen Manole-Martin really exists; maybe *she's* a figment of my imagination, too, like the memory of Mother. In my mind, Mother is distorted and unreliable. How much can I remember? How much of what I remember is true?

Entering a maximum security prison is like a trip to the hereafter. We get in with no earthly possessions, just one sheet of white paper (29.8/21cm) and a pencil (19cm). No belts, no laces, no jewellery. A stale odour floats around the interview room. A narrow window separates us from the rain.

Defendant (in Romanian): It's okay. I understand. Tell him to leave. I want to speak to you. In private.

Me: He says he understands and he wants you to leave.

James Hunter (laughing): Fair enough.

They shake hands. James Hunter knocks on the door.

James Hunter: The defendant would like a word with the interpreter. (To me) Careful. Don't go near that rail. It sets off the panic alarm.

Ten minutes later, he's waiting for me at one of the tables in the cafeteria. A cup of steaming coffee, black, just the way I like it, waits before an empty seat, next to a cup of bright yellow tea.

Me (smiling): Camomile?

Uncle Sebastian has aged badly. His hair thinned, and the freckles that gave him his unique look spread all over his face like eczema. There's white at his temples, and the forty-a-day cigarette diet shows in the deep lines around his mouth. Only his eyes are smiling, still alive with mischief.

Uncle Sebastian: Just like in the good old days. Mamma made me camomile tea with honey.

He stirs his tea, lost in his thoughts.

Uncle Sebastian: I couldn't even go to Mamma's funeral. You know how she always dreamed of me carrying her coffin?

Mitzi: Sebastian, you'll carry my coffin, you're my son, you must carry me the way I carried you in my womb. You nearly killed me, but you were worth it, I forgot all the pain when I saw you were a boy, and it was only my second try.

I could remind him that a life sentence often comes with major inconveniences, but sometimes the best answer is silence.

Me: Daddy had his probation interview today.

This makes Uncle Sebastian grin.

Uncle Sebastian: What exactly did he do to that guy? Slap him? Here you can go to jail for giving someone a slap. It's a fucked up world.

Me: He threw a pot of hot soup at him.

Uncle Sebastian (chuckling): Is that all?

Me: He was badly scalded. No injuries from the machete, thankfully.

Uncle Sebastian (shaking his head): Mad. What's happening to all of us. Mamma would say it's a curse. *Old Bailey*. Who would've thought I'd get to Old fucking Bailey! The guy in the dock beside me was sentenced to life in jail. The one before him got thirty years. If I don't get my trial transferred, I'll end up rotting in this place too.

Prison guard: Five minutes!

I sip my coffee. Uncle Sebastian slurps his tea.

Uncle Sebastian: Tell me about you. Are you sleeping with that lawyer?

Me (shocked): What? No!

Uncle Sebastian: He had his eyes glued to your bum, the dirty motherfucker. I told you, didn't I? They're all *please* and *thank you* and *how do you do*, but at the end of the day, it's all about their cocks.

Me (laughing): You don't change, Sebastian.

Uncle Sebastian: Look after yourself. If they move me, don't you dare come back. I'm not worth it. Be smart, Carmen. Don't come back, you hear me?

Tears well up in my eyes. I hold his hand. There's a pale mark on his ring finger. Uncle Sebastian notices me looking.

Uncle Sebastian: For every end, there's a new beginning.
I'm halfway across the cafeteria when I hear him shout.
Uncle Sebastian: Say yes, Carmen!
Me: What?
Uncle Sebastian: You always wanted a Beverly Hills wedding,
didn't you? James Hunter will give you one.
Me: I thought you didn't believe in love.
Uncle Sebastian: I believe in luck.

James Hunter's doing something with his shoes.
James Hunter: Still haven't learned how to do laces properly.
Wish my mum was here.
He laughs.
Me (smiling): I'll see you around.
James Hunter: You need a lift?
At that moment my phone rings.
Me: Excuse me. Hello?
Alex: It's me. Listen Carmen, I have a big favour to ask. I'm
on my knees, literally.
The last time I saw Alex on her knees, when I came home
early from my evening shift at the restaurant, well. It wasn't
such a happy occasion.
Me: I'm miles away, Alex.
Alex: We were meant to start at 12, but they're having some
technical difficulties. I'll be late. Probably very late. And my
husband is in bloody Leeds. Fancy him being around when I
need him most!
Alex is going to be on *Channel 5*, talking about her latest piece
of research on rheumatoid arthritis, offering insight into revolu-
tionary treatment. She's a hotshot scientist.
Me (to James Hunter): Can you drop me in Ealing?
James Hunter: Yes.
Me: How long will it take?
James Hunter: An hour, at least.
He doesn't seem disturbed by the thought. I remember what
an interpreter told me, that barristers, like criminals, don't

belong to anyone. They work the hours they choose.

James Hunter: I have the afternoon off.

Alex: Who are you talking to? You're not at the pub again, are you? It's two in the fucking afternoon!

Me: I can be at the school by three. You might want to ring them in case I'm late.

James Hunter (driving): He's not really your friend, is he?

Me: What do you mean?

James Hunter: I saw him looking at you.

Me (smiling): He says the same about you.

James Hunter (blushing): I was worried about you being in there with him.

Me: He was handcuffed to the table. Besides, he's harmless.

James Hunter: That's quite a statement to make about someone who drove a truck into a market with a pregnant kidnap victim inside.

A rush of heat. My skin is on fire, eating itself out; a wave of ice-cold realisation. Christina Petru is dead. Uncle Sebastian killed her. The madness on the news. Mother's brother, branded a terrorist until it was revealed that he wasn't Muslim. Ten people injured. I don't tell James what I know, that Orlando Batista is a stranger whose passport was stolen on a crowded Barcelona metro, and processed as part of Uncle Sebastian's new identity. I don't tell him that Christina was Uncle Sebastian's wife, but the baby wasn't his. None of them were; they couldn't, because a test result came back telling him that he was sterile, and a phone transcript proved what no one could ever had guessed. I don't tell him that the investigation into the disappearance of Giuliano Banu, a policeman's son, was reopened, stretching for months through the Romanian lazy justice system.

An hour later, James Hunter's Toyota stops by the school gates.

Me: Thank you.

I watch the black car swerving through the afternoon traffic. Parents and childminders stand in groups, young children crying in buggies. I've spent so little time with Alex's children. But would it have been wise to let them love me, knowing that I loathed their very existence?

Man's voice: Hi.

I turn around, slowly. The man I've been avoiding for the last ten years smiles his crooked smile.

Me: Hi.

Apart from the bright blue eyes, there's little left of Zamfir Boc in the well built man before me. He still has the dip in his cheeks when he smiles, I notice. He hugs me, tight.

Zamfir: It's been too long.

Me: It has. How have you been? I thought you were in Leeds.

Zamfir: The best part about my job is that I can be anywhere. I was never a "9 to 5" man, anyway.

Me: A film producer, eh? I always thought you'd be in a rock band.

Zamfir (laughing): Film isn't a straightforward career, either. It suits me, though.

The gates open and we follow the line of parents to the school-yard.

Zamfir: I've heard about the trial.

Me: It'll be all right. Daddy's on medication. He pleaded guilty. He'll probably get a suspended sentence.

Zamfir: I'm talking about Sebastian.

Me: Oh.

Zamfir: I've thought about him a lot over the years.

Me: Don't.

Zamfir (holding my hand): I thought about you too.

My belly flips. I want to pull my hand back, but I can't, I won't, not yet.

Zamfir: I thought about us. And I wanted to say that I'm sorry.

The children burst out of the classroom, nearly knocking over their teacher, a young petite woman with glasses. The buzzing gets loud, *loud*, LOUD.

Zamfir: Say something.

Sophia: Daddy!

Not yet. Not yet. Please, not yet.

Emmanuel: Auntie! Look, Auntie's here!

Emmanuel jumps in my arms and Sophia runs into Zamfir's crotch. He groans and bends over in pain. Our eyes meet. He's still handsome, a faded version of his younger self.

My phone beeps. *Going out for dinner with the crew. Can't get away. Can you stay the night?*

Zamfir (over my shoulder): Say yes.

Me: I really can't stay.

Zamfir: You wouldn't say that if you tried my korma chicken.

Me (snorting): You can't cook.

Zamfir: I'm pretty good for someone who spends his life on the road.

Alex's home is a two storey house in Brentford. Semi-detached; all cream walls and sofas and mirrors. The photographs tell the story of her life: Alex smiling on her graduation day at Cambridge, her wedding with Zamfir, her water birth of the twins. The air is heavy with the scent of pomelo from her favourite air conditioner, made by *The White Company* and no doubt expensive.

Daddy has gone to bed after insisting on washing the dishes, and by eight o'clock he was already under the effects of the Proxilin. The children are in bed, too: the soft, creepy notes of their bedtime music floats down the stairs. The kitchen tap drips, *drip-drip-drip.*

Zamfir pours me another drink, and then, of course, another. The wine, a beautiful French red, is cool from the cellar, the dark bottle coated with dust. I want to put my lips on the bottle's mouth and just drink and drink and drink.

The man I love licks his fingers. Instead of the 69 ring he now wears a silver wedding ring with my sister's name engraved inside. The korma sauce was delicious. The salad was delicious. Zamfir's lips as he sucks his fingers are delicious. His eyes, bright in the candlelight, travel all over my chest. Behind him, the garden begins to fade in the spectacular sunset.

Zamfir: Take off your top.

Me: Why aren't you in Leeds?

Zamfir: Finished early.

Me: Liar.

The floor moves. Zamfir catches the plate midair.

Me: Shit. That was close.

One hand on my waist. The other pulls me towards him by the waist of my jeans.

Me: Stop.

The walls are a carousel of shadows, turning round and round and round: Alex smiling in the photographs, in a past that should never have been. I should be living in this house; I should be Zamfir's wife; the sleeping children should be mine.

And then I'm in *her* bedroom. Not as tidy as it used to be, but I don't know if that's Zamfir or the fact that she never has any time. He's on top of me, just like all those years ago, his body strong, his fingers working on my buttons, quick, urgent. His hands on my breasts, his mouth on mine: I can taste korma and wine. On the bedside cabinet is a framed picture of my parents. I can't tell the year with certainty, but Daddy's middle-age charms were fading. The considerable age gap between them was beginning to show.

Woman at the beach: *Congratulations, you have three beautiful daughters.*

Daddy: *This is my wife.*

A pair of scissors: green handle, a curved blade with the label of a pair of M&S briefs still attached to it.

Me (holding out the scissors): Stop!

Zamfir (jumping back): What's wrong with you?

Me: I can't do this.

Zamfir: What's the big deal? We've done it before.

Me (sitting up): I'm seeing someone.

Zamfir: Who?

Me: None of your business.

Zamfir: You're lying. I mean, just look at you. Smelling of booze in the middle of the day, and you haven't brushed your hair in God knows how long. Who would want to sleep with you?

Me: The kind of guy who sleeps with both sisters for months before choosing the one who can support him?

Zamfir: You're out of your mind, thinking you can say no to a mercy fuck.

I burst out laughing. Suddenly I feel very sober. I leave the room, cross over the landing. My shoes are at the top of the stairs: I must have dropped them when Zamfir carried me up.

The dining room is the image of decadence: plates coated in fragrant curry, wine stained glasses, crispy discs of popadom shattered on the floor. *Let him explain.* I feel awkwardly strengthened, full of resolve. For the first time ever I feel sorry for Alex, having to walk into this prison, day after day. I yank open the door just as Alex's cab pulls over.

Alex: Good timing.

She's stylish in her pencil dress, a pearl necklace she didn't have on today around her neck. Alex spends so much time in her office that she keeps spare clothes and jewellery in a small *Ikea* cabinet.

Me: Should you be drinking in your condition?

Alex (pointing to Zamfir's blue Mercedes): What the hell is he doing home?

Me: You ask *him* that.

Alex: Why do you have to be so angry? You and Zamfir are history. Get over it.

Me: Gotta go. (to the cab driver) You free?

Alex: Daddy gave you everything, and what do you do? Still hover around people like Sebastian like a little fucking dog.

Me: Sebastian is your uncle. He paid your top private school fees when Daddy went bankrupt. And how do you repay him? By saying you don't know him when shit hits the fan.

Alex: I don't know Orlando Batista. Besides, I've a reputation to keep.

Me: Where was your reputation when you sucked Zamfir's cock every day while I worked my butt off to support you both? Who's the little fucking dog now?

I slam the car door.

Me: Let's go.

Alex (pulling the door open): You know what your problem is? *Mother*. You still can't get over what happened to her. It was her choice, Carmen! Her choice!

I give her a shove and she falls back into the mud. The rain drenches her in seconds.

Mother: Sometimes the best way to help someone is not to help them. I'm talking about Sebastian. If anything happens to him, it's all Mamma's fault, you know.

Alex once told me that some very aggressive forms of arthritis can turn a person into a tree. That's how I feel now: a deformed tangle of inflexible roots and knots and branches, hundreds of years old.

Cab Driver: Where to?

It's still dark outside when I wake up in James Hunter's warm bed. I'm drenched in cold sweat: the nightmare that tormented me all night starts bleeding its horror over my conscious mind. The words I refused to register yesterday now make perfect sense.

"Where do you think Zamfir was the night you were raped, Carmen? Why do you think he didn't turn up?"

"He was late. He was very late. When he couldn't find me at the bar, he phoned you."

"Bullshit. I was driving around, looking for you, when I saw him snogging some bitch in an entryway. I yelled at him to get the fuck inside the car."

James Hunter lives like a bachelor, with books, overflowing wash baskets, and two cats, snow white as camouflage against the bedsheets.

I take my time showering in his bathroom, lathering my hair with his *Jo Malone* shampoo, watching the sun rise through the fabulous glass wall.

When I go back to the bedroom wrapped in one of his fluffy towels, he's wide awake.

James: You cut your hair.

I run my hand through the shoulder length, damp strands. Zamfir was right. My hair was so long and tangled, the only possible solution was chopping it. Which I did, with an antique pair of scissors I found lying on a chest of drawers.

James: I know this isn't particularly romantic, but we're going to have breakfast with my parents. (He blushes) They're here for the weekend.

Me: *My name is Carmen, and I'm an alcoholic.*

Everyone: *Good morning, Carmen.*

Group leader: *Carmen, how long have you been sober?*

Me: *Three months, two weeks, four days.*

Alex didn't turn up at court. She blamed her pregnancy, as I knew she would. Daddy's lawyer built his defense on madness: according to him, Daddy suffered from treatable psychosis, which caused him to form an unhealthy negative attraction to Colonel Boc. He went as far as to say that Daddy imagined the romance between him and Mother, and he invoked the cocktail of medication Daddy took on a regular basis to manage his delusions.

Daddy (in the dock): Rubbish. Utter rubbish.

The prosecution, on the other hand, insisted the attack had been premeditated, their most crucial piece of evidence being the fact that Daddy boiled water at nine in the morning. I had to smile at that. Indeed, no one in England makes soup so early in the day.

The eighth hearing was also the last, and over within the hour. Daddy got a ten months suspended sentence, and was ordered to pay Colonel Boc a small compensation.

Defense lawyer: Do you have an income?

Daddy: Only my pension, £400 a month.

I knew what the lawyer was thinking: how can an engineer retire with only £400 a month. If only he knew that, in Romania, £400 was an excellent pension.

The view from the hotel stretches over the green fields of St

Albans. It's the kind of place where you expect to see horses, although the meadow is almost too magical to be anything but the habitat of fairies and elves. This perfect beauty is somewhat artificial. If it weren't for the aromas of cut grass and rain soaked earth, you could be looking at a picture: the picture of peace and happiness, a 3D snippet from some enchanted reality. And yet, beyond belief, this is my wedding day.

The reception is a discreet affair. Seventy guests only, mostly James' family and friends. No music, just speeches, and the cake is a tower of stinky cheeses: Gruyere, Raclette, Tomme de Chevre. At the top, ironically, sits the Stinking Bishop, made from the milk of the Gloucester cows. Cheese education was a compulsory part of my engagement, since stinky cheese is James' favourite dessert.

Daddy: You remember Auntie Nell?

Me: The one who has eleven kids? How could I forget her?

Daddy: Her wedding had no music, either. No music and no alcohol, because she turned Adventist. And they had no wedding bands.

Me: Well, there's plenty of booze here. And we have wedding bands, too. Thanks, Daddy.

Daddy kisses Mother's wedding ring on my finger.

Daddy: He's a great guy, James.

James: Are you talking about me?

He raises the flute. Golden champagne sparkles in the fading sunlight. It doesn't bother me that I'm only drinking freshly squeezed apple juice, mixed with the finest sparkling water.

James: You look beautiful.

Me: And tired.

James touches my stomach.

James: I thought tonight might be a good idea to tell everyone.

Me: No way. I'm not ready yet.

James: I wonder if it's a boy or a girl.

Me: It's going to be a boy. I already have the name.

James: Yes?

Me: Sebastian.

James: Mm, not sure about that. You know why? Do you remember that guy at Bellmarsh? *Orlando Batista*?

My blood runs cold. Goosebumps rise on my arms, spread all the way down my back. *Does he know? Could he possibly?* ...

James: Turns out his real name is Sebastian Petru. He was extradited back to Romania for the trial. Two weeks after he arrived, all the witnesses in the trial either died, vanished, or withdrew their testimonies. He was acquitted. It's unbelievable. I mean, he was in for so many offences: cigarette contraband, sex trafficking, drugs. The guy was a pro.

Sebastian Petru. Of course, Petru is Uncle Sebastian's married name. For the first time, this mysterious act reveals its significance. Uncle Sebastian didn't just want to protect himself. He wanted to protect all of us.

Me: Terrible.

Waitress: Mrs Hunter?

James (smiling): That would be you.

Me: Yes?

Waitress: Phone call for you.

Me: Excuse me.

James' fingers brush against mine. A sudden September gust makes me shiver. The skies are grey, bloated with rain.

Mother: Turner's skies are always grey. The colour of my moods.

Me: Hello?

Nothing but static at the other end of the line. Then the noise begins: slowly at first, then crescendo, until time rewinds to the night I'd rather forget, and yet I can't, *won't*, SHOULDN'T. I see myself waltzing with Sebastian. I see Mother stuck to Colonel Boc like a giant fleshy sticker. I see Giuliano Banu, frozen like a rabbit in the headlights.

The phone goes dead. The receptionist hands me a parcel.

Receptionist: Sign here. And, Mrs Hunter.

Me: Yes?

Receptionist: *Casa de piatra.*

She speaks Romanian with a Northern accent – Baia Mare, perhaps? The accent Daddy had before it was washed out by Mother's Southern slang.

Me: I'm very grateful.

I should've said something else, maybe given the girl a tip, asked her where she was from, how long she'd been away; the sort of questions one immigrant asks another. The unwritten rule of courtesy, but my mind was paralysed. I told James I had to lie down for a bit, that the baby made me tired. He gave me the key to the nuptial room. I wasn't meant to see it; not until later anyway.

My hands are shaking so hard I can't find the lock. Then at last, the door is open.

Strangely, the room is full of smoke. There's a man on the balcony, behind the white curtain. In the short time it took me to get here, the sun has come out again, and now it shines full force, but this is not unusual for England. I feel dizzy. Is this some kind of a joke? Was Daddy thinking of surprising me? And if so, how come Grandpa missed the ceremony?

Me: Grandpa?

Grandpa doesn't answer. It's him all right; in his Sunday suit, with the bow Mother got him for his sixtieth birthday, and his brown framed glasses, but the last time I saw him, he was in a wheelchair, living in the mountain home that Alex pays for. He just couldn't live alone in the house he shared with Mitzi, not after she was gone.

The curtain is blurry like steam rising from a waterfall. I get tangled in it, trying to find the gap, the parting that doesn't exist. I'm trapped on the other side of the see-through curtain, and the door to the other world has closed.

Grandpa: If you fall from here, salud.

Me: No. No, No, NO!

Grandpa doesn't hear me. He peeks down over the edge, to the sun-soaked playground where the men play chess in the shade of the dusty poplars. It's midsummer. Mitzi is washing her cup in the kitchen. I grip the curtain, ripping it with my nails, but it's solid and liquid all at once, something that doesn't rip.

Mitzi: I'm sorry, Stelian, but you called us here in the middle of the night. Now you need to hear us.

I turn around. Daddy is twenty years younger. He's wearing the purple shirt I haven't seen him wear in donkey's years. Grandpa is now in the room, too.

Grandpa: Don't you go defending her!

Uncle Sebastian: I have a better idea.

It's now. It's going to happen any moment. I can't bear it. I can't hear it. I can't ...

I've covered my ears, but I still hear Mother's scream; through my closed eyelids I still see the flash of her bright red claws on the rail as she slips away.

First I heard Mother's scream.

Then the thump, like the splat of a watermelon bursting open.

Alex and I race each other there, but it's too late. Mother's soul has already left. It smells of fresh warm pretzels, Mother's favourite.

James finds me in a pool of blood. The baby is yet another thing Mother took from me.

The cashier at Barclays stares at me over her glasses.

Cashier: Did you sell your car?

I smile.

Me: An inheritance. And in fact, I'd like to make an anonymous donation.

Cashier: How much?

I've never thought to count the 500 euro notes found in the parcel Uncle Sebastian sent me. I didn't know what to do with the cash until I saw an announcement on Facebook. A thirty year old Romanian nurse had collapsed at a hospital in New York. It was revealed that she had cancer, metastatic, no insurance, and she needed to undergo surgery. Not to save her life, but to make the rest of her life humane. It seemed as good a cause as any.

Mitzi: Blood money should be given away.
Cashier: Here.
She hands me a note she found at the bottom of the box.
Congratulations. P.S. I told you he was looking at your arse.

James and I bought a new house in St Albans, but that's not the first thing I see when I open my eyes. The walls are bright red, at least what I can make out through the lacy black bed curtains. James isn't next to me; a girl with the face of a doll sleeps with her head on my bare breasts.

It all comes back to me: this was our second wedding night, to make up for the lost one. A threesome is something both of us always wanted to do. Saiko is an escort we found in the photo album of a prestigious escort agency. I chose her because of my past; the half-Japanese aristocrat in the painting on Mrs Papp's wall.

I untangle myself from her, and for a while I watch them sleeping: her dark hair on my pillow, his hands on her breast, Daddy's wedding ring shining on his finger. *Sai-Ko.* It sounds almost like a lullaby. And then I know.
Me: If it's a girl, I want her to be called Sai-Ko.
James: An escort's name?
Me: A different name. Sai-Ko Hunter. When I was growing up, I was just a different girl with an ordinary name. I don't know what hurt more: that I was different or that my name wasn't. I want Sai-Ko's non-English half to be celebrated.
James: But it's an Asian name. You're European.
Me: That's beside the point.

I find Alex waiting for me in the new teashop in Ealing, in the mother and baby section.
Alex: About time.
Me: Sorry. Parking is a nightmare around here.
Alex: Can't believe you passed your driving test. Again, about time.
Me: So, what's the big news? Another baby?
Alex: I'm having a divorce. Sorry, I shouldn't really tell you

today.

Me: Why not today?

Alex: As in, you've just been accepted to University.

Me: It's not a celebration. I've a long way to go, still.

Alex: I always knew you'd be a lawyer.

Me: Don't lie.

Alex: You know how you always used to stand up for everyone?

Me: There's more to a lawyer than that.

Alex (winking): Apparently so.

Okay, so maybe it wasn't a good idea to tell Alex about the repeat wedding night. Chances are, she'll tease me about it forever.

Me: Good for you, by the way. You deserve better.

Alex: He was seeing some famous bitch from the *Game of Thrones* set.

Me: Some sex-on-toast cheapy, no doubt. Besides, you're also a famous bitch.

Alex (smiling): Congratulations. By the way, when were you going to tell me?

Me: How did you know?

Alex: I'm a mum, remember. Not the best mum, but I've been there. Can't believe she's one already.

She clips up her bra and places the sleeping toddler in the pram. Camille is the spitting image of Zamfir; so much that I can't look at her without a sinking feeling.

Me: You're a great mum.

Alex: Liar.

Me: By the way. There's something I always wanted to do. I take out the dollar note from my purse.

Me: Give you back your dollar. And this.

Alex holds the prayer book in her hands for a second.

Alex: I stopped praying a long time ago.

Me: That's why you married Zamfir Boc.

Alex: I agree. Besides, only prayers could've brought James Hunter into your life. A threesome on a repeat wedding night? Goodness me. These lawyers aren't as boring as I thought.

A Bright Day for a Funeral

The news travelled like wildfire.

Everyone agrees, Tanti Lucia's death had been predictable. Hadn't she lived her final years glued to the *chaise-longue* in the shadow of the old linden tree? More shrivelled up and quiet each day, as if she was already melting in the shadows.

The courtyard is still spectacular, a hundred years on from the death of its aristocratic owners. From the back orchard, the breeze carries the breath of ripe, bitter cherries. Their dark juice stains your fingers. A partly renovated manor with an ancient gold knocker gives everything the air of a ghost town populated by humans.

In the kitchen with vast windows overlooking the linden tree and Tanti Lucia's empty seat, Helga smokes a cigarette listening to the maddening drip of the broken tap.

Helga can't prepare wheat porridge pie. It's meant to be a secret, one of the many things she keeps from her husband. For years, her sister did all the heavy cooking – the Easter marble cakes that took two hours to knead and a whole day to rise, the baked sweet rolls, the leaves fresh from her tree filled with spiced rice, no thinner than a finger. The marvellous parties she threw were all catered by her sister, and almost always culminated in copious rows.

But for once Retta is unavailable. Gone to visit her grandchildren in England, and could barely make it back in time for the funeral – let alone cook for it.

Helga was furious at first. How was she to send her mother-in-law to the shadow world without a proper wheat porridge pie? No one had yet seen a funeral without a pie the size of a tyre, decorated with round mints or coated peanuts, powdered with icing sugar, a yellow wax candle burning on top. And what was wrong with Retta, getting on a plane at her age?

That picture of her on Facebook, drinking wine on some boat anchored on the River Thames. She wasn't wearing the floral headscarf Helga hadn't seen her without since they were children, and it looked like she'd dyed her hair. She'd be coming back with airs and graces. Before you knew it she'd want to go back, and it would just be a matter of time before she stopped cooking for her altogether.

The first visitor arrives holding a large bouquet of peonies and a bunch of candles.

"May her soul rest in peace."

"She's at the chapel," Helga replies, her eyes on the blood-red peonies. Her mother had a patch of peonies, crimson, violet, fuchsia, growing next to a shrub of wild mint. Helga liked to rub the hairy leaves between her fingers and chew them before a date.

The auntie gasped. "The chapel?"

It was unheard of, taking your dead to the chapel, not allowing them to spend the three required days on the dining room table. The heat, Helga thinks, fanning herself with a recipe book, is the excuse. It's true that she had a young granddaughter living in the house, but this is still her small revenge.

Her husband agrees. In the past, when his blood was hot, he knocked her about a bit, but their relationship was passionate, even scandalous. Old age made him docile, and he even finds it in him to praise her. In return, she cooks him his favourite meals, leaving the trays on the floor of his room, where he lives surrounded by cats and books.

Helga stirs her coffee and tastes it. The prints of her thin rouged lips stay on the cup, and she remembers all the love letters she signed with her lips. The coffee is just right, black and sugary, the kind of coffee that goes well with a cigarette. She takes a huge gulp of the cool morning air through her flowing nicotine stained curtains. A breeze blows from the sea, travelling up and down her thighs like a man's touch. The house is asleep, and the thought that her mother-in-law isn't here anymore is as sweet as young love. Helga is sixty years old, but as she stares into the misty September morning, she feels twenty again.

The church stands at the end of an unpaved road, its bells tolling in the serene sky, blackened steeples crumbling in the heat. It's a bright day for a funeral, with a little breeze to soothe the cheeks, shoulders and feet burnt to a reddish caramel by the midday sun. But the afternoon is charged with something evil, like the aftermath of war.

It's not such a bad thing, after all, allowing the dead to rest in church, under the watchful eyes of the saints. The dead with the dead, and the living with the living – isn't that what her sister always said?

"Mother, what are you doing here? Shouldn't we be getting ready? The mourners are on their way." Her daughter Octavia appears at the top of the stairs, a gown tied around her plump body.

"Why? She's at the chapel, here they have no one to mourn."

"And why are you not wearing black?" Octavia demands.

Her marriage is another thing she owes to her sister. As a young carer at the Municipal Hospital, Helga had nursed the hope of marrying a rich doctor. She may not have had a good dowry, but the gods had been kind. With her tar-black eyes and enigmatic smile, Helga was the cheap version of a movie star. No wonder her first mentor, a middle-aged physician, had taken a shine to her. The doctor wasn't interested in marriage, but he offered a stash of cash and moved to a different town.

It was Retta who'd arranged for an appointment with the village abortionist. They were five in total, the babies, one for each of her lovers. The last was a failed abortion. By the time she detected it she was almost dead herself. The thing was so big and looked so human, it had to be buried in the garden, by the fragrant roots of the peonies.

She would always remember the fifth: the tickle of its father's moustache on her breasts, the rough way his hands spread her legs, the cold sound of his zip in the silence of the woods.

She was twenty-one when she fell pregnant for the sixth time. Her lover was the only son of the richest couple in town. The

Stanniattis were landowners of old. At last, Helga had hit the jackpot.

Anghel and Helga were in love. There was only one problem. *His mother.*

Tanti Lucia had not always been the obedient shadow she became in the last years of her life. Once a fierce young woman with clown-red hair, pencil-drawn eyebrows and a diamond as big as a peanut on her finger, she made the servants stick to the wall when she stormed past. Helga saw the fury in her eyes the day Retta dragged her there, the baby ticking like a grenade in her belly.

"You may not disturb my son. He's resting."

Retta pushed past Tanti Lucia into a fabulous dining room, holding Helga's hand. The arrangement of furniture was different; the house, however, hadn't lost its aloof energy. The hostility lived in every crumb of stone.

Forty years went by, and still the crystal armoires gave Helga vertigo as if she was looking through the wrong pair of glasses. The old house was vivid in Helga's mind, as alive as when she first drank in the sight of it: the piano in a corner, large velvet drapes at the windows, antique mirrors and the rich tapestry she took great pleasure in ripping with her claws when they redecorated.

Helga and her daughter worked together to bring a breath of the *now* and the *new* into the grumpy old mansion. Gone were the squeaky floorboards, the Oriental rugs and the ancient coffee tables. The sofas with curly legs and the eighteenth century beds were sent to the tip in the back of a truck. The house was beginning to look young, even modern: an airy haven with freshly painted terracotta stoves, webs of iron roses on the windows and bulletproof doors. A beautiful prison, so decrepit you could never quite scrub off the scent of death.

Helga sniffs. It's there all right, an almost imperceptible whiff of naphthalene, mould masked by lavender cologne.

The sumptuous double doors, the twisting staircase, the children's theatre. Even in its old age, the place is as pretty as a doll's house, and just as unusual. To this day, Helga has not visited all the musty cellar rooms. The dark frightens her; it brings back the faces of her dead babies.

She'd have taken a hammer to the doors herself. It was the money to replace them she lacked, not the madness. And there was nothing she could do about the high vaulted ceilings, the cavernous servant rooms, dark as rat holes. She eventually put them to good use. For years, her lord husband and his lady mother nested in them, smelly old foxes in their rightful lairs.

The first time she met Tanti Lucia was the first time she'd ever been to her lover's house. That day, her sister gave her a lesson in combat. Holding a weapon didn't make you a warrior. You had to raise the axe. You had to bring it down.

That fateful day, Anghel's rooms were locked for over fifteen minutes. Tanti Lucia pounded on the wall with her jewelled fists. At last her son emerged, negligently dressed in a dark red velvet gown; his delicate feet in soft slippers, his fingers holding a cigar, his belly white and bald like a snake's. He announced the engagement in his nasal headmaster's voice, without even asking Helga. No one asks the apple if it wants to be eaten.

Helga sighs. Retta was a powerful speaker; very academic, in her few years at school. But for some reason her parents decided to waste the savings they had on the youngest, the daughter who wouldn't have been born if Jesus hadn't visited the family a night before the village healer was scheduled to arrive with her butchery tools. What a paradox, making the journey from unwanted to favourite in such a short time. She was born with natural charm, but an airhead. Retta was her brain, her oracle. Helga never made any important decision without consulting her. Sometimes Retta read her coffee cup, and Helga pretended to laugh at the complicated patterns where she saw nothing but Retta's eagle eyes unravelled mysteries.

She knows she should be in the kitchen, preparing the food, practising her tears, getting everything ready for the mourners. She checks her phone again. You can do anything with a smart-phone these days. She's become addicted to Facebook. And Wikipedia. She scrolls down the newsfeed and sees another picture of Retta dressed in a ridiculous outfit – my Lord, it must be an Indian sari. Getting drunk by the river, playing fancy dress while she's stuck here at the funeral with the cooking that was Retta's job – her responsibility.

She'd never admit it, but sometimes Helga wonders how far they'd have gotten in life if Octavian hadn't been born. Octavian and Octavia were twins; two peas in a pod. A miracle they were both born alive; the doctor offered to abort one of them early on to give the other a chance. He'd been a clingy child, and she favoured him over his sister.

Helga extinguishes her cigarette and is about to get up to make an attempt at that awful porridge cake when she sees a child at her gate. At first she thinks he's a beggar, but then, as her eyesight adjusts to the honeyed September light she recognises her grandson, Ali. He comes down the path towards her, smiling. Helga can see at once that he's hiding something under his T-shirt.

"What are you doing here?" Helga snaps, but seeing the boy's startled face, she softens. "Here, sit next to Nanny. Have you eaten today?"

The boy shakes his head.

"Isn't that granddad of yours looking after you, eh?"

"He's out," the boy replies.

Helga clicks her fingers and the old woman sleeping in the shadow of the cherry tree opens her eyes.

"Bring the boy some soup, and a loaf of bread."

"Yes, ma'am." The servant rushes to the summer kitchen.

Helga turns her attention to the boy. The spitting image of Octavian. Nothing from his mother; it's as if the father made him alone. She reaches out to smooth his hair behind his ears.

"You walked by yourself, all this way?" She clicks her tongue in disapproval. "Anything could've happened."

The boy grins and pats his belly. "Here. That's where I keep my iPad. No one stole it. That's the worst that could happen."

"No, that's not the worst. You could get hit by a car. Kidnapped. And if you're mugged, it's only your fault. You're eight years old, and shouldn't go round the streets alone." She sighs. The boy yawns. Helga notices the dark circles around his eyes.

"Goodness me. What time did you go to bed last night?"

Ali shrugs. "Mummy told me to sleep alone. I didn't sleep at all, not with the lights off." He bows his head. "It was a punishment."

Helga feels a hotness in her cheeks. "Punishment for what?"

"For not getting a full score in my maths test."

"So? It's not that she's some kind of mathematician." *Nor is your dad*, she thinks.

The soup arrives, steamy and full of flavour. Helga always makes cucumber soup this time of year. It's almost as refreshing as a shower. The boy wolfs it down with bread. He looks like he hasn't eaten in days.

When did the situation spiral out of control? They used to be a family. When Octavian married Olga, Helga swelled with pride. Not only did she come from a good local family, but she worked as an executive at one of the largest firms in Bucharest.

Then things went wrong. Octavian made bad friends. He slept around. He spent a year bedridden with syphilis. There were nights when she woke up to the giggle of the cheap whores he brought home when his wife was away on business. And he gambled.

They sold everything to pay his debts: the vineyards, the orchards, the cornfields. Without his inheritance her husband was like a snail out of its shell. Lord Penniless, she called him. He kept the pretence but he was powerless. And then it was up to her to deal with everything.

If only she'd known this as a young girl: rich men marry to be served.

Even so, Olga and Octavian would still be married if her cousin's husband, that damned Horatio, hadn't made it his life purpose to separate them. He gambled with Octavian side by side; he whored with him; and they worked together. Not only did he take over the business her son had set up with his brilliant mind and contacts – and which he was forced to give away cheaply to his partner to cover his debts. He also coveted his wife. Cursed was the day her cousin Cornelia ever married him.

The day he told Olga the truth, the castle of lies collapsed. Horatio was now installed in Olga's Bucharest flat, living a life of luxury, dining with celebrities. And, the cherry on the cake, Cornelia is still with him. How could anyone dare to tell Helga that this mad world made any sense?

The boy had never lived with his parents. When his grandmother passed away after a long battle with cancer, everyone expected Olga to bring Ali to her home in Bucharest. After all, how could a single elderly man care for a young boy?

And now she had the audacity to give him punishments over the phone. Helga will have a few words with VIP Olga when she gets hold of her.

"Have you finished? Would you like a main course? I've made rabbit stew. Your favourite."

"Rabbit stew is MY favourite, Helga. Not his." Her granddaughter Narcisse had appeared out of nowhere, swinging dangerously low in the wicker rocking chair, her bare feet on the table. She is buttoning on her iPhone.

Helga looks at her rounded hips, the large breasts, the waist-long hair sticking to her sweaty arms. When did she get so big?

"Get your feet off the table, and put something on, everyone can see your legs from the road! Goodness me, your grandmother is dead, and you're walking around with no clothes on! Have you no shame?" She sighs. "Where's your mother? Go and fetch her, tell her Ali is here."

"I'm too hot to move," moans Narcisse, uncrossing her legs and clicking a small hand fan on between them. "Can I have some stew?"

"No, you may not. You're on a diet, remember? Besides, didn't you proclaim yourself a vegetarian?"

"That was yesterday," Narcisse says.

Ali bursts out laughing. Helga smiles. She lights a cigarette. "Do you like rabbit, then?"

The boy nods vigorously. The servant brings the food. Helga leaves him sucking on a rabbit leg and she slips into the house. She sits in her favourite chair in her sanctuary, facing the ancient cooker and the chipped sink with a skinny tap whose shadow on the wall reminds her of a miniature giraffe's neck. At her feet sleeps a ginger cat and Helga dips a toe with a curved red nail in the fat furry tummy. The cat stretches and curls its body over her foot. Lady the bitch gives her a dirty look from the corner where she lies dying. The dog has served her well; better even than Retta.

She puts her glasses on to look for Christian's number. The phone rings and rings. Finally the old man answers. Breathless, the dirty old bugger. Having sex at his age, when he's got a serious heart condition, as if he didn't have any other responsibilities. Helga doesn't waste time with courtesies.

"Ali is here. He's walked all the way from your house. He's starving and has an iPad with him. And what's this about locking him in a dark room at night?" Helga pauses to catch her breath. "You need to come and get him, I have a funeral to attend to, the priest is on his way and nothing is ready."

"Yes, I heard. May God rest her soul. Listen, I'm a bit tied up right now."

Helga narrows her eyes.

In the background a woman's voice purrs: "Who is it, Chris?"

So the rumour *is* true. She knows that voice, she'd know it anywhere. Sanda's a new widow. An old schoolmate of her daughter's. She even had a fling with Octavian – but who didn't? Helga is not entirely surprised that she's in bed with her in-law. Didn't she always like old men? Wasn't she expelled when she was found astride her teacher on a summer camp? A hopeless case. If Helga would have a lover, would she choose someone who kept his dentures in a water glass on the bedside table? Certainly not.

A shiver of disgust shakes her to the core. What's wrong with these old people? Has the world gone mad? And still, she wonders ... no, that's impossible. Her husband stopped touching her more than twenty years ago. She stopped touching herself, too. Women her age are not meant to have sex. But ... the world is changing. If Retta had an affair in London, who would know? For a moment she feels savagely jealous of her sister.

"Hello? Helga? Did you hear what I said?"

"Listen. You come and get him in fifteen minutes, or I'll ring your daughter. I'd like a few words with her myself."

The old man sighs. "I'm not in town. I can make it there in half an hour."

"That's none of my business. *Fifteen minutes*. The boy is your responsibility. Why agree to look after him in the first place? You should've told Olga to pull her weight. She's not the only career woman in the country, you know. These days there are clubs, and nurseries, and nannies. It's ridiculous. Her married lover lives with her but her son doesn't!"

Helga almost screams when she sees the boy standing in the doorway.

"Stop sneaking up on me like that, boy! What are you doing, eavesdropping?"

"Nanny," he says. "Please don't call Mummy. She'll make me sleep in the dark again."

"She won't ever know if you sleep in the dark or not!" Helga yells. "She's a hundred miles away." Her hand trembles as she puts the phone back in its case.

Tears spring into the boy's eyes. "Yes she will. She can see me through the clocks. She's put cameras everywhere. And I have to keep the laptop open all night, so she can watch me on Skype."

Helga is filled with ice-cold horror. "Jesus Christ."

She takes the boy in her arms.

"Nanny, can I ask you something?"

"Anything, my love."

"Can I stay here with you? Can I sleep here tonight?"

Helga shakes her head. "You don't have your pyjamas. And how about your toothbrush?"

The boy grins and unzips his rucksack. "They're in here. Please, please, please, please?"

"What's that? You came all prepared? Don't I have a say in this?"

The boy wraps his arms around her neck.

"Doesn't that grandfather of yours look after you, eh?"

"He sits in the dark with his rum."

"The old bastard," Helga grumbles.

But deep down, she's used to it. Her house has always been a full house. She lived with her parents-in-law and when her daughter married, the young couple were installed in one of the house's many wings. She had brought up her granddaughters herself. Tatiana got married young. Narcisse still lived with them. She was friends with Ali. She supposed it might work. The only thing was, the mother had custody. Social services couldn't care less if she neglected him. They punished the poor, not the rich.

Helga is all in black when the priest arrives. Even at sixty, she is stunning, with her arched eyebrows and porcelain teeth. She wears a veil over her face, lace gloves, silk stockings. Her husband is in a dark suit, shiny shoes, and a black tie. Bright blue eyes sparkle in his pudgy face. Who would've thought that he'd turn out so obedient? She can barely remember the vicious lover with raised fists who terrified her in her youth.

He did everything she said. He even agreed that his mother be kept at the chapel. Their daughter and her daughters walk side by side in their dark dresses, carrying bunches of flowers and candles. How plain those girls are! Plain, just like her husband and his mother. Of them all, only Ali, the boy, inherited her charm. He would be the unlucky one. The gods can be cruel like that.

Her son Octavian is missing. He was already on the circuit when the death occurred. He'd rung earlier from Austria.

Octavian is a truck driver in Europe. It's the kind of job he loves: being on the road, picking up whores, earning. She supposed she ought to be pleased. If only her son hadn't once been professor of Political Science at the top university in the country, she could even find it in her heart to accept it.

In the church, she listens to the priest's singing and smells the incense as if in a dream. Helga watches her daughter. At least *she* is happy. At first Helga was worried when Octavia married a jobless writer, but they are happy and heavens, doesn't it all come down to that? She can hear them at night, making love in their quarters. How unhappy beautiful people are! How much bitterness in vanity! And how it all fades!

The mourners offer their condolences and place money in a tray near the dead woman's head. On Tanti Lucia's chest is an icon of Our Lady, and fragrant flowers surround her body.

"This is the best porridge pie I've ever tasted. Much better than the one you made for your father-in-law, God bless his soul. And look at this, how ingenious. You put all these lovely candies on top. Never had anything so fine! What are they?"

"M&M's and Skittles," the small boy answers.

Helga winks. She didn't really know what to say when Ali bragged about having made funeral porridge pie before, in a summer camp.

"It was a workshop called Little Masterchef," he explained.

"And they taught you to make funeral pie? Isn't that a bit morbid?"

The boy laughed. "We made rabbit and soups and cakes. By the way, your rabbit was overcooked."

Helga sucked her teeth. The world was changing all right. In her time, little boys knew nought of cooking.

She assisted her grandson in making the porridge pie, and it came out wonderful. Sprinkled with cocoa, not icing sugar. When it was done the little chef reached in his rucksack for a bag of sweeties.

"Lordy!" Helga's mouth dropped open when she saw the finished product. She would never need Retta again.

Rain pours down as the procession follows the coffin to the graveyard. A summer storm blackens the sky. Thunder erupts from deep inside the bloated bellies of the rain-filled clouds. A flash of lightning narrowly misses the priest as he holds the holy book over the grave.

By her side, Ali stands still. Helga feels a tightening in her chest. There were times when she pictured a hole in the ground and her mother-in-law lying in it. The old woman made her life hell. She had to work her way up to love, to acceptance, but, forty years later, her power was complete. If only Octavian hadn't ruined everything with his gambling, maybe she could have travelled the world with Retta. How she wanted to go on a cruise, have affairs and cocktails!

It was possible. Her kids were grown up. There was enough money in the land, and neither her nor Anghel were land people. There was enough life in her to pack up and start afresh. She'd never divorce him, of course, but that would have been a goodbye. In her reveries, her fifth lover, the pilot, welcomed her on the plane – a private jet. Even as a grey fox he'd made Helga catch her breath. Lucia's diamond necklace would be at her throat.

She's never been on a plane.

The necklace? Sold cheaply, to pay off the officers who dealt with Octavian's case. Diamonds could buy justice, especially in a shithole like this.

Who would have thought Retta, little old Retta, with her simple ways and that excuse of a husband, would be pampered like a queen and photographed in places Helga only saw in her dreams. London with those red houses and the luscious green parks and that famous river.

When they get home she heats up some dinner. Tomato soup, potato stew, fried pork. She smokes a cigarette while the kids eat around the kitchen table.

The boy watches the rain. "It's easier for a body to decompose in the heat," he says. The braces fit tighter on his teeth now, Helga has seen to that. She wonders how long he'd been wearing them the wrong way around, and how no one noticed. The deep cuts in his mouth bled; Helga rubbed glycerine on them, round and round and round until the boy bit her finger to make her stop.

Narcisse throws a slice of bread at him. "Shut up!"

"You're a clever clogs, aren't you?" laughs Helga, startled by her own voice. *An old woman's voice.* "What do you do all day, read?"

The boy nods, his mouth full. "Nanny, promise me you won't bury me when I die. Can I be cremated, please?"

"I won't have to worry about that. I'll be dead long before you."

"Nanny, how did she die?"

Helga busies herself at the sink, sponging the dirty plates with a wet cloth. Her nail varnish is chipped; her engagement sapphire embedded in her tanned, swollen finger.

"Tanti," the boy insists. "How did she die?"

Helga's eyes narrow. She stands at the sink, soapy water dripping from her apron onto the steps of the pedestal where the sink sits; the mocking throne where she wasted her life bent over a pile of filthy dishes.

She's sent the servant home. She can't afford a domestic, but Irina is a drunk, and she pays her in leftover brandy and food.

"Nanny?"

No one had asked her that, not even the pathologist who wrote the death certificate without even looking at the body. Everyone just assumed it was old age.

"She was old," Narcisse explains. "Everyone dies when they're old."

"There's always a cause of death," says Ali. "Always, always."

Thunder rumbles around the room, making Helga's heart beat faster. She watches the shadows around the darkening windows. In her feline eyes dances a glimmer of fear.

The kids go to bed and she stays to finish tidying the kitchen. She collects her husband's plates from the foot of his bed, covered in patterns of calcified food. Ten years ago, he diagnosed himself with chronic fatigue, but Helga knows better. She's too old to be fooled by these phonies.

Her eyes fall on the half-finished porridge pie. Why, they were just like that, *men*. Attractive on the outside, but inside they were nothing but plain wheat, only fit for the dead.

The kitchen is spotless when she finally retreats to her room.

She opens the door to refreshing coolness, the air vibrant with the whirr of the air conditioner. Her parents-in-law's bedroom. How she coveted it. And now she was here, and everything was hers. An elegant boudoir with high arched ceilings and extravagant French doors overlooking the garden.

Even after all these years, she still feels like a servant sneaking to the master's bed. But she insists on sleeping here, killing the shadows with violent artificial light, teasing the walls with her rude laughter, raping the bed where her husband raped her, with the weight of her body, sweating like a sow in the fine sheets. Helga is a hooligan in a sanctuary, a vandal lost in rapturous wrecking.

She closes her eyes. The bar had closed, but Helga is used to falling asleep with the sound of the game machines under her window. Like an amputee hurting for missing limbs, she still hears the reassuring buzz of the poker games, the whoosh of the roulette wheel, the shuffle of the playing cards. The bar kept them alive when all the money had gone; even though Retta said that owning a gambling business could only bring misfortune.

It all started with the gunshots she heard one night. At first she mistook them for champagne corks but when she peered out of the window, she saw the commotion. She barely had time to duck before a fourth bullet smashed her window.

Then Hortensia, her barmaid, was arrested for smuggling drugs to her boy in jail. Helga was astonished. Hortensia – the most honest person she knew.

"He made me do it," she wept when Helga visited her in prison. "A last favour, that's what he said."

Helga understood all too well. She knew what it was like to burn with love for a son. She knew what it meant to be judged.

A knock makes her look up. She pulls the nightgown over her legs. Her lips are parted.

"Yes?"

The door opens a crack, and the small boy creeps in, dressed in his pyjamas.

"What is it? Can't you sleep?"

"I just want to ask you something. I have to know."

"What?"

"Can I live here from now on? Please, Nanny. If you send me back to Granddad, I'll kill myself and then you really will have to worry about cremating me. It won't be easy. Our religion forbids it, Nana told me before she died."

"What's this? You're a blackmailer, just like your dad?" She sighs. "I said you could stay the night. That was the deal."

"I can help you in the kitchen," the boy says. "You do everything yourself, I saw it."

Helga's eyes fill with tears. She promised. She vowed, she'd never fall in love with a child again. Children are crueller than men. But this one is as persistent as his father. He sucked the love right out of her soul, the way his father sucked her breasts until there was no milk left for his sister.

She holds up the duvet and the small boy crawls in. The house is quiet and dark – so much emptier without the queen mother. She might have wished her dead, but her death meant that there were fewer people to go before it was her turn.

The boy was right. There must be a cause of death. But it wasn't her idea. Lucia had been nagging her about it for a while. It took her months to gather up the courage to enter the pharmacy and ask for a repeat prescription of sleeping pills.

"The other one was lost," she lied.

Behind the glasses, the chemist's eyes smiled.

She'd left Lucia with a large glass of water and the tiny pill jar. Just as she was closing the door, her mother-in-law called her back.

"Look after yourselves," she whispered. Her hands closed around her daughter-in-law's.

Helga found it in her to return the touch. Just a little squeeze, but the old woman received it as a blessing.

The next morning she woke up at dawn to remove the empty jar, wipe the froth from around the dead woman's mouth and close her eyes. She'd even felt sadness. But when her time came, she wished someone did the same for her before old age took away her dignity.

The warm weight of Ali's head presses on her chest. If anyone would do that for her, it would be him.

The sound of his breathing makes everything fall into place.

That old bastard hasn't arrived to collect him. But when he does, she'll tell him to leg it. From now on, she's in charge. She'll take the mother to court. This would be her last battle. She doesn't need allies. She learned to fight alone.

Glancing down at the small boy's sleeping face, she doesn't know which is worse: to be loved desperately or not to be loved at all.

Helga takes another long look at the portrait of her twenty-year-old self as a beauty queen on the wall, before she turns off the lamp and savours the silence.

Army of Angels

They lay down on their stomachs, fifteen, maybe twenty of them, two neat rows lined on the ground behind the cars, their hands on their rifles.

If I go now, I may have a few seconds before they start firing. The silence echoes in my ears. One second, ten, twenty. Black holes left by bullets in the distant walls look at me, hundreds of eyes waiting for my move. I crouch behind a van. Petrol drips on the cracked ice.

I wait.

If I go now, maybe they won't shoot just as I'm walking through them.

I run.

When I'm close enough for them to see me, I slow down. My right foot on the road. The snow sticks to my soles. *My left foot, heavier. My right foot. My left.*

I walk, looking down at my feet.

Emil is going to fire. He's suddenly gone very still. *The snow falls.*

He was wearing a mask. The man was wearing a mask. There, the snow is not yet red. I'm not dead, either. The air is grey and the gunpowder falls from the sky. Debris falls. *Tiny bits of wood and metal.* I sweep them off my coat. Pull my hood on.

The General looks old and tired. Something hangs from his hand, brushing the ground. *Is it a stocking?*

"You were wearing a mask, you bastard ..."

The General is crying. Large tears fall down his cheeks like ice drops. He pulls out his gun.

"You're making a mistake."

The man looks at me, cool eyes enlarged by the glass of his

spectacles.

"Millie, tell them."

The glasses slip down his nose; his bare eyes are frightening. His face is framed by snow-white hair.

Is it made of snow?

He removes a squashed pack of cigarettes from his jeans pocket – *contraband jeans* – pulls one out with his teeth and lights it from a trembling blue flame.

A black shadow grows in the empty white space. Shadows are bigger than the things they shadow. I close my eyes. A rhyme comes to my mind.

Crispy white hair, crispy white snow.

What are you? What are you?

I don't know.

The bullet whistles. I watch it spinning in the air. A small, fast bird.

The unseen bird flies right into his neck. Disappears inside it. I wait for it to come out from the other side.

But something else happens.

A purple spot grows on his skin. He can pretend he's been stung by a wasp, or that he had a penicillin injection. Maybe he can spit out the bullet and everything can be like before.

But something else happens.

His eyes lose focus.

He falls.

First to his knees, then to one side. His hands are now caught under his body. I think it would be okay to hold his hand, and yet it wouldn't. The smoke of his cigarette is the colour of winter.

His hair is snow-white, or the snow is hair-white.

I step back to keep the blood off my brand new boots. German boots are hard to find, even on the black market.

Grandma takes hold of my hand on the escalator. It froze overnight and now the mechanics are gazing at the bowels of it like surgeons into an open stomach. Their smiles are all bare gums and broken teeth. All of them are missing teeth.

Grandma's body swings from side to side. Her weight presses on my wrist. Is she pulling me along, or am I pulling her? Her carrier bag is orange today.

I'm late for school again. It took her too long to boil the two eggs, to spread the butter onto the thin slices of bread. We ate in the tiny warm kitchen, watching red cockroaches race each other across the brown and white squares of the linoleum. A cockroach game. I'm still trying to figure out the rules; the ball is a grain of sugar or a coffee bean. The stakes are high. If they are detected, their bellies burst open like fish-oil capsules.

Grandma stamps her fat foot on top of the winning cockroach. She removes her slipper and peels the dead thing off her sole.

"Bloody cockroaches," she mumbles, her mouth full of egg.

"The Chinese eat cockroaches," I say, thinking of what Mother-cockroach will do when her child doesn't get back home. But maybe cockroaches have so many eggs, that they can't keep track of all their children.

"Well we're not Chinese, are we?" Grandma spits in a tissue. "Hear the things she says, Cornelia? Someone should rip her head off and give her a new one."

Auntie nods. She drinks her coffee like an addict: her hands shaking, her eyes shiny. She always comes and drinks our coffee – real coffee, you can tell it's genuine by the silver stamp on the back. Grandma has good connections on the black market.

I drink coffee too. This is the real stuff, not chickpea dust. Grandma makes it milder for me, with milk and sugar. We have milk and sugar. We have books. We have foreign salami and Mozart chocolate and Palmolive soap.

For Auntie, she makes it black. Grandma says she never buys her own coffee. There are forty families living in our block, all of them well connected. Every day, she does her morning tour.

I stood on my toes to reach the top shelf of the cupboard for my Moo-Moo cup.

I ate the soft eggs and couldn't help noticing something different about Auntie. Was it her smile? Her smile wasn't more than another wrinkle on her yellow face.

Her head and Grandma's were so close together they AL-

MOST touched. They whispered, their hands holding mugs of steaming coffee. A brownish membrane bubbled on the hot surface.

Something blasted outside. I ran to the window.

"Just fireworks," Grandma said.

"What's the celebration about? Is it New Year's Eve yet?"

"Freedom," Auntie answered.

"I don't know what freedom is," I said.

"Neither do we," Auntie replies. She sipped her black Nicaraguan coffee. "But I'm having a taste of it. And it's worth dying for."

Auntie's eyes snapped open and shut. Grandma's eyes snapped open and shut. OPEN AND SHUT, like the doors on the 117 bus we ran to catch the other day. It should have been packed, the 117 always is, but that day there were seats. Grandma spoke to the lady in the fur coat and she stayed silent for too long. I saw the blood in her hair, even if the blood and the hair were almost the same shade of wine-red.

I said nothing, not even when Grandma sent me to speak to the driver. He'd died with his hand on the controls and the doors opened and shut, opened and shut. Grandma screamed because the dead lady had fallen in her lap. I wanted to scream too, but if I did, it would make everything real and that's when the doors of the bus shut and stayed shut because the engine was frozen. Grandma screamed blue murder; she pounded on the doors with her fists. It's embarrassing when someone so old wants to live. Daddy says it's because life is like Austrian chocolate: the more you have, the more you want.

"Have you finished your homework?" Grandma's voice. "What if the teacher picks on you today?"

I shrugged. "What if a Molotov cocktail hits me today? Then I'd be dead. No more homework."

Grandma slapped me so hard I bit my tongue. Her friend sipped her coffee. Imagining the blood in my mouth, tasting it with her eyes.

"Your nana is right, you know. You can't put your life on hold just because of this silly war."

"It's a civil war." Grandma slurping the coffee sounded like water going down a plughole. "*A revolution.*"

"What's the difference?"

I swallowed the soft creamy yolks, too bored to wonder.

There are no trains, it seems. I'm hot. I remove my scarf, my knitted hat, and my head still feels like a roasted pumpkin. Grandma's face is sweaty and red. She fans herself with the electricity bill.

"Put your hat back on. We're underground, remember."

"So?"

"It's very draughty. You'll get an ear infection."

"Mrs Barbalata says that's all nonsense. Infections are caused by viruses, and viruses are everywhere. Like germs. Your mouth, for example has more germs in it than a public toilet. That's even when you brush your teeth, and you don't."

Grandma raises her arm to hit me. I jump out of the way.

"Who do you think you are, telling me my mouth is a toilet! You fucking little cunt!"

She takes a deep breath like a dragon about to blow fire. Her breasts look like two deflated footballs in a wool-coat. If I could make a wish, I'd wish that I don't have to see Grandma naked again; her saggy stomach, her hairy nipples, the bird nest between her legs.

"Where the hell is this motherfucking train? Thieves!"

Her hat blocks her view so she pulls it off. Oily curls and the smell of her head: boiled cabbage, mould, naphthalene.

"Motherfuckers." Grandma peers inside the tunnel, stepping over the yellow line and dangerously close to the gap. I picture her cut in half by the train. Moving around on a skateboard like the little Gipsy beggar whom everyone calls Half.

"I hear something."

"What?"

"Shush!"

Her hand has frozen in a funny way, with her index finger pointing sideways to her bright red lips.

Not wheels. Footsteps. Lots of them. Running. Thumping the

ground like the herd of buffaloes in a cartoon I saw on the Bulgarian television channel we stumbled on by chance, pressing all the buttons on the black and white Diamond TV. Sometimes I pressed two at once, sometimes three at once. Some you press harder than others. Everyone cheered, the neighbours muttering the new language like schoolchildren learning to read.

Grandma's eyes grow wide.

"Aaargh!" she yells.

Their faces appear in the mouth of the tunnel; flags in their hands, blind rage in their eyes.

"Death, death," they're chanting.

"Aaarghhhhh!" screams Grandma. "They're going to kill us!"

She drops her carrier bag and moves sideways like a crab. The men are everywhere. They step on the bag, smashing the eggs. I didn't think I could see so many smashed eggs at once and still be alive. The yolks flow very slowly until they reach the sharp edge of the platform where all the baby mice are waiting. There are mice in the tunnel, I've seen them running on the tracks like tiny acrobats. Mice can even crawl upwards on walls and they can fly if they have to. Grandma says it's because they have no souls.

The flags have a round cut in the middle where the Communist coat of arms is missing: the scythe and the oil well and the mountains, I know them all because it's the only picture in my classroom, apart from the portrait of the Comrade. When you get picked up and don't know the answer that's the only place to look. And I never know the answer; it only comes to me when I've sat down with my ears on fire, my hands stinging.

The coat of arms is more sacred than Jesus, more sacred than the priest's cold cross Grandma makes me kiss on the secret house-blessing days. And now it's gone.

One of the boys pulls out a gun. "Death to the Party! Out with the Communists!"

My heart races. No one can say the word "Communist" out loud without dying on the spot. Something to do with militia or black magic, or both.

Grandma is lying face down on the ground. A giant cockroach.

106

The escalator is a gaping, rat-smelling hole.

I stand all alone in the crowd.

For three days there's been nothing but shooting. Our lights were off and the curtains drawn, but last night our window got smashed. We're now sitting in the frosty lounge with our coats and gloves on. There's a piece of cardboard where the glass had been, but the bullets pound on it like hail stones.

"Get under the bed," Mother orders. When she's at home, Mother is the boss. No one dares talk back to her, not even Grandma.

Mother watches TV. Something is wrong with it because it's been on for hours. The image is blurred and shaky. None of the people in the central square are waving or holding out carnations.

The gunshots sound like corks popping out of bottles. You don't know if they come from outside or from the telly. Every time a cork pops someone falls. 'Don't shoot me, brother!' wails the cameraman. Then the image of the central square gets even shakier, until the only thing on the screen is a brick wall. A trickle of something dark enters the TV and flows to the brick wall. We follow the blood trail until the image goes blank.

Under the bed, the floor is bare and dusty. I find an old toy bird and that furry slipper I'd lost.

"My name is Millie," I say. "What's yours?" I press the toy's belly hard and it cheeps.

"My name is Alice." It's still me, Tweety doesn't speak. It's all shabby and dirty. "You have very big eyes, Alice. But you don't have a tongue, do you?"

"I only have a beak," Alice says.

"Stupid, stupid," Mother mutters. "Where are they? God, where are they?"

Our flat is dark. Even the sunlight is grey. Everything is as black and white as the Diamond TV. It smells of old wood and dust. A bullet hits the glass cupboard where Mother keeps her precious tea set, but she doesn't seem to notice.

"I have to go. Don't answer the door. Millie, stay under the bed."

Grandma pleads with Mother not to go. She can't fit under the bed so she's wrapped herself in the goose-down duvet, huge as a whale; a whale with a sheep's head. It's all the Mozart chocolates she eats. It's the contraband salami. It's the double ration of bread she gets from the Party's bakery.

Mother doesn't kiss me goodbye.

I crawl to the window on my knees, just in time to see her walking quickly out of the building. Her footsteps are loud. The space between the tower blocks is an open deserted space. The burning car is now a blackened carcass of metal. The end of Mother's headscarf touches her waistline. Her coat brushes the ground …

The telly's loud, *loud*, LOUD. Grandma's telling me to turn it off; her voice strange as if she's talking through water. THUMP. Sharp pain in my shoulder. My finger stabs the button on the TV, and the screen is now a black mirror. I can see the room: the bookcase, the sofa bed, the table. Something that shouldn't be there stares back at me.

I remove the cardboard.

"What are you doing?" screams Grandma. Her wrinkled head pops out of the duvet like a baby being born.

Then something speaks with my voice. "None of your fucking business, you stupid fucking cunt."

Someone's shaking me awake. *Not yet.* I've dreamed of my real mother, I must have because her memory is sweet like the aftertaste of Mozart chocolate. My eyes snap open.

The man is looking at me and through me at the wall where the clock ticks an unknown hour. He smells strange, of blood and tobacco and sweating gun metal.

I blink at last. I must stay cool.

The General is half naked. When he switches on the light, the drawings on his chest and stomach come alive: the church with the three domes for the three years he spent in prison and the three skulls for the three people he killed. My legs hang in the air; woollen socks with my big toe popping out. I'm still wearing the nail varnish my-real-mother put on the day she died, but the red is dying too, fading to reveal the bare, ugly nail.

He presses his hands on my knees. The mermaid on his arm smiles at me.

"You have to remember."

He clicks his lighter and holds it so close to my eye that my lashes begin to sizzle. The stench of burnt hair fills the kitchen.

I shake my head. The flame is now close enough to peel my eye like an onion.

Grandma's smoking. A thin black veil is draped around her head and shoulders. Her silver corkscrew curls creep out like snakes. She stuffs them back in and rearranges her scarf, knotting the two ends under her chin.

"Tell me."

I wonder if he learned this trick in prison, burning someone's eyes while they're still alive.

Emil is standing in a corner, his arms folded on his chest.

All of them are waiting.

I gaze at the big clock on the wall but can't read the time. A wristwatch for giants. I know that God is watching me through the faces of clocks. I see my cup in the cupboard behind the glass. From where I sit, all I see is Moo-Moo's tail and the letter "o". I can easily stretch my arm and turn it round, I think. I can reach it now.

Mother is walking out of the building. She steps on a canal grill that goes *cling*. A metallic noise ...

The General puts out the flame.

"Tell me," he says, more gently.

The telly is buzzing like a bee. Grandma wails. She tucks her head inside the duvet.

"Turn that shit off," she yells.

Then, again, louder: "Turn that fucking shit off, you hear me, Millie?"

Millie doesn't move.

"You have to remember!"

The white sheet is almost shapeless. It's the ironing sheet, on

which Grandma straightens my shirts and skirts and collars.
Shapeless.

I see the yellow prints the iron left behind. And the brown
burns. The dried blood of a spider I'd squashed. It came out of
my school uniform, racing on the sheet. I killed it with one finger.
"Speak!"

Shapeless. Almost completely *shapeless.* Except for one small
detail. *That arm.* A long arm with fingers curled in a loose fist.
"You have to remember, Millie."

I'm not on the table anymore. I'm on a boat, bouncing on
waves. I swing and swing. The waves throw me higher and
higher. I almost reach the sky. My cup is sitting on a cloud. I
look at Moo-Moo and she blinks, just like a real cow.

"Moo-Moo! You're alive!"

I fall back on the wooden deck, seawater bursting out of my
lungs. Only it's not seawater; I've just been sick all over myself.
The mermaid on the General's arm laughs and laughs and
laughs. In prison, tortured people vomit a lot. I wish he could at
least let me wipe my face, but he saw the truth in my eyes and
won't give me any time to hide it.

"You have to remember, Millie. Who killed your mother?"

His hair is oily and black. If I look hard enough, I can see his
beard growing, fast forward, like in a dream.

Emil's eyes fill with tears.

In the silent room, the giant's wristwatch clicks its tongue:
Tick tock, tick tock, tick tock. I smell coffee. I smell Grandma's
cigarette. The lit butt is abandoned in an upturned jar lid. It
won't stop chewing on the metal, like a rat with fire teeth. The
curtains are moving softly. I catch a glimpse of the old playground. The monastery on the hill is the size of a finger. The
snow falls.

For the first time in days the shootings have stopped. Silence
has fallen over everything. The silence of a house where everybody is lying on the floor with tape over their mouth and hands
tied at the back.

The black neck of the rifle pops out of the window, pointing down, following a small spot that is moving across the play-ground.

A few flights above me, a masked man disappears in the gloom of his apartment.

Grandma missed it. She's used to the shooting by now. Her ears are stuffed with cotton wool but still she ...

"Turn it off!"

She's shouting, of course. The book hits me hard on the shoulder.

I go and turn the telly off.

And I scream, breaking the damned silence.

"None of your fucking business, you stupid fucking cunt."

The world is still. The twin towers are still. The body in the playground is still. The riffle in my hand is still. The thought of my-real-mother takes away the fear.

One of the skulls on Daddy's chest has her smile.

Countdown

That we call each other Mummy and Daddy isn't even the worst thing.

Here I am again, awake with the kids while Daddy's sleeping off a hangover.

"I could do with a coffee!" he yells from the master bedroom, at the ring of the kettle.

I take a moment to snort through my nose, in and out. Sharp bits of Lego are embedded in my knees so deep that I might need a surgical intervention to remove them. My hair is sticky from the cup of milk Elena threw at me.

"Get up and make your own coffee!" I yell back. "I'm too busy picking up toys!"

A door slams upstairs, followed by more shouting. Laszlo covers his ears. No one understands our through-the-wall, mumbled language, no one but me. I know how Daddy's mind works. He would've said something like: "They're old enough to pick up after themselves!"

To which I reply: "So are you! I could make an escape rope from all the soggy long johns you dump around this place!"

Sophia is my saviour. She's more than a childminder; she's my angel, my confidante, the other mother. I fantasize about her moving in with us, always there to rescue me from the sleepless, tireless monsters.

The monsters have gone, immaculately dressed, with neat hair and brushed teeth, not a hint of their inborn talent for torture in their angelic features.

Nights are no longer long stretches of peaceful rest. I'm their prisoner, waitress, maid, pet; like vampires, their thirst for attention begins in the dead hour and only ends when, exhausted, they fall asleep at the precise moment I'm serving dinner.

Skipping dinner is a blessing and a curse. I can have an hour's rest with a glass of wine before I, too, collapse into unconsciousness. But if they don't eat, they don't sleep; if they don't sleep, I don't sleep. If I don't sleep, I'll miss another day of work, chipping away at the academic career I've worked towards all my life.

Angels and monsters. Aren't we all the same?

I've read about parents returning adopted children they can't bond with. There's a novel about it, a book I read when I didn't spend every waking moment in the service of tiny humans. *Lily Aphrodite.* But what do you do when you can't bond with children you created yourself?

I've stopped feeling a sense of guilt. If it makes me less of a mother ...

"Kate!"

Someone's knocking on the bathroom door. By *someone* I mean Daddy. Who else can it be? I don't know how long I've been here, telling this hollow-eyed beast to get the hell out of my mirror. In the end, I flush the empty toilet, wash my face – but I can't wash *her* away.

"Marry me, Kat."

No.

They all come to me in the wrong order. This is not how it was. This happened later. The proposal, I mean.

I blink. Still seems surreal, the lounge of our 2.5 million house in Hampstead. I suppose we've made it in life. Daddy's real name is Alexander. Alexander Wyatt, the novelist. If you're one of those people who think you should go to bed with either a book or someone who's written one then, trust me, the book is your best bet. Books smell nice and they can't make you pregnant.

It was Daddy who had the last say on the house – since he was paying for it. Six bedrooms, a well-trimmed English garden, the woods on our doorstep, yet if you think it's enough to satisfy our selfish sense of freedom, you're wrong. Recently, while visiting a furniture store, we bought a new king size bed and separate duvets. The idea of meeting Daddy halfway under the sheets lost its appeal years ago.

Sometimes the glow in his eyes, a small smile, a tender gesture, touches my heart in an unexpected way. It's immaterial though, an aftertaste, like a sudden scent you catch on the breeze, something wild, something you can't hold, capture or even understand. *Something like love.*

Things were so different before *the children*. We still dated, Daddy and I. We bought presents for love, not a sense of duty; he called me Kat, I called him Daddy Bear. He never called me Kate when we were in love.

"Kate, I'm off."

He bends to kiss me on the cheek. And that's when it strikes me. Daddy brushed his teeth. He's been brushing his teeth for weeks. And, come to think of it, he hasn't been in the mood for quite a while. I always say no, but it's kind of nice having someone to say no to.

First, we went to a movie. The cinema was very old. I filled my mouth with popcorn so that he couldn't kiss me. He put a shy arm around my shoulders. The scent of his skin, now the core of our home, tickled my nose. Crawled to my heart. Nestled there.

Not a day goes by without me wishing my life was different. In the morning, I have my coffee and buttered croissant sitting on a stool in the kitchen, looking out over the city. Am I a bad mother for hiding my children here, in this solitary wildness? Should I tell anyone that I regret having them?

I sit back on my chair, *The Guardian* open in front of me. They've published a story about a hermit found in the woods of Maine. One day, he walked into the forest, and didn't come back out for twenty-five years. I raise an eyebrow. Really, everyone's branded him a weirdo, but I can kind of see where he's coming from. "I became irrelevant," he told the press. I wonder what it must feel like, the relief of ceasing to exist and yet still be alive. Retreat and inaction are, according to Tao philosophy, the key to achieving true wisdom. But how do you escape from a prison you built yourself? How do you shed the chains of modern, middle-class life?

Daddy's car is only a dot on the snaking road. I throw open the window. But instead of the cut stone steps overgrown with wild mint, lavender and rosemary, I see something else ...

I see the church. I see young Alexander. I see myself. I see love just beginning. Cinnamon, mulled wine, flavoured love.

My mum sings the Christmas carols. She gives a little cough at times, like people always do in concert halls. The church is decorated with flowers and the air heavy with candle smoke.

My cheeks are hot and I'm singing very loud.

I'm standing in the door of Daddy's office. I don't normally come in here; I respect his privacy. He writes books. People buy them. Okay, a lot of people buy them. The end result is, we have money. A lot of money. But I'm home alone today. Off sick, *again*. The head of the research team was understanding. But it's only a matter of time until my project goes to someone else.

It's true, though. I'm sick. Sick of everything. I start opening drawers, look through Daddy's files. Call it curiosity. Call it a sense of entitlement. Daddy has been here for so long, that he ceased to exist. His private life, too, became irrelevant, although it's clear he has one. His scribbles are everywhere.

Unintelligible.

My mother warned me about that. "He's a dark horse," she said, squinting at his love cards. "Look at the way he writes his g-s and j-s. Look at how he hides their tails under the line ..."

That's when Robert calls. It turns out, I still have to do the Skype session I've booked months ago. There's no one else available. I sigh and fire up Daddy's Mac.

We kiss. I've just broken my leg at the Alexandra Palace skating rink and we're together in the back of the ambulance. I'm crying. I can taste my own tears when he kisses me. It's not because of pain I'm crying, but of shame. I told him that it wasn't my first time on ice. And it was.

I'm reading the Harvard International Law Journal in the lounge when he comes in. My hair is in curlers, every single strand. The children, asleep in their rooms. They even had dinner – beef sandwiches and a cup of milk. Sophia has gone. The house is warm and cozy, the fire roaring; a perfect place to spend a winter night.

Daddy walks in, sits down in his chair. Lights a cigarette.

"Shoes off," I snarl. "Sophia's just done the floor. And I thought we agreed not to smoke in the house. Jeez. You stink. Have you been to a kebab house again?"

He smells of cigarettes and smoked meat and ...

"You smell of Chance."

"Pardon?"

"Chanel. *Chance.* Is that what she uses?"

Daddy sighs. "Mummy ... er, *Kate*, we need to talk."

I put down the journal because my hands are shaking. I cross my arms. And I give Daddy my most intimidating glare – the one I normally use for unprepared students.

"I've been thinking. I'm not happy and neither are you. I mean, you're always complaining. When was the last time we even had meaningful contact? When was the last time we didn't talk about the children?"

"What are you saying?"

"I'm saying that we should consider separating. And before you say anything, Kate, think about it. You know it's the right thing to do. Think of the children. It's not fair that they grow up in a loveless home."

"I see. You've thought of everything."

For a brief moment, a memory trails in my mind like smoke.

We sit in the box and we can't have wine. I left my *Victoria's Secret* gloss on his lips. When the lights are off, his mouth is still visible in the darkness. Before the show, people talk softly in the shadowy hall, everywhere. The twilight is full of their voices dropped to whispers. They sound like crickets, I think. And they look like crickets, I think.

He takes a silver flask out of his inside pocket and smiles. He opens it with his teeth.

"Whisky?" he says.

I'm already drunk with the smell of it.

I blink. Daddy's still talking.

"You can keep the children and the house, mortgage-free. I'll also give you a generous allowance."

"What if I don't want to keep them?"

"Excuse me? But I assumed ... as they're very young ..."

"Why shouldn't you have them? Or at least one of them?"

Daddy looks shocked. "One of them? Kate, would you have the heart to separate them? Knowing they are ... *twins?*"

He stands up, glaring down at me from his intimidating height. "I really don't know who you are anymore."

I burst out with laughter. "That's okay. Neither do I."

"The courts would never allow it. You should have the children. You're their mother. When they're older ..."

"Is there someone else?"

Daddy says nothing.

"There is someone else," I screech. "A bitch you can screw until midday on Saturdays, while I look after your fucking children. You fucking bastard."

My soon to be ex-husband sneers at me. "Enough. Yes, there is someone else. Her name is Victoria. She's a journalist."

"Aha. We're making progress. For a moment, I thought you'd say you're screwing Sophia. That would've made more sense. But it seems you have enough zest in you to hunt outside the home. I'm impressed. Maybe if I sat on my ass all day writing novels, I'd get laid too."

"Kate, please. I've felt alone for so long. We haven't had sex in ..."

"I thought writers *want* to be alone. I thought you needed space. And maybe I don't want to be your in-between-chapters shag. Assuming you are writing. For all I know, you could be locked in there all day watching porn."

Daddy laughs. "That would be a fine way to pay the mortgage."

"Stop reminding me you pay the fucking mortgage."

"Stop reminding me you look after the fucking kids. For God's sake, you were the one nagging me about kids all along. And now it's too much for you?"

"Your mother said you first slept through the night when you were five. Don't you think you should've told me that when we were trying to conceive?"

Jesus, am I still wearing my curlers? I touch my head in horror, and start pulling them out of my hair. You ought to look pretty, at least, when a man is leaving you.

And then a horrible thought chills my blood. Just as we're splitting up, our clothes are still together in the laundry basket; my lipsticks sitting peacefully with his electric razor by the mirror. His coats on top of mine. My skirts hanging with his shirts in the dark.

It's dark. Hand in hand, we go up the stairs. My evening gown reveals my naked back. My scarf is fluttering in the sweet July wind. I leave a trail of perfume behind me.

The night is as warm as a breath.

A curler lands in the bin, loud in the heavy silence that hangs over the house, creeping unseen along the corridors.

"A journalist, then. Is it that blogger who always retweets your posts on Twitter? BookFanatic29?"

"Kate, this isn't about her. This is about us."

"Very well. Who is going to tell the children?"

"They're three, for God's sake. And it's not that I'm going anywhere."

"But you're *going* to leave the house." I sigh. "Oh, whatever. I'm off to bed. If you still want a divorce tomorrow, get a good lawyer. I'm not giving this up without a fight."

"Kate, you're being unreasonable. I fell in love with another woman. I'm moving out. Why complicate things?"

This makes me pause on the stairs. My fingers grip the banister so tight my knuckles turn white. For a moment, I want to take off my engagement ring and throw it in his face. But then I remember it's worth a good few grand; if Daddy is leaving, then I'll probably have to start counting cash. I have divorced friends. Generous allowances tend to drop after a year or two, and the courts are too much of a gamble. "I won't give

BookFanatic29 the satisfaction of going out with a single man."

"Kate ..."

"I got you first, didn't I? I had to deal with your dirty socks when you were Mr Nobody. I made you into Alexander Wyatt! Me!"

Alexander Wyatt the novelist smiles. I know it now, that bitch Victoria hasn't fallen in love with my man. And I don't love *her* man either.

I throw my chin up. "One more thing. Call me Kate again, and I'll put all your precious videos on YouTube. Or, better still, your shitty website."

Daddy's face turns white. "Excuse me?"

"You heard me. I hacked your Skype account. Oh, it wasn't intentional. I'd locked myself out of my account and needed Skype urgently for a tutoring session in Dubai. That's when I saw that your last Skype call was to a woman, and it lasted an hour. *One fucking hour.* So I pre-recorded all your video calls. I must say, BookFanatic29 has a most impressive collection of underwear. And toys." I laugh. "It'll be a hoot for your fans. Especially the 11 to 13s. That's your age group, right, *Daddy*? Look on the bright side. You might get a book deal with Mills and Boon." To my horror, tears spring in my eyes and a loud sob escapes from my mouth.

Daddy holds his head in his hands as if he has the worst headache in the world. He drops to a stool and sits like that for a long time. I wait, feeling like I've just thrown myself off a cliff and someone pressed *pause.*

"Name your price," he says at last.

"Tomorrow, you'll buy me dinner and apologise for being such an ass."

"Kate, I'm talking about money."

"And I'm telling you I'm priceless. Isn't that why you married me?"

Daddy says nothing. Damn his fucking silence. He looks overwhelmed by sadness, his head bowed, his hands in his lap. For a moment I think he's sorry, but then I see his phone. He's writing a text message to that Bitch Fanatic. They've made a coalition against me. Two snotty brats vs Agent Provocateur underwear. Dry breasts vs full breasts. Middle age vs youth. Housework vs sex.

Daddy took me to the middle of the ocean and now he's going to leave the boat.

Before sleep, I observe myself in the full-length mirror by the bed. I'm old. Or at least, I look old. My eyes are puffy, their colour changed. Am I standing in the wrong light? Or is it something else?

Our conversation is still floating in my head but the words are meaningless. I feel a sort of relief. Nothing else.

When I lie down the sheets are cold and fresh. The bed feels like a coffin. His voice echoes up the stairs. The alien happiness of another love fills the room, creeping over the memories of our own happy years.

And then again, we go up the stairs. In front of us, but still very far, is the lighthouse. A thin fog floats over the sea. It smells of pine trees and the ground is crawling with the shadows of the agaves.

Soon our table is surrounded by people with trumpets and violins. They shoot their songs to my heart. I listen. I lick the last bits of tiramisu from my spoon. I sit back in my chair. And finally, I say yes.

The front door slams shut. The black Audi opens its big eyes in the darkness. The night is blue. And he drives off.

I'm lying perfectly still when he comes in, his shadow moving across the room, from the walls to the ceiling and on the bed.

He undresses. His clothes smell of cigarette smoke, his breath stinks of beer, his skin reeks of the other woman's perfume. He's drunk. But, tonight of all nights, I don't care. He lies down next to me, pulls his own duvet up to his chest.

Silence.

But he's not asleep yet. I know. I'm wide awake and he probably knows, too. I want to move closer. I want to ask him, *Do you really not love me anymore?*

I want to ask him many things.
Instead, I say something stupid.
"Good night."
Even to this, he doesn't reply.
Maybe I was wrong.
Maybe he fell asleep right away.
Or maybe not.

Yes. They clap their hands in delight. My mum is wearing one of her funny hats. Dad looks a bit sad. And, underneath my white wedding dress, my belly is swollen. I'm nervous and, because of this, the twins are doing a little dance.

My heart drums. Will he notice that I'm naked? Will he even care? My hand hovers against his chest. It's been years since I touched him other than in passing. His skin feels feverish against mine. He takes a sharp breath.

I'm close. So close I can smell the other woman. So close the old lost magic begins to bubble in my blood.

And then, just as I'm about to straddle him, I see Elena's face in the dark.

"Mummy!" she whines.

"MUMMY!" her brother shouts from the bedroom. "COME!"

"Get up," orders Elena, her voice like ice.

"NOW!"

My separate duvet is pulled off me. Tiny cold hands grip my ankles. In the moonlight streaming from the window, Elena's blue eyes look white. Her mouth curls downwards in a chilling grimace.

"I'm gonna count to five."

"MOVE, MUMMY!!"

"One, two, three ..."

Emilia's Heaven

I emigrated to Canada on the 17th of December 2004, two days after my mother's birthday.

The morning before my flight I strode down the stony path in the Orthodox graveyard. I like graveyards. They're quiet and peaceful. In winter, when the tree branches are bare and the ground is too hard for any plants to come to light, you wonder if the dead aren't lonely. Just imagine, being locked in a cold grave with no one but the grounds' caretaker for company. The man's half mad and he curses the dead, but there's one good thing about him: he forgets your face the minute you're out of sight.

The graveyard was locked, but I slipped a crumpled note into Izidor's hand and listened as he grumbled something through his teeth. He shuffled his bad leg across the driveway. A moment later, he was rattling a set of rusty keys.

I walked in, breathing the still air, which in the gentler months is fragrant with the scent of lilac and roses. The tombs were all frozen, silenced by the blizzard.

I won't be here to see them come back to life, I thought, scraping snow from a stone where Mother's yellow photograph smiled at me from the folds of time. The roses, or the dead.

As a child I used to lie down on my mother's tomb and try to catch the beating of her heart from inside the mushroom flavoured earth.

"The soul never dies!" I told the guard who grabbed my arm and threw me outside the gate.

"Bugger off," he yelled. "You sick little brat!"

I lie down between the twin gravestones, Mother's and Daddy's.

I light a cigarette. The smell of the smoke brings back a memory of another winter night.

Daddy and I were sitting in the filthy kitchen, the leftovers and bones from the last meal cooked by Mother, now buried, still on the stove. Daddy had been drinking all day. He sipped the cheap vodka straight from the bottle, his bloodshot eyes on the small TV where football players rolled around the pitch like tiny elves. The image flickered. Then it went blank. Daddy picked up the TV and bumped it against the wall.

"Stupid thing!"

I played with the laces of his shoes.

"Daddy."

"Hmmm."

"Do you think Mum is really in heaven, like Father said?"

"What?"

"In heaven. Do you think she's already gotten there, or is she still on the way?" I lowered my voice. "It's been three days."

Daddy bowed so that his greasy head was at the same level with mine.

"Let me tell you something, puppet." He took a long sip of his vodka, his eyes closed. I hated when he did that. It's as if he was slipping into another world where I didn't belong. "There's no such thing as heaven."

I got up, headed for the door.

"And anyway," he coughed, choking on the smoke from his cigarette, "even if there was such a thing as heaven, your bloody mother wouldn't be in it, that's for sure!"

His peals of laughter followed me down the corridor with striped wallpaper, all the way to my freezing bedroom.

Emilia was praying. I laid down next to her, shivering. Rolled on to my side and closed my eyes.

But I couldn't sleep.

"There is no heaven," I said. "Daddy told me."

Emilia slapped me. I slapped her back.

"There isn't, there isn't!" I screamed, crossing my arms over my face to shield it from her fists. The blows fell over me like furious rain, leaving me breathless.

We waited for sleep, curled around each other, Emilia's hot head on my chest. In the silence of the night I heard Daddy snoring in the kitchen and my own stomach growling. It was the third night we'd gone to bed without supper.

"Lily?" Emilia said in the dark.

"Yes."

"I don't want to go."

The next morning, a fat woman in a suit pushed her in the back of a car. She slammed the door shut and Emilia pounded on the window.

"Lily! Lily!" she cried.

I didn't say a word. The car drove off and the noise of the engine drowned her voice. Her crying face disappeared in a cloud of smoke. I caressed the glossy prayer book she slipped in my hand before that woman took hold of her arm and dragged her away.

"Millie, I promise you ..." I whispered, and a cold dizziness came over me. Everything went blank.

The reason I went to Vancouver was not to get over Danny's death, or to find work as a waitress. The true reason behind my decision was the hope of finding Emilia. Maybe it was written in the stars that we'd be together again, or maybe I owed it to my son, who wandered out the back door to send a paper boat to his auntie Emilia in Canada, only to find his end on the murky shores of the Danube River.

I didn't know her telephone number, or where she lived, not even if she was still alive. All I had from her was a postcard. The photo of a lake, shiny like glass. If you moved it the water rippled, as if it was real.

Dear Lily,

Hope you're well. School is so much fun, all French. My parents are good but they're very old. Fifty, I think. They love God a lot. They buy me everything I want. I'll write a real letter soon. Love, Millie.

I read it lying on my bed at St Ann's Centre where no one ever prayed and they all dreamed about this miracle called adoption.

I took the cap off my pen with my teeth and wrote: *Dear Millie*. A thumping sound made me look up. A seagull had flown into the window, and was watching the deserted dormitory through the pane of dirty glass. The rows of beds lined silently, white pillows, brown blankets, all the same. Blue wedges of sky radiated through the skylight.

I live in a lovely centre on Winter Road and I have my own room.

My eyes stung. I didn't want to cry, so I ripped the sheet of paper off and turned it into a white, crinkled ball.

I looked at the postcard and had another drag from my cigarette. It said Vancouver in black letters underneath the lake. I put it back in my bag and feeling the prayer book with my fingers, the book she gave me all those years ago.

"I promise you, Millie." This time I didn't collapse in the patio and wake up to find Daddy still asleep in the kitchen.

This time I stood up, stepped on the cigarette butt, glanced at my watch and walked away, crushing the snow with my boots.

How I found Charlotte was the funniest thing. It was my first month in Vancouver and I had just enough money left for another week, a vegetarian week with no cigarettes and no beers at night, just one week between me and the gutter. I ran up and down the streets, my pockets stuffed with newspaper ads and coins for the public phones, my heart full of misery and the growing certainty that Emilia must be dead clawing at my heart.

I was treating myself to a much needed milky coffee in a central café when a woman called me by a strange name, greeted me in a language I hadn't heard on the streets of Vancouver, or anywhere else. I looked at her and she blinked in surprise.

"Oh, I thought you were someone else. I beg your pardon, you just look so much like somebody I know," she said in perfect French.

She continued to watch me, her eyes like laser beams beneath the rim of her green velvet hat.

"You just ..." My heart leapt, the penny dropped. I stood up and grabbed her hand, my own hands shaking.

"Please. Help me. She's my sister, I haven't seen her in twenty years."

The woman measured me up. With my unkempt hair, missing teeth and husky voice, I must've looked more like a drug addict. The woman opened her leather bag, soft as a fold of old flesh, and took out her phone. She held it to her ear and for as long as I could hear the ringing, I stopped breathing. Then the ringing stopped, dropping down like bowling pins at the end of a lane.

Crash.

"Allo?" A shiver ran down my spine.

Two days later I stood waiting in a small airport, my bag on my shoulder, hair brushed, stinking of the wet wipes they gave us on the plane. I hadn't eaten, only had a strong coffee and whisky on the rocks.

"If you ever find yourself on a bloody plane," Daddy always said, "don't forget to get a drink. Drinking is better in the clouds. It makes you twice as high."

Daddy had only been on a plane once, being flown back from France in handcuffs to be transferred to a new jail. He was proud of his mugshots. They were framed on the wall of his cell until the day he died.

I stood in the arrivals zone, my heart thumping madly in my chest. I must have looked just how I felt, like a leopard in a chicken coop. Polite announcements were made through loudspeakers, the air was rich with the scent of well-fed bodies, the floors sparkled like ice. When I saw her, a stain of colour in the black and white crowds, the hand of a little girl in hers, I just watched her for a few moments. The sounds around me froze to silence. Her body moved in slow motion, shifting to the smiling image of the short-haired girl, the girl who disappeared in a cloud of smoke all those years back.

An adult version of that girl was next to me, the thin body of her daughter glued to her own. The kid smiled from under a mane of curly blonde hair and I saw she was also missing a tooth, one of her fronts.

"Hello, Lily."

A Canadian accent. Her voice was old, seductive, like that of a woman who had known love.

"Hello," I said, looking down at my dusty boots.

I didn't know what else to say so I just said: "You must be Millie." Stupid, I know.

"My name's not Millie. Well, not anymore." She smiled. Her teeth were so much whiter and straighter than mine, none of them missing.

On her head she wore a black bandana, the glittery edge just above the curved black eyebrows. We didn't look so much like twins anymore, I thought.

"She's called *Efrat,*" explained the little girl. She must be Sophie, the daughter Emilia said she would bring along.

"I see. A Jewish name."

"We're Jewish," Sophie said. A bright light flowed from their identical eyes towards me like a magical bridge of love. And for the first time since Danny died, drowned in a few inches of muddy water on that damned riverbank, I felt at peace.

Daddy was wrong, I thought as Emilia curled her fingers around my arm and led me through the parking lot to her car. Sophie walked ahead of us, skipping and singing.

"Auntie Lily," she chirped, her toy bunny dangling upside down in her hands. "Do you want to drive our car?"

"I don't know the way," I murmured. Emilia smiled as she handed me the keys.

As we approached the car an image of a just awakening city flashed before my eyes through the windows flooded by sunlight. The tall buildings, the sharp roofs of cathedrals, outlined on the smoky crenels of the mountains. Somewhere close by was my sister's house, a beautiful brick box surrounded by trees and flowers, with creaky stairs and children's toys scattered in the back yard. And for the first time in all those years, I thought of Daddy without hate. For the first time in all those years, I was happy he signed those stupid adoption papers.

You're wrong, I wanted to shout.

There is heaven, but not beyond death like everyone thinks.

I took a deep breath and looked at Sophie, standing by the silver 4x4 Porsche.

I saw the light growing brighter behind the glass and the rooftops floating in the golden air.

Heaven is for those who believe in it.

Heaven was this beautiful morning in the town of Red Deer, Alberta and what was to come: the drive, the smells and the sounds.

Drinking coffee from thick carton cups, Emilia and Lily would avoid each other's eyes, knowing that the grief they shared could break loose. A grief that was their bond forever, beyond love or blood.

"Come on," cried Sophie, kicking the ground with her little foot. "Come on, Auntie Lily! I'll show you the way."

I'm Not Talking About Tea

The cottages on her left and right are identical, mirror reflections of trimmed lawns and lacquered brown doors. Cold sweat forms on her brow.

She knows she should talk to someone about it. But who?

Her GP, that Northern lad whose Lancashire accent makes her stomach ball up like when she was a young a girl on a date? Rosemary Woolbridge isn't ready to admit she's that old, not to someone she fancies. Not yet.

The kindly nurse? She looks too young for her age, a clear sign that she couldn't even begin to evaluate bitterness. She'd only do her job, refer her to some dementia specialist. She's been to one before, with a friend. And no, she couldn't go through the humiliation of singing a nursery rhyme back to front, or recite what she had to eat at Christmas – and in what order. Rosemary needs more than that. She needs someone who really understands; someone she can talk to.

And yet, she's been wandering for at least an hour, drenched through by the October drizzle. How long can she keep going? What if her house no longer exists, what if she's forgotten years of her life? What if – and it's a big if, because Rosemary suspects her age by the ugly hands clutching the Hermes purse – she's a fugitive from an old people's home?

Fear makes her weak at the knees. She takes deep breaths, but there's something in her chest – an obstruction. *It's all in your head*, she tells herself, *all in your …*

There's the clock tower, at last. The photograph of the dead girl is there, solid proof that Rosemary hasn't somehow somersaulted into the future. A tramp sleeps curled up in the warmth of the candles. She resists the impulse to kick him. How dare they make this place so filthy? The houses on her road are detached, each with its own driveway and garage. And yet this is a part of London where the local library stinks of feet and bottoms. Worse still, the council cut the funding for the mental health unit across the park, and now you couldn't even enjoy an evening walk without seeing a man wank in the bushes.

A girl is dead. The community is fuming. All the politicians talk about is human rights. Her mother said that it only takes one rotten apple to spoil an entire basket. And wasn't she right?

Flowers – so many flowers. There are freesias and roses and lilies – and chrysanthemums, her favourite. Autumn is her season, and October her special month.

Gathering the waterproof cloak around her, Rosemary flicks open her umbrella. Head bowed, hood drawn against the furious sheets of rain, she heads home.

The house would be warm; the smell of the soup she made in the morning, welcoming. She's not demented yet: she knows what she put in the soup, and in what order: squash, sweet potatoes, carrots, onions, grated nutmeg. As a child, she drank this winter warmer from a cup with cinnamon on top. Ah, and there'd be hot Assam tea which, since George's death, she's taken with sugar, and from her best china.

Alison Garr, the girl in the photograph at the clock tower, had gone missing on 6th October. She'd told her parents she was going to meet friends in the park, but she went for a stroll along the canal instead.

Rosemary's house is beautiful. She reckons it could be sold for a pretty sum. Two million, maybe more. Despite the stunning view of the park, the garden of luxuriant plants swept by the cool breath of the river, and the ideal location close to the heart of the city, *The Lodge* has always felt like a prison to her. Rosemary was the wife of a doctor; a stay-at-home mum to her twins, Samuel and Ethan. Stay-at-home mums were common on her street. She'd have been a doctor herself if she hadn't dropped out of university in her second year, when she fell pregnant. When her kids grew up, she often thought about going back. But could she have coped with a demanding study schedule as well as maintaining a mansion? Her house was spick and span but, without her care, wouldn't stay that way. And *The Lodge* was her pride, the only thing she could hang onto.

Her neighbour, Philip, waves. "Miserable day, eh, Rose?"

Another bloody doctor. His wife is a Russian ballerina, although she suspects that the only ballet she was famous for was around a strip pole. Their son – an artist. Rosemary helped deliver him one winter night in their conservatory. He's now a grown man, a silver fox, as they say. He's got a wife, children and a mistress. The apple doesn't fall far from the tree, does it, now?

"Hi, Phil!"

God, he looks ancient. When you see people every day you don't realise how they age. But every time she wakes up from her amnesia episodes, she's in shock at how old her friends look. She feels younger than all of them, as if life is only just beginning. At 70, it's not too late to date. Maybe even someone young, like Reuben – her GP.

Who would stop her? She's single. She's rich. To be fair, her body is deteriorating. The corsets keep all the skin folds in place, the cashmere cardigans hide them. Not even the expensive push-up bras can conceal the hideousness of her skinny breasts.

But one can still make love in the dark. The last love is as deep as the first – isn't that what they say?

Philip is piling up the half-logs inside a niche.

"Getting ready for winter?"

She might have fancied him once, but she likes to aim high – and high for her is not a man in dungarees and a woollen vest. He'd be a polite fuck, and Rosemary wants none of that.

She wants …

The lights are on. Her hat is on the stand in the hall. The reflection from the hallway mirror stares back at her. For a moment her old self, the young blonde with Mediterranean skin, flashes in the cool waters of the mirror. Her father was Greek, though it's not something she's proud of; a secret her mother whispered with her last breath. A one night stand; there was no name, no address, no way she could get hold of him – not that she ever wanted to.

She should've suspected it, really; none of her siblings were as good looking as her; none of them married so well; none had her tragedies. Would she change it all? Perhaps not. Beauty was the devil's gift; it came with the devil's hold.

The alarm goes off. Rosemary taps in the code. No one knows the four digit combination, not even herself. Her brain forgets it as soon as she's typed it, but thankfully the muscular memory remains. She is a blonde, after all, as her husband liked to remind her. *"Why can't a blonde cross the road, Rosie?"* He *always* chuckled before delivering the punch line: *"Because she gets run over by a truck!"*

The echo of his voice makes the silence unbearable. She turns on the upstairs lights and calls out, "George?"

Then she laughs at her own foolishness.

George is *dead*. No more jokes. No more dinners. No more lying in the dark with her eyes closed as he groaned on top of her. Death makes everything seem so futile. In the kitchen, she admires the furniture she bought with the money her husband left her. In life, he'd been a stingy bastard: scouring the shops for the cheapest children's toys, the "on sale" perfumes, the two for one deals. But in death – oh, in death, he was so generous. Rosemary enjoyed shopping for the new kitchen: the induction hob, the futuristic sink, the oven big enough to roast a human. And now she was sitting on a bar stool with a glass of champagne from the bottle that had sat in the wine fridge for twenty years. No special reason, other than celebrating life, or *death*. Talking of death …

The day following her disappearance, 7th October, Alison Garr was reported missing.

Rosemary finishes her drink and smashes the glass on the floor. She takes great pleasure in crunching it underfoot: it's real crystal, hard as steel; she groans as it breaks into shards, too sharp and brittle to ever put back together, if she changed her mind. But she wouldn't. How many years did she spend without using the crystal flutes, without even seeing them?

Why miss them now?

From the kitchen, where she stands at the sink filling the kettle, she sees a picture of Alison glued to the bark of an oak. She puts the kettle on. With a delicate pair of tongs, she extracts a fragrant tea bag from a jar. The park has disappeared under an avalanche of leaves: pale green, rusty, crimson, *golden*. The colours of October. October is a significant month in Rosemary's life: the month she had given birth to her first child. It's her birthday, she remembers, *today*. And, oddly enough, it wasn't long before her third birthday, forty-seven years ago, that Olivia, just like Alison Garr, went missing.

Alison was short and slim, the perfect target for an attacker. In America, for instance, a hundred missing children every year fit the profile of a stereotypical abduction. Two thirds of those victims are ages 12 to 17, and among those eight out of ten – an alarming number, Rosemary thinks – are white females.

George did nothing to help with the children. He stank of booze even when he wasn't drinking. Rosemary did her best to keep their life afloat: the perfect, riverside fantasy bubble that was her marriage. It had been exhausting, debilitating. Living with a manic-depressive is like living in a tiger's cage.

The light is fading. Rosemary switches on the lamp. At the bottom of a chest, she finds a photo of Olivia. The same one, in fact, that Rosemary and a team of volunteers had glued on all the walls and shop windows in the area.

Olivia went missing from her bed at home on 29th October 1955, when she was almost three years old. The twins were unharmed. It was supposed that Olivia had woken and walked out of the family home alone, through the back yard and into the park, where she vanished forever.

The search teams combed the park, a thousand square meters of woodland, just as they did now in search of Alison Garr. Divers searched the river. Sniffer dogs arrived in police vans. The houses in the area were searched. Finally, an arrest was made.

On the tenth of October 2014, four days after Alison Garr went missing, police arrested a 24-year-old man. After forty-eight hours in custody, he was released without charge. The following day, a 40-year-old man was arrested, but he, too, appeared to be innocent.

Olivia followed her everywhere; she was a clingy, sickly child who woke up every night tormented by nightmares. "Come to bed with me 'fore the giant comes and gets me, Mummy," she used to say.

"Forgive me, Livvie," Rosemary whispers. "Forgive me. I couldn't keep the giant away."

She opens the box where, for forty-seven years, she kept the hospital bracelet and the umbilical cord – withered like a vanilla pod. Olivia's DNA is in there: her cells, her blood, the proof that she existed.

The man arrested in connection to her disappearance was released after three days. No further arrests were made.

It wasn't until two weeks after Alison Garr went missing, that the first mention of a man called Lucian Bolt appeared in the press.

"Where were you on the evening of 31st October?" The question tolls, clear and loud, in the interview room.

"At home." Her own young voice rings in her head. "I nursed my twins at ten o'clock. At twenty past ten I went to Olivia's room to check on her."

"Was she in bed at the time?"

"Yes. Fast asleep."

Alison Garr was found on 25th October, nineteen days after she went missing. Her body was wrapped in plastic sheets, lying at the bottom of the river, weighed down by rocks.

"What time did you realise she was missing?"

"Not until the morning. My husband, George, raised the alarm. We searched the house, every nook and cranny, before ..."

Rosemary clutches her chest. What is grief but pain beyond imagination? An eternal labour of the heart?

She remembers George's frantic scramble around the cottage. The twins screaming. If anyone had seen her turning beds upside down and emptying wardrobes, they'd have said she was either mad or a good actress. Deep down, though, she hoped to find Olivia, curled up with her teddy bear in some unlikely corner of the house – the playroom, the washroom, the shed. If only she could rewind time to before her life slipped into the darkness of this nightmare. But not even God can change the past.

She sits back in her armchair and mops her eyes with a handkerchief. Her tea is cold. She unlocks the drinks cabinet and pours herself a cognac. It tastes like wood. She pushes it away.

"Why was the blonde confused after giving birth to twins? She couldn't figure out who the other mother was!"

Rosemary covers her ears. If only memories could die, too.

It had been ten o'clock when Rosemary checked on Olivia. It took her less than a second to see that she wasn't breathing.

Four days ago, on 27th October, two days after Alison Garr was recovered from her underwater grave, Lucian Bolt's body was found hanging from a tree. He didn't leave a note, although it could be presumed by his suicide that he experienced some sort of remorse. Rosemary knew, however, that this was little consolation for Alison's family. They'd have to live their entire lives haunted by the images of her last moments, horror scenes they would turn over and over in their heads: her last words, the look in her eyes, the ring of her strangled cries. The autopsy proved inconclusive. Sadly, or maybe mercifully, the cause of her death would never be known.

Rosemary had taken a lie detector test at the time, as did her husband.

"Do you have anything to do with your daughter's disappearance?"

"No, sir."

Alison Garr's body was changed beyond recognition. She could only be identified through dental records. On finding her body, the police also discovered a handful of fragmented bones.

"Is she asleep?" The lights of the television flickered on George's face.

"Yes," Rosemary answered. "Fast asleep."

The rain fell heavily as twenty-three-year-old Rosemary

walked her way down the canal path. She could make her way through the wilderness with her eyes closed: it was their route to the local pub, when they met Philip and Martyna for a Sunday lunch – although Philip always seemed hungrier for her curves than for the roasted bird on his plate.

The night of her death, Olivia had been restless. It was only, Rosemary thought, wishing for the thousandth time she could turn back time, going to be a small dose to help her sleep. Her husband was a manic-depressive, and they always had Prozac at hand. Sometimes she managed to convince herself that it could have happened anyway: Olivia might have stumbled over her father's drugs and overdosed herself.

Rosemary shed no tears as the small body was lowered into its grave. She was running on adrenaline, fuelled by a frightening mixture of strength and logic she didn't know she had. It was only afterwards, when she remembered how the water's skin closed over the tiny fists, only when she was alone in the darkness of her daughter's empty bedroom, that she allowed herself to grieve.

It had been October, too, a year after the twins had gone to university, that George found a bag while digging out some roots. In the last years of his life, he was sober, but that only made her hate him more. How convenient for him to sober up when all the kids had gone. Now that she didn't need him anymore, he remembered that he was her husband.

The cloth bag contained Rosemary's old diary, with one incriminating piece of evidence. A Polaroid picture of Olivia, taken after her death. On the back she had written: RIP, my angel.

Rosemary watched him from an upstairs window. When he walked into the room, he looked as if he was already dead.

"How could you, Rosie?"

Rosemary caught a reflection of herself in the Victorian mirror above the fireplace. Her eyes were cold and sharp: two sheets of broken ice.

She grabbed the poker. Now she knew what he felt when he hit her: the tingle in her fingers, the warmth in her belly, the trickle of excitement down her spine. She could choose to stop, but why would she? It was now or never.

George drew back. He cowered in a corner, and for a moment Rosemary saw herself, three hysterical children by her side, trembling in her husband's shadow.

It was now or never. She raised the poker. The silver glinted in the fading October sunlight.

"Not too bad for a blonde, eh, love?"

It was a perfect blow. Rosemary estimated that it cracked his skull, pushing the tiny bone fragments into his brain. How wonderful to know that in his last moments of life, George didn't think of her as a stupid blonde.

It's getting late. Rosemary feels hungry. Killing takes a lot of energy; thinking of it does, too. If she had been convicted, prosecution would have argued that it was premeditated murder. If it ever came out that she took a butchery course on dismemberment, her defence would fall like a house of cards.

She looks for the prawns, then remembers she put them in the freezer. They're in a bag labelled *Waitrose Finest* next to the organic peas and the ice cream. She doesn't eat peas anymore, not since she used them as ice packs for her bruises. She only takes them out when the twins come to dinner, which would explain why they're past their expiry date.

Rosemary takes out the prawns. For a moment she stands mesmerised, surrounded by the misty breath of the freezer.

"Hi, George," she says.

She knows it's risky keeping George in the house. He looks beautiful, like a work of art: frost on his eyelids, eyes like frozen scallops, his skin like marble. He looks trapped in eternal winter. But where would she put him? It's been five years, and she hasn't come up with a cleverer idea. After all, this was his home, too. No one could argue that she drove him out of it.

"Mrs Woolbridge?"

Rosemary slams the freezer door shut. *Shit.* What the hell is the doc doing here? She reaches in her gown pocket for her Guerlain lip gloss, runs it over her cracked lips. She now seems to remember that she gave Reuben a key. Why, of course; he's her next-door neighbour. He has children, young children, and a wife who looks like a troll.

"There you are." Reuben appears in her kitchen. It's like a dream come true. He's in his cycling gear; she likes the way his leggings stick to his muscular thighs. Rosemary wants to drop to her knees and …

"I've been knocking … Are you okay?"

"Yes, erm … I was just about to fry some prawns. Chilli and …" No, not garlic. Not tonight. "Fancy a cuppa?"

Reuben seems unsure.

"Come on, a cuppa won't hurt. Been for a bike ride, have you? Bit of a miserable day for that. Go on, grab a seat. I won't bite."

Reuben sits on a bar stool. Rosemary nods. She's no fool. She's seen the police car parked outside, the lights flashing on her lawn.

The kettle whistles. Rosemary places two immaculate china cups on their saucers. "How do you take it?" she asks.

"Milk, no sugar."

Rosemary takes a deep breath. It's now or never. She lets her dress slip down her body. From the mirror atop the fireplace, where the children's photographs are lined like tin soldiers, her younger self is smiling. Naked. Beautiful. Lustful.

He's everything she ever wanted. Because you should always want what the moment gives you. Always say yes. Never say tomorrow.

She steps out from the circle of cashmere and merino wool at her feet, until their faces are inches apart. The sweet scent of his sweat floats in the air between them.

Her smile is wide, confident, sexy.

"No, *sugar*," she breathes. "I'm not talking about the tea."

Psychiko

Psychiko, Athens, Greece

The Macedonian whore was dead. Her mouth – a tight purple line. The fabulous breasts flattened with cling film. Her damp hair sweeping the marble patio.

They loaded her in the back of the truck like a sack of rice. A gun barked. As the engine whirred into life, and the Army car began the descent of the steep hill, its lights off as it slipped through the orange trees in bloom, I realised with a jolt that Babis' face had vanished from the window of his tiny hut.

Hana De Ville knelt on her bedroom floor, the reflection of the blue flame flickering in her eyes. The foil curled and twisted, before vanishing into thin air, where the white powder floated, fine as dust.

"One, two, three!" She closed her eyes, inhaling deeply. Her nostrils flared.

In a few seconds, Hana sniffed around her. She glared at Dakini. Her eyes narrowed and her mouth twisted downwards.

"You bitch!" she snarled. "It was my turn!"

Dakini giggled. She scratched her thigh under the skirt of her uniform, until the goose pimples on her skin started to bleed.

"Come on, Hana. Get a grip. We're partying. We're all good."

I stood by the window, watching the dusk set over the city. In the distance, the outlines of the dog-eared Acropolis seemed to float in the shimmering clouds. The sound of shattered glass exploded in my ears, but my body reacted in slow motion. My limbs were heavy; I felt like I was treading water with leaden arms and legs.

To my side, the sofas were moving. They blinked through

heavily lashed, chocolate-brown eyes, snorting through their noses. Camels, the lot of them. And someone had murdered the footstools. The seals just lay there, their throats slit, their blood a gush of partially digested fish. What a mess. One of the seals gave a guttural shriek and offal bubbled from the hole in its throat.

Then I realised the sound I'd heard wasn't shattered glass, but a slap. What had crumbled to the floor was Dakini's face. I didn't know she had glass eyes – they'd smashed into sparkling shards that caught the sunlight sifting lazily through the De Ville's orange orchard. Soon, the night lights would be on, and the new watchman would sit masturbating in the tamarisk shrubs, spying on the naked bodies splashing about in the swimming pool.

Hana's daddy was the French ambassador, and together with his Greek wife Eleni, held magnificent orgies on Saturday nights. Hana's mum would spend days looking through CVs and arranging interviews with swingers. Demand was high; everyone wanted to spend a night in Psychiko, Athens' richest suburb. Drinking free French champagne straight from the mouth of the ambassador was something worth fighting for.

Dakini's figure was materialising before my bleary eyes – an hourglass body growing from a handful of sparkling dust.

I blinked, and Dakini fell into focus. She was in one piece after all, holding her hand to her cheek.

"You bitch! Get out of here! Out!" Hana landed a fist in her stomach.

On the floor, Dakini laughed hysterically. When the vomit came out in a violent stream, she made a funny face. She gagged with her mouth like an "o" and her tongue out like when you have a hair stuck to the back of your throat.

Everyone was quiet. Seal blood, and puke. Eleni will go mad at Hana. But then I remembered they had a maid. She was called an *au pair*. They couldn't tell seal blood from real blood. The police might come. I had to get the hell out of there, but instead I stood, transfixed, watching Dakini die. She rolled over, her knickers in full sight.

White knickers just aren't cool. All knickers should be black. Black knickers make even fat bums like Dakini's look good.

The skirt of her uniform was held up with safety pins to make it shorter, even if just by a few inches. It didn't even show, and there was no real point, because boys didn't have a chance to look under our skirts anyway. We all went to Saint Eulalia Elementary, an all-girls school. Thousands of square meters of woodland, bright green cricket fields, kept alive with expensive bottles of Evian, and the ornamental lake, full of salty seawater turned sour from sitting still for too long.

I tried that water once. It was cool as death, even in the scorching August sun.

Everyone ran wild behind the nuns' backs. Hana and Dakini were the worst. Hana made Dakini put chili powder in Mother Eulalia's underwear drawer. At least that's what she said when Father Benedict came out of her cell sneezing. Babette returned from the Christmas holidays with a suitcase full of sexy lingerie, and stayed up late so that, during midnight prayers, she could swap some for Sister Ephraimia's beige and boring grandmother panties, only to discover that she already had numerous pairs of very provocative thongs, and even a pink bullet that, after much examining, we concluded wasn't used for stimulating prayer concentration.

As for me, the bravest thing I'd done so far was swim naked in the lake with the bust of Saint Eulalia. The bust looked like a mermaid turned to stone by a spell. I even pretended I was Saint Eulalia rising from the water – only a saint would never pose topless. The caretaker caught me. He might have been a man who looked like a woman. She was actually a woman who could pass as a man. Or whatever. That was before I met *Hana, Hana the Fabulous, Hana the Bold* and *Untouchable Hana*, and my world turned upside down.

"Password!" Hana was shouting at Dakini.

"Chicken soup!"

"No! It's chicken soap!"

From the table laid with silverware by the pool came the murmur of adults' voices and the clinking of plates and wine glasses. Hana's mother was talking, laughter trailing her words like fireworks. It was early still. Later, we would hear the splash of water in the moonlight, and Eleni's shrieks of pleasure as yet another young playboy nibbled her breasts. Hana swore her baby brother Achilles, fast asleep one floor below, was the spitting image of the hunk who was fired after slipping some crucial information to the press.

"You can't be serious," said Babette, rolling her eyes. "You can't just kick her out of here in the middle of the night!"

"She knows the password," I whispered.

"Chicken soap, chicken soap, CHICKEN SOAP!" yelled Dakini, frothing at the mouth.

Hana eyed her coldly. "I'm Hana De Ville," she said, switching to her posh accent. "I can do whatever I want."

There was no other way to climb the metal ladder but crawling up like a cockroach. Each time you moved you heard the screeching of metal and the wind made your body feel like a paper plane. The height was terrifying. Hana had pulled the yellow sign saying *Fire Escape* off the wall and was sitting on it, cigarette in hand.

"Come on," she called, and as much as I hated her for making me go up the ladder, as soon as she opened her lips in a smile the familiar, irresistible desire to please her took control.

I went further up, trying not to think of why she made me go first, or how much like a cockroach I really looked. I didn't ask myself why not Dakini, or Babette, or even Hana: Hana would only go first on a drinking competition or when sniffing crystal meth.

I thought she hated Dakini. Only a couple of days ago she hit her and asked her to leave the ambassador's villa in Psychiko. We called it *The Castle*, but only when Hana wasn't around. If she heard us she would probably smirk and say it was just a doll's house.

Hana was the biggest snob I'd ever known. When I first met her in Year 8 – only a few months back – and she rolled her eyes and spoke in that funny French accent, I thought *She isn't for real.*

"It is my house," was her favourite expression.

She sometimes said it before downing her daily shot of scotch, standing naked at the end of the curved staircase, on the last glass step. Her chain necklace fell over her breasts like the armour of a warrior. Then she turned and walked back to her bedroom, wig in hand, slowly, so that we could admire the tattoo on her shaved head. I wondered what Sister Efigenia would say if she knew Hana had Satan tattooed on the back of her skull.

"Are you there yet?" She shook the ladder, and I felt like a cockroach more than ever, clinging on for dear life.

I walked against the wind on the roof of that twenty storey building. Adrenaline pumped through my veins. A rainbow stretched like a bridge on the sky. Pink gold, yellow gold, blue sapphire, emerald. I could walk on it straight into the sun. I could …

"Lexi!" I was surprised at the strength in Hana's grip. Her knuckles were white; her hand on my arm like a cuff. The rooftop's edge was slippery and sharp. The rainbow was dissolving, effervescent in the air. I caught one of the sparkly particles on my arm. It was a feather. I touched my face with it: it smelled of dead bird.

We were out of Psychiko. It had been an adventure to take the bus to one of Athens' poorer neighbourhoods. That's where Hana found the building site. She'd been obsessed with it ever since she read about the murder in the papers. The murder had occurred three weeks ago. The leftovers were everywhere: from the yellow police do-not-cross strips ripped by passing vandals, to the blood on the sandy floor strewn with rotting rubbish.

"Do you think he raped her before, or after, he killed her?" Hana picked up a handful of dust and took it to her mouth. "You could get Aids just by licking this," she said.

"Not everyone who lives outside Psychiko has Aids."

She inhaled deeply through her nose and narrowed her eyes. "Daddy has alligators in the basement. Just hatched. The *baths* are perfect for them. Wet and warm. Alligators like that."

Just hatched. The thought made me smile.

Being so high was amazing. I'd never been higher than the rooftop terrace of Hana's villa, where the old Macedonian butler filled Eleni's cups with Martini while she lay baking in the sun, her diamonds forming rainbows of colour around her. She was like an exotic animal in a scintillating cocoon, as separate from us as if she existed in a different universe. Once a stupid little girl from our class saw a small resemblance between the butler and Hana, and joked that the butler was her real father. That was the last time she was invited to *The Castle*. We all dreamed of having secret fathers, more interesting than the ones we already had. *Fathers who loved us*. But what if instead of diplomats, our dads were butlers? Wasn't it better that your daddy was an unloving ambassador than a loving butler?

Midday. The sun was shining, hanging so close in the sky that you could almost stretch out your hand and pluck one of the golden rays.

The rows of cars streamed along one of Athens' main traffic arteries, all following a massive truck billowing ash-grey smoke from behind. I thought of the swans I saw in Regent's Park with Daddy the week before. They rumpled the surface of the water, the mother with her head curved like a question mark and the small ones, one of which was jet black and kept losing direction. Daddy gave me a present carefully wrapped in silver glittery paper. I opened it. *A doll.*

"She can speak English," he said. I chucked the doll in the nearest bin. Daddy would forget about it by the time our jet landed on the private runway outside Psychiko. Marcel, Daddy's bodyguard, caught my eye and smiled behind his dark glasses.

From the top of the building everything looked so neat and orderly. The traffic signs, with all the precise instructions, SLOW, FAST, 30, 50, STOP, GO. If only life could be like that.

"What are you doing here all alone?" Hana's hand was on my shoulder. She smelled of cigarette smoke and her skin had the faint aroma of *Magie Noire*, Eleni's sex perfume – the same one that wafted from her crumpled sheets. She closed her eyes: the mascara on her eyelashes was the blackest black, the powder on

her eyelids electric-blue, her lips full and glossed. I could kiss
her on her heart-shaped mouth. But then I remembered her
mumbled apology to Dakini.

"Sorry babe, I'm just so messed up ... I hate myself, really I
do ... See, this is why I think we shouldn't stay friends, I'm
driving you astray, I am, Dakini, I know I am ... Get away,
please, I couldn't bear leaving you ..."

My cheeks burned. My eyes burned. Dakini was crying on the
phone. Hana smoked and smoked and smoked.

"Of course, darling. Of course, of course, I love you too."

"*Idiot!*" Whisky tumbled into her mother's heavy bottomed
crystal glasses. She stuck her pierced tongue out. "We need her,
though. I get her to steal her mum's doses of morphine. The
bitch is dying, you know. It's cancer."

My blood ran cold. Dakini hadn't said anything about the
cancer. We were in Eleni's bedroom, where the curtains blew in
the breeze from the olive grove and the burgundy silk cords
knotted around the intricate headboard caught the light of the
sun. From the floor beneath, her baby brother babbled. It was
then that I saw Hana's mobile on the floor. Still ticking away
the seconds of the conversation. On the other end of the line,
Dakini was sobbing.

Hana moved away from me and flung her arms in the air, her
pretty mouth curved in a cheeky smile. Her cardigan opened
and her low-cut blouse slipped to one side to reveal her pear-
shaped breast, with a small ring through the tip of her brown
nipple. At that moment, I knew that would be how I'd always
remember her: her arms outstretched, her long legs bare and
only partly shaved, her blue hair ruffled by the wind.

"I'm so fucked up, man!" she screamed. "I'm on top of the
fucking world!"

When we came back to *The Castle*, everything was silent. We
weren't meant to be here; Hana had faked her father's signa-
ture on the slip. The convent school was atop a hill in Psychiko,
so we walked the distance to the villa across the narrow pebbled
roads lined with orange and lemon trees in bloom. The alley-

ways were littered with the white petals, which were growing by the second in the sweet night wind, like a fragrant snow.

The aroma of food crept on the patio. Kostas, the night guard, was mopping his sweat with a large handkerchief. The Mediterranean nights are sly: they deceive you with the promise of coolness when they only give out more heat. It was cruel that he had to wear his suit on a night like this, with the tie tightly wound around his neck like a noose. We waited behind the myrtle bushes with their blood-red berries, until he left his post to use the toilet. Then we sprang out of our hiding place and into the house.

It was quiet inside, cool from all the marble floors. Perhaps no one was at home. The ambassador's villa was a doorless labyrinth of columns, the walls smooth and white like carved bone. Statues jumped blocking my way in the dark.

We knew there was something wrong with Hana. She had been throwing up all the way back. I'd seen blood through the rancid remnants of undigested food that ran in rivulets down the pebbled alleys.

Dakini, Hana and Babette had gone upstairs, to Hana's bedroom, and I was left alone in the unusual silence of the house. I entered more rooms softly lit by *abat-jour* lamps, golden light spilling over the spines of leather bound books. Suddenly the books sprang wings and fluttered above my head, ugly bats with vampire fangs and red eyes, but I blinked and they were gone. With time, I'd learned to discern between what was real and what was hallucination, the effect of whatever drugs I could get my hands on at Saint Eulalia's. Through the glass walls I saw the blue surface of the swimming pool, gleaming behind the palm trees whose shadows trembled on the water. The blue was an incredible colour, as if the pool had been filled with heavy rolls of velvet that rubbed against each other like bodies in the throes of love. The glass wall dissolved into a storm of glittering particles. *Snowflakes.* I could feel their cold breath on my skin. I shivered, and the glass wall came back into place with a thud like a falling guillotine.

Thud.

Then I saw *it*. The door. I'd never dared open it before but tonight I felt invincible. I crept towards it in the darkness. After a few twists of the key I found under a slab of marble on the floor, it gave way.

It was w*et and dark,* just as Hana had said. The stairs were cold on my feet. From somewhere came the sound of rippling water. The Roman baths were forbidden territory. As sacred as a catacomb. Eleni bathed here with her friends and lovers, in the green soapy water where the musty walls and the tall slender columns projected their hideous reflections. It was here that something had gone wrong that night with the Macedonian prostitute.

The lights switched on, and I gasped at the expanse of water around me. Venetian lanterns hung from the ceilings, pouring their light in the cave's deep, murky swamp. My feet were ankle deep in the lukewarm mush. It was ugly and green.

The gunman wore a fighter's mask. His face was caged, and maybe his soul, too. Babis had frozen at his post. I said a silent prayer when the truck started. But then it stopped, as I knew it would. The driver climbed out. I could tell his gun had a silencer on because of the long shadow it made on the ground. The shadow crawled over the potted azaleas and over the rectangular hut where Babis sat motionless.

The gunshot sounded like another bottle of champagne opened by the pool. More red droplets sprinkled the myrtle bushes. I made no sound. On my skin, Babis' blood was as warm as the night.

The ripple was close, deafening. Something was floating at my feet in the green water. It took me longer than usual to register that it was a mutilated human hand.

And then I saw *them*. The dirty green of the water wasn't the aquamarine reflection of the marble. The pool was a tangle of green bodies, whipping tails and snapping jaws. *Alligators.* The sounds they made as their strong jaws crumbled bones were intoxicating. The limbless body floated face down in the water, inches away from a circle of hungry snouts. Then, with a swish of scaly tails, the bodies lunged forwards, and the shearing resumed. One of the alligators snipped the body in half. The other ate the leg stumps. A third finished off what was left of the arms. And the largest broke the skull like a nut. The pink brains leaked through its teeth like a ripe, shredded kernel.

I scrambled up the stairs and back into the house, locking the door safely with the key. I was on my way upstairs, still shivering, when I heard the moan.

Eleni's voice. I followed it to a room at the very back of the house, where antique furniture dressed the walls. I recognised Eleni's camisole, the one I'd seen in her bedroom, and the burgundy cord which now hung from her waist. Her olive skin gleamed in the moonlight; her closed eyes looked like tulip bulbs on a face transformed by ecstasy. At first, I thought the man standing behind her, pushing her harder and harder into the bookcase behind the cabinet her wondrous body was slumped over obscenely, was the ambassador, but then I saw his silver hair sprouting from the deeper darkness. Sat in an armchair in the shade of a potted fig tree, he was so still he could have been one of the many statues that populated his home. Only the penis in his hand wasn't made of stone. Liquid spurted in the dark, arching over the top of the fig tree and dripping from the startled leaves.

Tomorrow, the maid would have to wipe the plant with a damp cloth. Eleni would bathe in the hot water pools at the basement of the villa. Maybe she thought that bathing in human blood and brains would preserve her youth.

The ambassador's eyes glinted as silver as his hair. For a moment it seemed as if a giant snake was slithering around the fig tree. Eleni gave out a savage grunt and her body shuddered against the bookcase.

I turned and ran. I ran through and around the columns, knocking over a couple of statues on the way. The statues were all naked, with beautifully sculpted breasts that seemed to follow me from the gloom like the barrels of loaded pistols. I locked myself in the luggage lift. It took forever to get upstairs. The lift was made of glass, too. At the first floor, Hana's *au pair* gave me a frightened look as she held a screaming baby, trying to feed it a bottle of milk.

I stormed out of the lift and into Hana's room. Hana was lying on her bed, curled into a ball, her hands holding her stomach.

I started stroking her hair. This is how I wanted to see her, helpless, quiet, mine and only mine.

"I am really not feeling well," she murmured. The cheeky tone of her voice had gone and, with all the dark rings under her eyes and her blue lips she looked younger than ever, almost a child.

"Try and get some sleep," I whispered back and got up to pour myself a whisky.

"I'm not feeling well." She sounded desperate. "Don't leave me, Lexi. Please stay with me until I feel better."

I patted her back. "I won't be long," I said. I felt sick, like after every fresh dose of heroin. I went to the bathroom and before I could switch on the light, I was sick on the floor.

I wiped my mouth with toilet paper and put my head in the cool toilet bowl. I brushed my teeth with a random toothbrush from a crystal glass. The whiteness of the sink flashed on and off. I let the water run over my head. I was still in the bathroom, my face buried in a snow-white, fluffy towel, when I heard the scream.

Back into the room, Dakini and Babette were bending over the balcony. The bed was empty.

"Where is she?" I grabbed Dakini by the shoulders and started shaking her. "Where is she?"

From the corner of my eye, I saw Hana's parents walking over the *chaise-longues* like zombies. Eleni tried to scream, but she was so full of coke it came out like a choked moan.

"It was an accident," Babette said. On the floor was a puddle of puke.

"Hana!" I called. Panic hit my bloodstream like poison.

A baby's cry echoed in the house.

"We need to get the hell out of here." Dakini's voice.

More voices rose from downstairs. With a fat moon and a dusting of brilliant stars and the acacia creepers filling the room with their delicate perfume, it felt like nothing could go wrong. Yet, there was something down there that gave the innocent May night a new, invincible power, as if the devil on Hana's skull had suddenly come to life. Because there, floating on the incredibly blue water, surrounded by orange blossom, was Hana's body. A black pool of blood surrounded her head, and her wig was a dark patch a few inches away, a hairy spider in the shadow of a palm tree. The edge of the pool was red where she'd smashed her head in the fall.

"She was dead when she hit the water," Dakini said.

I grabbed my bag and hat, flung the door open and stormed down the stairs. *Hana's dead*, I heard myself thinking. *She's dead.*

I ran through the doors and onto the patio, while the ambassador shouted, his voice heavy with tears and the haze of some unknown drug. "Who the fuck are you? What are you doing in my house?"

A gunshot, ricocheting off the column behind me. Another, blowing Adonis' penis into pieces. And a third, making a whole glass wall collapse in a rain of singing shards.

I ran down the narrow pebbled streets littered with citrus blossom. Lemon trees, orange trees, grapefruit trees shook their flavoured branches from the patios of bigger and fancier villas. I ran until my lungs burnt, until I could see the hill with the convent school emerge from the darkness. But no matter how fast I ran, I couldn't get those words out of my head:

I'm Hana

Hana

Hana

The words swarmed in my mind like frantic wasps, going round in circles, tireless, dripping their wet venom with every step I took, every syllable I heard, every letter of the name I wanted to destroy.

I can do whatever I want.

Hana's sarcastic laugh filled the sleepy street. It seemed to be coming out of the trees that rustled gently in the breeze. I felt weak. What was dripping from my head was not the sticky venom of memories, but my own blood.

And then I remembered. The gleam in Dakini's eyes as she stood, her arms crossed, on Hana's balcony. The devil on Hana's skull had found a new home in Dakini's nut-brown eyes.

Reconciliation

The worst thing about a nice cup of coffee is that it gets too cold too soon. I watched the dark, fragrant surface, stirring it unnecessarily with a spoon.

Around me, laughter, chatter, the scraping of food off plates, cooks in white turbans making simple and vulgar dishes: chips, beans on toast, omelettes. The *Arianne* is not exactly a Michelin restaurant but it's where I spent my afternoons, writing my never-ending twenty-act play that I like to start from scratch every winter as a New Year's resolution.

The truth is I'm a bad writer. I'm the kind of writer who's always looking for inspiration. There's nowhere I haven't been: the five continents far and wide. Boy, I spent a fortune on those travels. Not that I couldn't afford it. I'm rich enough to live off my assets and I haven't done anything to deserve it. Yes, I'm one of those people who everyone hates. Not someone you can look up to. Not one of those who worked hard for what they have. And this is why I'm fundamentally different from the masses. From those who, to be like me, would have to be born all over again.

Hate me already, don't you? Why? You haven't heard anything yet.

Writing. For some it's easy. Some can write a whole poem on a toothpick. Some can even finish novels that started out as jokes. Some – and these are the worst – can actually write on the spot. This is what they do at those evening writing classes. Thing is, they look absolutely normal. *Writers.* I always thought, well, that they'd be the stand-out-in-a-crowd type of people.

The night this story starts, I spent nine and a half hours in the bath with a few bottles of champagne and some readymade lines of coke. Crystal had gone; her pink G-string was hanging from the ceiling lamp, over Smiley's web, looking like some kind of strange insect captured there. Smiley is my bathroom spider. Marietta, my maid, is not allowed to touch him.

At about midnight I called my ex.

"Hello?" She was wide awake.

"Are you drunk?" I shouted over the noise of the water cascading from the tap between my feet.

"Hello?"

Music blasting in the background.

"HAVE YOU BEEN DRINKING?" I shouted again, loud enough for the neighbours to hear, if I had any.

I live in a mansion by the woods, in the wildest countryside you would never expect to find only a couple of miles away from London. *Buckinghamshire* – quiet, wild, quirky. I could kill someone and bury them in the woods and no one would ever know.

"Go to hell," she said but didn't put the phone down. She wanted to hear the knife plunging in my flesh, twisting and turning.

"Put Charlotte on."

"No."

This time she hung up. My wife – I still think of her as my wife – isn't exactly the most polite person in the world. The phone slipped through my fingers into the bath, where I was lying in about a ton of ice. I looked at my bright gold wedding ring. I never used to wear it when we were married. I'd always find the craziest excuses, like it's too tight or too loose.

I was counting the bottles of champagne lying on the marble bathroom floor when this brilliant idea struck me. One of those "Eureka!" moments. I jumped out of the bath, stumbled down the hall to my bedroom, dripping wet, my gold silk gown flying behind me. I heard my Venetian antique vase crashing, but I didn't bother to turn around. I was in such a state of excitement that my hands were shaking.

And then I was in my bedroom, searching feverishly for the laptop and knocking down a crystal carafe with my opium-water, and my thousand mils bottle of *Star* perfume.

Ah. *My bedroom.* Designed to seduce women. An Aladdin's cave with expensive mirrors, burgundy bedspreads and a bar where I keep, apart from fine wine and refined spirits, my potions and drugs. *Black balls of opium, cocaine, antidepressants.* All around the room, in elegant silver pots, grow my magic mushrooms and my peyote cacti. And, the last and most perfect touch, black satin sheets.

Frankly, it looks like the lair of a rapper, the kind of sex nest 50 Cent might make for himself. But, in truth, one can get bored of sex, even of the hottest women and the wildest perversions, something ordinary men see only in movies. At the end of the day, all we ever really want is love. Even the worst of us.

Even someone like me.

I threw myself on the bed and lit an apple-scented cigar: two hundred quid a box. I was smiling so widely my cheeks ached.

Room to let, I typed furiously, my smile getting wider and wider, almost breaking my cheekbones.

Room to let. I don't think many people could even afford to live in my hallway. I have an amazing detached house, one that seems to have been cut straight out of a magazine.

Room to let. This is how I got to know Paquita. That day at Arianne's, it was her I was waiting for.

"Mr Anderson?"

When I looked up from my now cold cup of coffee, I saw her: a fiery brunette, all legs and lips and hair. I wolf-whistled in my head.

"Ben," I said, grinning like an idiot. "Just call me Ben."

Paquita nodded appreciatively as I walked her around *The Chateau,* showing her the music room and the billiard room and the basement cinema. Her eyes caressed the exquisite furniture, the Persian carpets, the moon-shaped windows, the spiralled flights of stairs with their gold-plated banisters, the lemon trees where my blue and green parrots roosted.

"It looks like a magician's castle," she said, without the smallest spark of greed in her eyes – eyes the colour of roasted almonds. She did not regard *The Chateau* as something that could be hers one day. Here I was, ten minutes after bringing a woman into my home and she wasn't down on her knees giving me a blow job.

I kept the cost low. If I gave her the room for free, she'd get suspicious, and the last thing I wanted was for her to know how crazy and lonely I was.

"Do I have access to the Internet?"

I just gazed at her.

"I talk to my sister," she explained. "In Chile."

"Of course," I muttered, feeling like someone just woken from a long sleep. I felt as if I'd slept for a hundred years – and now I was being kissed awake by a Chilean princess.

She moved in the next day, her belongings stuffed in an old leather suitcase that I carried for her to the room next to mine.

"The first landing is the only one in use," I lied.

"What's wrong with the second floor?" she asked.

"Haunted," I winked, and, to my delight, Paquita smiled.

I loved her indifference. Being rich makes you want things you can't have – and you want to have *everything*. We're over-dosed by women who try too hard. And we get bored with those who don't try at all. Two things I thank heaven for: being born a man, and having met Isabelle. Okay, so maybe the second floor *is* haunted. Sometimes, in the dead of the night, I hear the clink of *her* bracelets and see *her* standing in the shadows. *Poor old Isabelle.*

To Paquita, I might as well have been the kitchen tap, or the battered old suitcase which, incidentally, was the ugliest thing I'd ever seen. I could probably sell it to one of my friends as an antique. Hey-ho.

That night I listened to her chatting on the phone. I spoke Spanish, something I omitted to tell her – my Mexican, low-life father was yet another secret I'd kept even from my wife, Mandy. When she went quiet, I imagined her taking off her jeans and those filthy boots, unbuttoning her shirt and dancing around the room, moving towards the *en suite* bathroom, step-ping naked on the cool marble floor.

And, when I went to bed, there were no tears for my wife. For the first time in months the toilet roll by my bed remained untouched.

In the morning I was woken by Marietta's vacuuming. She'd brought her eight year old daughter, Federica, with her. They were on the landing; through the door left ajar I could see Marietta's long slender arm on the banister, wiping away, and remembered the time right after Mandy left when I dragged her into bed with me, the hot Marietta smelling of bleach and lemon floor cleaner.

"Mummy, why do you clean *his* house, but not ours?" little Federica was saying.

"Does your room clean itself, Federica?" her mother barked, and I knew she'd seen Paquita's things in the hallway from the furious scraping that accompanied her voice. "Are there any plates in the sink, Federica?"

"Sorry, Mummy."

I turned on the other side and slept. When I woke up, it was late morning. I opened my remote controlled heavy drapes, and brilliant sunlight cascaded over me like a waterfall of gold. The trees were emerald green, the birds loud, the air sweet and fresh. Paquita had gone off to work, so I picked up the phone and called Chris.

"Are you free today?" I asked, while Crystal, my Friday date, massaged my shoulders with aphrodisiac oils.

"It's rather short notice, but ...?" I waited as he pretended to consider his options. It's not as if he could say no – I had shares in his company and I could withdraw them just as fast as I could poke him in the eye. I muttered the words even before he said them: "What do you need, boss?"

"I want you to cut a door in my wall."

Chris laughed. A chainsaw whirred in the background and a rude voice shouted orders.

"I'm serious. Whatever it costs, as long as it's finished by four."

"Yes, sir."

By the time she came home the new door had been fitted in the wall, looking like it had always been there. Paquita walked past it, dumped her bag on the bed, and opened the windows.

On her way to the bathroom she stopped short.

I watched from the hallway where I pretended to fix a cupboard's handle. She'd seen the door, because now she was creeping towards it as if it was something that might spring at her. She touched it, and as it slowly opened with a creak she jumped – she must have caught a glimpse of my luxurious bedroom where, I remembered with a jolt, the stripper, Crystal was still asleep, her black skin shining like ebony in the last of the day's sunlight.

"Everything all right?" I asked.

"Yes, just that, well, I ... I didn't realise you had a door here. Ah, well."

She just shrugged and went to have her bath.

Blimey. I love it when women are so laid back that being with them is as easy as breathing. Nothing like my Mandy – oh no, her every breath felt like you had a fish bone in your throat. Though deep down, I know, no woman is ever that easy. Some of them are just cleverer than others.

That's the only downside of being wealthy. Your life's a detective novel where everyone's a suspect. Not that I complain. When you've got nothing to do to pass the time, it can be kind of nice playing Sherlock Holmes.

"How come you got to be so rich?" she asked me once, over a dinner of fried beans and chicken – her favourite. "You don't do anything all day."

The memory of how I got to inherit a fortune turned like a knife in my heart. A dark secret that never sees the light of day. Something that lives within me, an evil seed that never grows and never dies.

Vegas, 1989. I'd gambled my weight in blood, and now I was hanging around the roulette tables, watching the wheels turn with an explosion of colour. Have you ever wondered about the red in the casinos? The red walls, the red carpets, the red tables and wheels. *Blood-red. Murder-red.* The colour of passion, and of the wounds it leaves behind.

I was actually hungry when I saw her, and the remaining

hour until I had to check out from *The Palace* was ticking in my head like a time-bomb. I had no money left – *nothing*. I'd spent my family fortune on gambling debts – most of which haven't even been paid. Back then I was still using my real name, one I won't mention in this journal in case it falls into the wrong hands. Far as I know, there are about twenty angry Russians looking for me, not to mention the Chinese and the Albanian. My friend Cipri didn't make it. He'd be meat for the rats by now. They found a watch on the bank of the Thames that might have been his, but who knows? The Thames is full of unpaid gambling debts.

There was only one thing left – my body. I was a good-looking chap and when I was high I dressed like Elvis – white studded trousers, jacket with frilly arms, my hair black and slick.

The woman noticed me – in my peculiar clothes, I must have stood out like a sore thumb. She wasn't a spring chicken, by any means, maybe forties or fifties. You could never tell with these rich madams. There might have been a lot of plastic surgery there, or just the effects of a light life having orange juice served in bed and bathing in goat's milk and a diet of young men on toast. She was even beautiful – though probably the best thing about her was her classic *Chevy* parked out back. We sat in it for a smoke – I'll always remember the sparkle of her diamond jewels in the moonlight. She'd had no children, I could tell just by looking at her narrow hips. She told me her name was Isabelle.

Isabelle. I always say she was my lucky charm. Because, after I met her, and she invited me to join her table, I started winning.

"A ghost of the past, Mr Anderson?"

I quickly wiped away a tear. Paquita was behind me, peering over my shoulder at the photograph in my hand, a photograph of Isabelle as a young woman, one I'd found in her Arizona home when I was sorting out her things.

"She's beautiful. She looks just like ..."

"Marilyn Monroe? Everyone told her that. She was my mother."

"Ah. May her soul rest in peace," said Paquita, crossing herself.

Indeed, I thought. Although I don't know how a soul can rest when the body is dismembered into a million pieces, and your blood is feeding the cacti in the Nevada desert.

A fine mist was floating over the garden. Another day was dragging to an end, a sweet end because I was to see Paquita, watch her prepare supper, inhale the steam of her chicken curry.

She loved chicken – especially on the bone. I told you, there was something feral about her. She would have looked so hot in a loincloth, dressed in feathers, with a bow and arrow on her back.

She ate the bones too – the thin ones at least; the grinding of her teeth loud and spooky in the silence. Outside, the darkness fell ever so gently over the magnolias, slowly obscuring every shape and colour like a creeping illness. In the garden, the stone statues peered out from the rosemary and thyme bushes like nocturnal creatures, while the fountain with the peeing angel that came alight at nightfall illuminated their bald heads and limbless torsos.

The house phone was ringing.

"Yes?"

"Hey, stranger. How's life?"

I cleared my throat. "How much, Mandy?" I asked resignedly. I'm a generous bastard, like all of us gambling men. Easy come, easy go. We know that better than anyone.

"Oh, no." Mandy chuckled. She sounded tense, like someone at gunpoint. "Don't be silly, darling. This is just a courtesy call. To see how you've been."

"*Darling?*" I erupted. "*Courtesy call?* Mandy, you should really stop getting high. What the hell are you on?"

Mandy faked the retreat technique.

"Never mind. If I knew you'd be like this I wouldn't have bothered. Good-bye!"

"Cirio."

Just before I put the phone down I heard her say something at the other end of the line. Then Paquita's key turned in the lock.

"Wait, wait," Mandy was pleading but I could barely hear her. All I heard was Paquita's footsteps on the stairs, small and quick like rainfall.

Mandy was sinking her venomous claws into my heart. "Charlotte wants to see you. We could come over tonight, if you like. Grab a movie or something."

"I don't know, I don't know," I muttered, all eyes and ears. Paquita gave me a tired smile as she walked into her room.

"Patrick? What's that supposed to mean? CHARLOTTE WANTS TO SEE YOU. DON'T YOU WANT TO SEE HER?"

She was really shouting now.

"Mandy, I have to go. I'll call you later. To explain ..."

"Patrick!!!"

I put the phone down. She seemed so far away I couldn't grasp the meaning of her words. As though she was talking in a different language I translated word by word in my head: Charlotte, Mandy, Paquita. Mandy, Charlotte, Paquita. Paquita, Charlotte. Charlotte, Paquita. Paquita, Paquita.

That night I lay in bed watching her sleep. She was holding a teddy bear, and her two long black plaits had curled through the iron headboard like ropes. I picked up the remote, set to rewind whatever happened in Paquita's room that evening. I argued with Chris about where to fix the camera. He thought the Big Brother option was the best – who would think to look behind a mirror? But I insisted it should go under the reading lamp – a better angle. It finally went behind the mirror – Chris advised that women like applying their body cream while looking in the mirror. She came out of the shower without wiping herself – that was another thing we had in common – and, I could've kissed Chris – she sat on the stool by the mirror, oiling herself with Johnson's baby oil until her skin shone like fish scales, even through a screen. I was watching her, so close I could hear her breathe. She smiled. I stiffened. Did she know I was watching her?

When she lifted her arm, I thought she was about to wave, my heart jolted but then ... then she started feeling her breast with circular moves. *Phew.* Her armpits were clean-shaven. I touched the screen and traced them with my finger, up and down the side of her body, counted her ribs in my head: *one, two, three.* I thought of the bones she was chewing every night at dinner – it was as if those bones had grown back inside her body, new, strong, perfectly arched. Saliva pooled in my mouth. I loved her so much I could eat her.

She stretched her arms and her hair cascaded over her shoulders, covering her breasts with a flurry of curls – so dark they shimmered blue in the light. I watched her putting on unattractive white briefs – which, by the way, should be illegal – and a pair of huge reading glasses. I smiled. Only I knew what her comfort book was. A big dog-eared volume she'd borrowed from the children's section in the library: *A Hundred Classical Fairy Tales.* She was dreaming of her prince. Not knowing he was right there behind the intricate tapestry on her wall, lying on the bed in his underwear, smoking Havanas.

That night I dreamed of Isabelle. The dreadful events that happened after we left *The Palace* in the early hours of the morning unfolded slowly, painfully slow, in the film of my memory. It was two in the morning when Belle and I scrambled into the Chevrolet. The car was a beauty – slick and shapely, with mirrors like a lizard's eye-slits and immaculate leather seats.

"I'm lovin' it, baby!" The car moved under me like a lover, a spectacular dancer in a bright red dress; I'd never driven a car like that before, and whether because I was drunk or because of its powerful engine, it felt like all I had to do was touch her, and *she* moved. I sometimes think I was more attracted to the car than to Isabelle; it was *the car* I was having the one night stand with. Though now I know that the *Chevy* was for me what the topless siren is for the sailor – fool's gold, a chimera, a beautiful bridge to hell.

But then, while the whisky still bubbled in my blood and the adrenaline bloated my veins, her every roar roused me like a love moan; and when I look back I realise that was the start of a mad death dance.

We swerved our way around the traffic lights and colourful signposts. Isabelle was laughing – I can still hear that laugh in my head, loud and tinkling, the sound of a thousand bells. She laughed like a rich woman – all her good life and power encapsulated in that laughter.

In the morning, I cracked the door to Paquita's room ever so slightly, popped my head in, ever so slowly, slithering around the wall. She was sighing in her sleep – kicking her long, splendid legs like a mare, neighing softly. I gasped for breath at the expanse of all that young, smooth skin, emitting a low hiss from the back of my throat in reply, like a viper anticipating the taste of its prey.

Back in my room, I opened the window. The squirrels hung from Marietta's bird feeders like acrobats. I took a large gulp of the fragrant air, and made my decision. Today, I would take Paquita into London.

I stood in the black marble bathroom, shaping my hair with strong gel to get that Elvis look, though it came out looking more like a Japanese roof. Once I was dressed I knocked on Paquita's door. She was applying make-up, a tango playing in the background. Around her neck was a scarf, knotted like a noose.

If you haven't been in a speeding Ferrari, you can't know how much like a plane taking off it feels. Some woman told me it's just like childbirth, the dizzying sensation of having your insides pushed down to the floor.

The countryside flashed past us, my roof was down, the engine was roaring, so it took me a while to hear Paquita screaming.

"Slow down!"

I pulled over in a cloud of dust, down a secluded driveway, between trees and fields. A smell of wet forest was in the air: mushrooms and rain-soaked wood. Paquita was retching, and I pushed her out just in time for the jet of vomit to ricochet off the nearest tree.

We had lunch in a crammed restaurant in Chelsea, our table practically in the middle of the pavement.

"This is my first time in Chelsea," she said, a strip of lettuce dangling from her lip. A tiny dog with a diamond studded collar began to lick my Armani boots and I remembered I used my aphrodisiac oil to shine them.

"I'm so awfully sorry," the dog's mistress squeaked as she unglued the dog from my shoe.

I added two extra monitors to my bedroom. The same night, I sat there on my sumptuous bed smoking cigars and watching her undress.

She wore black lace underwear with embroidered cherries.

I drew myself closer to the screen, spat the bitter tobacco into an ashtray and took in the sight of her, as if by staring at those firm thighs and breasts and curves, I could absorb all that youth back into my body.

The cherry knickers, I decided, had to be mine, and it wasn't without a sense of sheepishness that I extracted them out of the laundry basket the following morning, and put them in the safe next to Isabelle's charred shoe.

One night I was so depressed, I decided to keep the monitors off. Once again I was remembering Isabelle, and how her voice had exploded in my ears, all those years back: "Don't stop, Ben! Keep going!"

We had both seen it, the kangaroo, frightened in the head-lights, a baby in her pouch. I was driving at unimaginable speed: the impact would kill them both instantly. Weirdly, a line from Sunday school came to me, a parable about how animals are loved by God because they are without sin. How animals don't think bad thoughts, like people do. *Sunday school* – courtesy of my Catholic mother.

"Ben! Don't stop!"

And in that moment I was seized by anger, anger at the old rich woman who thought that what was left of her easy life was more precious than a mother and a baby's and, almost without thinking, when I was so close to the kangaroos I could see their eyes wide in the headlights, I stepped on the brake.

My phone was silently flashing by my side. *Bitch calling* – twenty missed calls. The house phone was ringing, too. I was feeling downright miserable and missed Charlotte but still couldn't bring myself to see her. She'd be fourteen soon, or was it fifteen?

Why was Mandy calling?

Another scene from long ago came to mind, another type of silence, and the loneliness of knowing that you've lived on the other side of reality. That you've been on a distant shore all along – watching the world go by, just like a ghost who doesn't yet know that it's dead.

On that hot summer afternoon, the silence in *The Chateau* was broken by sighs and moans, a man and a woman, a baritone and a soprano singing a love duet and me, the only audience, the cheated husband. Mandy's body under a body that wasn't mine, all sweat and muscles and scars. The bright sunlight gave her face a honey-like shade, he'd sunk his hand into her long crimson hair; his dreadlocks were on my pillow.

The worst thing still, Charlotte was home. She knew all about it. When I charged through her door like an enraged bull, she took off her headphones calmly, a defiant look on her face.

"Are you going to get divorced now?"

My heart dropped into my shoes when I realised it was not only Mandy I hated. I hated Charlotte, too, really hated her and this freaked me out.

What kind of psycho wants to see their only child dead?

Someone was knocking on the *inside* door. I quickly wiped a tear from my eye, and went over to open it. Although it could be no one but Paquita I was still surprised to see her standing in the doorway, her face swollen and red from crying.

The next moment, she was in my arms, sobbing loudly, wrapping her arms around my neck. I cuddled her back, and she made the fatal mistake of wandering into my territory.

We sat side by side with a bottle of brandy and some Marlboros, playing strip poker. When she was down to her bra and knickers, while I was still fully clothed, I said: "Does this guy not realise how lucky he is?"

Flattery. The only thing women can't resist. Only thing more powerful than money.

"He left me," she sighed. "For a fifty year old woman with kids." Tears were rolling down her cheeks, dropping down on her queen of hearts.

"Pick up your cards," I said. "Go on, I'm not looking."

"What do you think? *Why?* I mean, look at me? I'm twenty! And I'm gorgeous!"

I gave a small meaningful cough, and said gently: "Paquita, let me ask you something. How old is the guy?"

"Well, he's almost fifty, but ..."

"And is that fifty year old woman ... *his wife?*"

"They were going to divorce ..."

"Are her kids, well, *his?*"

"That's what she told him ..."

"Life is to be enjoyed." When I kissed her, I slipped a pink pill into her brandy.

As I was making love to her that night all I wished for was for Mandy to see me. I hoped that through some kind of miraculous coincidence she would walk in on us, just as I did on her, and find me cloaked in the black, silky sheet of that Chilean hair.

The house phone was ringing, ringing. At the other end of the line, Mandy was sobbing.

"It's Charlotte," she said, and my stomach dropped. "She ran away four days ago. Heard she's over in Brighton, living in a slum with that drunkard boyfriend of hers. That Italian. I didn't call the cops." She sighed. "I'll kill her. I bloody well will! First her grades drop, then she's bullying kids, and now this! *A boyfriend!*"

"Do you really want to play the blame game, Mandy?"

She said nothing, just wept in silence. *A-ha,* I thought, not without a twinge of satisfaction. The Jamaican bloke was gone. I knew it.

"Mandy, listen. Are you listening?"

"Yes."

"Put down that phone and dial **999**. Report her missing."

"No!"

"Mandy, gossip spreads. Yeah? Think about it. I bet everyone knows by now anyway. You know what, fuck your stupid friends! And fuck you too! I'm calling the cops myself."

"No, no," Mandy said. She sighed. "I have an address."

"You know the address?! Then say so! I'll pick you up in ten minutes. And if you're not ready ..."

"What? Drag me out by the hair and lock me in the boot? It wouldn't be the first time."

"I didn't lock you in the boot ..." I protested.

"You locked me in the car. *Naked*."

"It was a hot day."

Okay, maybe I'd gone a bit too far when I soaked Mandy's ripped camisole in chloroform and put her boyfriend to sleep, then grabbed her and drove the Ferrari as fast as it would go over a bridge, but I was hurt. *Hurt.*

I was putting the phone down when she suddenly said my name in that warm, cosy, long-forgotten way.

"Patrick?"

For some strange reason my mouth watered.

"Yes?"

"Are you living with a girl?"

For the first time since I'd woken up I glanced over to the bed. Paquita was asleep, her skin fair against the black sheets, and that last night exploded in my mind, the cards, the brandy, the sex.

"No," I answered.

"No, what?"

"No, no ..." I stammered.

"Patrick, I know you're living with a girl."

Out of the corner of my eye, I caught a glimpse of a rather ugly mole I hadn't noticed before, hidden in the curve of Paquita's underarm. She looked kind of ordinary in daylight, as if the magic spell of the night had worn off. Even as I stood there, undressed, the euphoria of having had her at last was slipping away, dripping into the fog of memory, and the contours of her body seemed to vanish in the shimmering sunlight.

"She's just a lodger," I mumbled and, after hanging up, I headed for the shower.

It was going to be a hard, awkward day.

What a relief to drive to Brighton with no traffic. It felt like I had my own private highway. I had the music on *loud*.

"Can you put the volume down?" Mandy pleaded. "I can't hear myself think."

"What?" I barked. "Don't you like rap?"

She said nothing, and for a while it was just the grey-blue ribbon of the road and the buzzing of other speeding cars and Snoop Dog's voice yapping away.

"Hey, whatever happened to that fucker?" I heard myself saying. "The Rasta playboy. Is he still around?"

"No." Mandy's voice was quiet.

"Oh?" I gazed at Mandy's forlorn face, sucked in her grief, enjoyed it; a balm for my wounds, sweet old revenge.

"It just didn't work out."

"I see."

We spoke very few words on the way, each one of us deep in our own thoughts. She didn't mention Paquita and I was relieved. It must have been Marietta, the maid, who told her. She'd remained faithful to Mandy despite everything – despite wanting me for herself. Women are funny like that.

The misty haze of the sea air hovered over Brighton in the warm, summery morning, almost like something you could touch, something that obscured the view and clung to you like a diaphanous web. It smelled of sea and the sound of the waves flooded the narrow streets. I thought of Charlotte, living with a man, her designer clothes hanging on lines with his filthy rags. It made me feel sick. I opened the window and spat outside.

The navigator guided me to the beach.

"Are you sure you've got the right address?" I asked Mandy, peering around at the neat terraced houses and their occupants, drinking their morning coffees out on high, elegant balconies in the sun. "This is ... *nice*. I doubt Charlotte has any taste in men. If she took after you ..."

To this Mandy bristled. "I've chosen you, haven't I?"

I had to laugh. "Precisely."

Mandy looked down at her lap.

"I'm sorry," I muttered. "I didn't mean ... But really, I don't know what you were doing with someone like me, anyway. I'm an idiot."

"No, you're not," she said quietly.

"I'm not?"

"No."

"But you said I made your life miserable. That I drank too much. That you hated my mood swings."

"You're generous," Mandy said quickly. "And loyal. And ... and you don't have any chest hairs."

We looked at each other, enjoying, after what felt like a century, but in fact wasn't more than a couple of years, a private joke. We both remembered the Harley Street clinic, where I endured excruciating pains to have my chest hair removed by laser. For Mandy. I emerged, reborn, looking like a shaved gorilla.

"There's somewhere I'd like us to go and I won't take no for an answer."

We sat down. It was the place where we first met, a beautiful Italian restaurant facing the beach. The memory nibbled at my heart. We were both seventeen, having brunch with our families and respective dates, I with a girl whose name I can't seem to remember – was it Lisa? Or Lizzie? – and Mandy with a guy she'd never admitted sleeping with though I knew she did, having heard it from the horse's mouth and seen it on video, too. Soon afterwards, we moved in together and had Charlotte. I found myself having to make a living, and when I started gambling, I realised I was a natural.

The waiter handed us the menus. Mandy looked at me with a spark in her eye and I knew what she was thinking. I know Mandy better than anyone. She wanted exactly what we had that first day.

Ten minutes later the waiter returned with milkshakes. Mandy beamed at me.

"For old times' sake," she said, raising her glass.

I looked out at the calm grey sea, and then ...

"Mandy! We have to find Charlotte!"

I leaped up, wiped my mouth with a tissue and signalled to the waiter to bring us the bill.

"Are you ready to order, sir?"

"We're leaving," I growled.

Mandy put a soft hand on my shoulder.

"Give us a few minutes," she told the waiter. Then she squeezed my hand. "Patrick, the reason I've brought you here is ... well, to tell you that I love you."

Bang. Just like that.

"I thought you loved Bob."

"Pardon?"

"*Bob*," I spat. "Your lodger."

"He's not my lodger." Mandy turned pink.

I remembered how flushed her face was that day, making love to him on a torrid afternoon, in our bed. Her feet in Jimmy Choo, high heeled sandals. Those sharp, slender heels. The marks of those heels are in my headboard even now, the ultimate, everlasting proof of her infidelity.

She pulled herself together and had another long sip of her milkshake. Then, her chin in her hands, she fluttered her fake eyelashes. "Anyway! What makes you say that I love him?"

"You told me so yourself," I cornered her. "Said that you loved him. That you can't live without him. That you wanted a divorce."

Mandy seemed to recoil at the memory.

"I'm sorry."

"You're sorry?!" I was yelling now, and some of the people in the restaurant turned to look at us.

"I am," she said in a loud whisper. "And I want us to get back together. I love you, not him."

"Oh!" I was getting angrier with every word she said. "Do you have any idea what you've put me through? I've turned into a freak, thanks to you!"

Paquita's face flashed in my head, her cherry knickers and those bloody monitors.

"Let's give it another go ... Please, Patrick! I'm begging you."

"I can't believe this. And how about Charlotte? Shouldn't we go and find her?"

Her eyes twinkled.

"What?" I snapped.

"She's in Watford, spending the weekend with Patricia."

"Patricia? *Patricia Adams*? Her school friend?"

"Yes."

For a moment I felt as light as air. It felt as if Mount Fuji had been lifted off my back.

"Then what ..."

A cheeky smile was on her lips.

"You made it all up?"

She sighed. "What could I do? You wouldn't see me. You wouldn't talk to me. You wouldn't take my calls. And I wanted you so badly."

"Yes, but why this disgusting blackmail? Why drive all the way to Brighton for God's sake? Why not go somewhere in London?"

"Because," she explained, "I wanted us to do something special. Something we've never done before." She had a sip of her milkshake, licking the rich froth from her lips. "And besides," she smiled, "love is a war."

Love is war. Well, my house sure looked like a battlefield when I returned home from that day trip to Brighton. The place had been vandalised, and I laughed out loud at the bare walls, the slashed paintings, the ruined curtains lying on the floor in pools of exquisite fabrics. The stairs were bald, bits of ripped carpet hanging from them like a flaking scalp, exposing the raw wood beneath. My silver was gone. So was my *Monet*. I walked through puddles of water and turned off the taps. In the sink was Smiley, or what was left of him and his glorious web. I stood in the too silent corridor and knew something awful had happened to my Tanzanian parrots.

They were hanging from their cage swings, strangled. And, in an upstairs cupboard, I found Crystal, tightly wound in rope, tape over her sobbing mouth. I'd forgotten that today was Friday.

I suppose, it saved me from telling her she had to move, that, in real life, Cinderella's days in the prince's palace are numbered. In my room I found the monitors were gone, all three of them. On the bed was a little note.

THAT DOOR WAS NOT THERE BEFORE.

I sat down, and amidst all the devastation and Crystal's incessant sobbing, the night Isabelle died came back to me one last time.

It had been a wild night at the casino. We made some money, a neat stash we kept between us in the car speeding through the desert. I couldn't help touching the crisp notes; ah, the smell of them, a smell old and new all at once, of pain and joy, of love and hate. The *Chevy* flew like a bullet, and I felt on top of the world. That was before the damned kangaroo appeared out of nowhere, and the baby reminded me of Charlotte, the toddler I'd left behind for an indefinite period of time, for a gambling diet in Vegas, after one of mine and Mandy's many rows.

And I stepped on the brakes. The car gave a shrill cry, as if strangled. Isabelle screamed, and that terrible noise before anything happened, the fraction of a second before time moved again, towards certain disaster, haunts me even today.

Isabelle flew through the air like a rag doll, in a motion so fast and violent her white sequined dress was stripped off her. Then it was all a blur; I knew the car was rolling around from the sharp pain in my bones every time it hit the ground. I prayed for death but consciousness stayed. I was lucid when the car landed back on its wheels. And sober, too. For a few instants all was quiet. The cacti stared at me from the dark desert, lonely and erect like giant cocks. It was hot and smoky, and I was immobilised in a carcass of metal; Isabelle lying next to me, *dead.* She was completely naked, her body covered with a pink dusting from the scraped metal paint, drops of blood glimmering on her face where the blue eyes were wide open.

"Isabelle!" I croaked. "Wake up!" I turned her around, and

that's when I saw the iron bar. Her insides fell on me, warm and soft, like a hot dinner spilled on my lap. I was crying. And then, amazingly, mercifully, just before I had time to realise that the army of fireflies advancing towards us were the eyes of hungry hyenas, just as one of them tugged at Isabelle's limp hand, I slipped into sleep.

The next thing I knew, I was in a room with a glass wall overlooking the Grand Canyon, and everyone was calling me Mr Anderson. I was in a wheelchair, and a hot nurse was feeding me chicken soup through a straw. Later that day some lawyers came to see me. A murder of crows, they were – all in black, with faces carved in stone, and sinister beak-like noses. They told me how sorry they were for my loss, and then they babbled about an insurance policy, and how because I had been severely disabled by the late Isabelle Debaussy-Anderson, I was to inherit her vast fortune. I stared ahead, listening to the list of properties, shares, and goods, just stared in disbelief. Then I nodded. I didn't let slip that I was the one driving the car – they supposed because Madame Debaussy had so many drink and drive convictions, and even a pending jail sentence, it could've only been her behind the wheel.

As the Barbie doll nurse let the gents out, I remembered. *The white chapel. The drunk Elvis priest. The pews, empty in the candlelight.* Isabelle and I had gotten married. I had murdered my own wife. For a fleeting moment I thought Mandy, whom I was engaged to, would kill me but then I remembered I was already widowed. A plan so perfect it could've been sketched in heaven. Or *hell.*

It sure is nice having money. It makes you feel you never really lived when you were ordinary. Crystal's whimpers brought me back to reality, and a feeling of shame washed over me as I recalled the night I met her – how I'd grimaced with contempt at her cheap necklace. I went over to the safe, where I kept all of Belle's jewellery, everything I found when I was tidying up the house once I recovered – fully apart from *my leg* – and I opened it. The code, one I didn't even reveal to Mandy, was the date of the accident. I started putting the bracelets and the necklaces and the tiaras on Crystal. When I finished, she looked like a Christmas tree.

"Take it," I said. "A goodbye present. No more Fridays from now on, I'm afraid, love."

I didn't add that with what she was going to get on the jewellery, she needn't fill her Fridays with work for the rest of her life. But of course a girl like Crystal will spend everything and still be a stripper.

At the back of the safe, hidden under the cherry embroidered knickers, was Isabelle's shoe, all that was left of her after I was rescued by the truck driver, who found nothing but a pile of bones and some hair after chasing the hyenas with his shotgun.

"My lucky charm," I said, kissing it.

Mandy and I got married again. A small wedding, nothing like the glamorous affair we'd had the first time; just a small reception with family and a few friends.

As we lay down together that night, her face smelling of make-up remover and toothpaste, she snuggled up to me.

"Do you remember our first night together?" I said.

"At your parents' house? How could I forget? I puked all over you."

"Well, actually ... you didn't. It was me. I lied because I was too embarrassed to admit that I was sick in the night ..."

Mandy slapped me. "You're an absolute jerk. I was mortified for months!"

"You'd be even more mortified to know I watched you fucking Pete."

Now her mouth was hanging open. "I should've known that loser taped it." She swallowed. "Did I look absolutely ridiculous?"

"Drunk," I said. "Best body I'd ever seen."

"I agree," she grinned. "Pete was voted Mr Sexy Bum by all the girls in my year."

"*Touché.*"

She smiled, and snuggled closer to me. 'I want another baby,' she whispered.

I cupped her face in my hands, the memory of her making love to Rasta-Bob now as thin as a wisp of smoke. Soon it will be inconsistent and then vanish altogether. I'll give her another chance. We'll have another baby, live happily for a while. I thought about my dream of being a writer and how nothing ever came of it. I'll give that another go, too.

"You never told me what happened to your foot," Mandy said suddenly in the darkness.

"My foot?" I felt for my prosthetic leg on the bedside table. You know what they say about amputees feeling their missing limbs itch? Well, it's true. I sometimes forget my right foot isn't there anymore. I can even still wiggle my toes. "I told you. A hyena ate it."

"Be serious."

"I am serious. A hyena ate it. Best meat it's ever had, I bet," I grinned.

"And I suppose *Ben Anderson* is the guy who lived here before us, and never got to change his mail address?"

"I told you why – he's *dead*."

Mandy sighed. "Yeah, right. And I'm the queen of the universe."

I turned to look at her. "So you are." As I kissed her, caressing her breasts underneath the silky night gown, I couldn't help thinking, love is all about staying put. The less you do the more you do. This war called love was all about strength, just like everything else.

Silver Bells

"I think I'm wearing someone else's coat."

The man appears out of nowhere, in such a great state of agitation that the look between Lucien and me goes unnoticed. The swivelling doors are still turning in the nippy breeze, carrying the smell of snow – crisp and fresh like the starched napkins we're folding for tomorrow.

It's past midnight, and the streets are glossy with sleet. The spectacular Christmas tree twinkles in the window, decorated in Angelino's favourite colours – blue and silver. A jazzy carol oozes from the bar, where the American bartender polishes glasses, whistling a merry tune.

This had been happening for a while – more precisely, in the three weeks since I started working at Angelino's. People left in other people's coats all the time. Only the other week one of our regulars, Sir Allastair Knight, walked off in his own cousin's minx fur. They were in the road when they realised, and the pair of them rolled about laughing, finishing off the night with a good snow ball fight that made the countess bleed copiously from a split lip. Then the limo arrived, and the lord climbed in, his stripy trousers around his ankles, a cigar between his teeth and his manhood in his hand while the countess giggled hysterically.

The customers were misbehaving, no doubt about it. Last night I found the cloakroom unattended and several gentlemen having a hoot trying on other people's hats.

"Sorry!" a young man in a pompous, feathered hat chuckled.

"We're being naughty!" his friend shrieked, staggering on his feet in a head to toe fur. "Are you going to punish us? You're not thinking of smacking us with that awful thing, are you?"

I was holding the toilet brush with a special hook for collecting

175

the bloody tissues left nightly by the rich cocaine sniffers.

"No, I'm going to stick it up your bottoms," I grumbled, and left them kissing passionately in their ridiculous disguises.

"You make me look like a *cunt!*" the manager hissed as yet another inebriated customer stumbled out in a spectacular polar fox coat.

But what was I to do? Wealthy drunks are like children, cruel and reckless, ready for a tantrum at the drop of a hat. When I handed in my CV at Angelino's, what I had in mind was a job in the kitchen, anything for a pip at the fantastic cooking going on behind the scenes. I'm an aspiring chef, and Angelino is one of the top food writers in England. Word went around that he'd personally chosen the head chef.

Maurice (that's the manager), though, thought I was too pretty to be scrubbing dishes. His sister (the assistant manager) helped me prepare for my first shift as a hostess, and when she held up the chipped mirror shard she used for sniffing her lines, I had to agree I looked like the hot Italian whore they were making me into. Now I smiled until my cheeks ached, walked in high heels with bleeding toes and babysat expensive coats that made the cloakroom smell like an Egyptian catacomb. I was lucky enough to be out of Angelino's radar.

"Not my type," he'd told Maurice over dinner one evening. "Too scrawny. I'm not a fucking paedo. Is she Chinese? Some of my mates will think they're in Thailand, I swear." He laughed. "How old are you anyway, *bambina*? You look about twelve."

"I'm nineteen." I cleared my throat. "I should get back, sir, Trish is on her own."

Angelino narrowed his eyes. Trish, the other receptionist, was giving a customer one of her huge sleazy grins.

"Where did that monkey come from?" Angelino cried. "This is an Italian deli, not a banana market! Get rid of her."

"She dresses well," Maurice, who screwed Trish in secret, murmured. "Our image ..."

"Fuck that. She's a dressed up gorilla, for God's sake."

"What happened?" Trish whispered, slipping the tip we were meant to share in her trousers.

I didn't notice Maurice behind me.

"What do you think happened? Lord Reginald Purchell's coat went missing! He's going to comb the place until he finds it, but oh, fancy that – I have a feeling it's not here anymore! He'll be back any minute, didn't even realise he walked out undressed, thanks to that bottle of champers we gave him for FREE!"

I swallowed. My eyes misted over.

Trish smiled.

"You're sacked," she sneered. "Now who will give you money to pump up those tits? Gosh." Her eyes went up and down my chest. "I thought my boobs were small."

I'd kept quiet about Trish's horrible manners for a while. I even put up with her stealing my tips, but this was too much. I narrowed my eyes and bent until my face was level with hers. She smelled nauseatingly sweet, like the perfumes she stole every day from Boots. The first things I saw were her earrings – cheap Primarni glass adorning her ears. "If those diamonds were real," I spat, "I'd have some respect for you. And now –" I grabbed her belt and slipped my hand inside her knickers where she'd hidden the money. "I think you'd better share this." I took out the tenner and threw it in the tip tray under the desk.

"You're a freak, man," she grumbled. "I'm reporting you for abuse, you're a fucking …"

I blocked out the stream of insults to greet another customer, and then another. The lunchtime madness had begun: more coats, more scarves, more swearing.

Lord Reginald Purchell made his entrance, enigmatic as ever. I still had his business card in my wallet. He winked at me as I helped him take off his scarf.

The man looks like he's just seen a ghost. Something's not right. He's shaking – his face as white as the snow clad London streets.

"We apologise, sir. If you'd like to accompany me to the cloak-room, I can help you look for your coat."

I grab the black mackintosh – Lord Reginald's. *Phew*. At least we have an important customer's coat now. Maybe I won't get the sack after all.

But then I see the small, leather bound, gold embossed diary. "You don't understand ... this is *really* wrong ..."

Without another word, the man slips out into the cold wearing nothing but a shirt, his tie fluttering in the icy breeze as he turns the corner and vanishes from sight.

"Isn't this Lord Reginald's diary?" Lucien asks.

I nod. What a laugh we had when I'd lost the diary while carrying the black mackintosh from the cloakroom through the busy lunchtime buzz. Maurice was mortified when another customer brought it back, but good old Lord Reginald laughed heartily.

"Oh dear! My private diary! I wouldn't want this in the wrong hands!"

We assumed it was a joke – after all, who wrote diaries these days?

But as I open it, something really disturbing catches my eye. The pages are covered in the same spidery scrawl as the business card, and every few pages there's a title – a woman's name. And ... here comes the creepy bit.

Each name is scribbled in blood.

We're sitting at the same table that Angelino shared with a pop diva in another era – a time when he didn't look like a shrivelled prune in a Gucci suit. Well before my time, but it still made good gossip. Bob the bartender deactivated the smoke alarms and a mountain of cigarette stubs is growing before us.

"So what do you think?" Lucien is the first to talk. "Could this be red ink?"

"Unlikely," Bob shakes his head, holding up the diary in the light.

"I think we should put some rat poison in his food," says Trish.

"No, seriously." Bob, usually so composed, looks scared. "I mean, this could be an important piece of evidence. We must hand the diary over to the police."

"Shouldn't we tell Maurice first?" I suggest.

"And what will that cunt do?" snaps Trish. "Sack all of us and give the diary back to Lord Reginald."

I have to admit she has a point. You can't trust Maurice more than you can trust Angelino. And Angelino ... he's Italian. Well connected to the mafia that is, and what the mafia hates more than anything, is snuffers.

"May I remind you something?" Lucien takes out a slip of paper from his wallet. "We all signed a confidentiality agreement."

"I'm sure it doesn't cover MURDER!" Bob shouts. "We keep quiet about the coke, okay. But, we're talking TEN dead women. One might still be alive."

"Her eyes gouged out of her sockets." Lucien's face is grim.

Jesus. I down my wine. I wish I was home, snuggled up close to my one year old son, Riley, but the thought of walking alone through the empty streets gives me goose bumps.

I wonder if any of those women had children. According to the diary, Lord Reginald picked them from expensive bars and restaurants, gained their trust and lured them to his lair, where he tortured and killed them.

Banging coming from the basement makes us all jump up, and Trish's scream bursts my eardrums.

"Paulo," Lucien whispers. A chill spreads around the room. The restaurant suddenly appears cavernous without the fancy customers, the chandeliers, the glistening silverware. "Is he still here?"

We creep down the serpentine steps to the kitchen. The lights are off, but the noise wasn't a mouse. In the dark, refrigerators purr, a tap drips, unseen water travels through a labyrinth of pipes.

Someone turns on the light.

And there, in the middle of the industrial kitchen, legs sprawled, his chef apron on, lies Paulo.

"Oh my God!" screams Trish, her hands flying to her mouth. "He's dead!"

That's when I see the knife and the thick blood dripping onto the tiled floor.

We all sit around the body in a daze. Paulo's blue eyes are wide open and his purple tongue is lolling out grotesquely.

And then ... his hand shoots up and grips Bob round the neck. There's an explosion of screams and laughter as Paulo charges around the kitchen growling, stabbing everyone with the trick knife from the Halloween costume he'd worn at the staff party. The blood is probably pig's from the bags he keeps in the fridge for black puddings.

"You nutter!" Bob screeches, rubbing his neck. "You nearly gave me a heart attack!"

When he's had enough of laughing, Paulo says: "And you're fucking stupid. I heard you lot, reading that diary aloud. All crap. I bet it's all made up. The guy's odd, but a murderer? No."

I sigh with relief. Paulo is a good judge of character, despite being gruff and rude and stinky most of the time.

We're turning the lights off when the figure walks in. I've just gotten a text from my mother. Riley is awake and crying. She won't be looking after him in the morning while I nurse a hangover, she warned.

In the doorway, a hand takes off a hat and I catch a glimpse of the shiny bow under the long, white scarf.

"Ah," Lord Reginald Purchell sees me holding his diary. "Just the thing I was after."

There's a stunned silence around the room as he tells us the plot of his latest novel, gesticulating with his notebook. It's going to be a modern retelling of Jack the Ripper.

"Only with a twist," he teases. "You'll have to read it once it's published."

Then, with another unctuous smile, he turns and leaves, the diary tucked safely in the pocket of his mackintosh.

"I should've realised he was a writer," sighs Lucien. "He just looks so arty, and he's nicer than the rest of them. Let's look him up. What publisher did he say he was with?"

"Penguin," I reply quickly. The same publisher I'd sent my cookery book to and got an instant rejection.

Bob fires up his phone. "There's nothing on their records. But maybe he's using a pen name? Did you find anything?"

Lucien's face is pale. "No. But this is interesting."

He holds up his tablet. The blurry picture of a girl comes into focus. No one I knew, but I hear Paulo taking a deep intake of breath.

"Angela," he breathes. "The girl from Uruguay."

"Isn't she the one who went missing?"

"They must be desperate if it's in the papers. She was here illegally."

"What happened to her?"

"One day she just didn't turn up for work. Strange, not unusual. They're always in trouble with the authorities, illegal immigrants. She worked under a fake Spanish passport."

"Angela went missing the night before Halloween." I scroll down and read the article aloud.

30th of October. The day before I'd been offered the job.

Angela's job.

I feel sick.

"That was the last name in the diary," I mutter. "I'm quite sure."

"Folks, how about we all make our way home? Let's sleep on it, shall we? We've had too much wine, damn it, and wine blurs the mind." Paulo throws his coat over his apron and makes his way down to the kitchen to close up.

It's three a.m. before I finally exit the restaurant. Bitterly cold too; the few cars parked along the road are covered in frost. At the next corner I say goodbye to Lucien and hurry down to the bus stop. The street before me is black, a faint line vanishing in the eerie mist.

I don't notice the car until its lights snap on, blinding me. The face behind the wheel is concealed by the deep shadows, but I already know.

"Fancy a ride?" Lord Reginald Purchell's voice rings out in the cold winter night.

Something Trapped

It had been raining for days, and Fiorella felt her depression deepen. She watched the rain flowing on the curved window, and it made her want to blink back tears. The park was deserted; the playground drenched and dead. The climbing frames, dripping wet, looked as if they were bleeding.

There is no joy in the world, thought Fiorella.

She'd been sitting on the bed for days on end, not eating, sleeping with her eyes open in case she heard the door. She missed the cats. How they burst through the cat flap with their noses and tails, hungry for food and love.

Fiorella sighed. She remembered the first time she arrived at this home, along with her new mother. Everything looked so big and beautiful, although now, after watching so much television, she saw it was actually small and dull. Sixteen Glebe Court was a tiny, cosy flat, sufficient for a single woman and her daughter. The cats were in and out; they didn't really count. She had once gotten a scratch on her cheek from Toby, the ginger, that never quite healed. It would be a scar forever.

At first, Mother had changed her nappies and soothed her in a sweet, sing-song voice. Sometimes, she liked it. Other times Mother simply got on her nerves, and she hoped the woman would just put her back in her cot and let her sleep. She'd take her out in the baby pink, fancy pram, show her off to relatives, friends, neighbours, *strangers.* Pretending this was her real child, and Fiorella pretending back, not that she had a choice. She had never learned, and perhaps never would, how to speak.

Mother liked it that way.

"You'll never grow up to be a naughty child." She breathed the smell of her dinner over Fiorella – kebab, onions, cheap wine. "You'll never answer back, will you? No one can take you away, my sweet, sweet baby."

And she kissed the baby on her red, wrinkled mouth and gazed into her sky-blue eyes, trying to straighten out a crease on her forehead that wouldn't straighten. A birth mark? A defect? Mother frowned, and checked again the adoption contract. It didn't say anything about any marks. An accident in transit? Maybe?

The rain won't stop. The room smelled strongly of linden flowers, grass, wet soil. In the branches of the fir tree a blackbird pecked at its feathers. When the blackbird looked inside the house through the naked window, Fiorella's heart beat faster.

What if the bird flew through the glass and took her away, somewhere she'd never be found, to devour her entirely? She was in no position to defend herself. In her dreams, she was always running.

Fiorella glanced away from the rain and the fir tree and the bird. She felt trapped inside her body, trapped inside a house she called home.

She woke up with a start. How long had she been asleep? An hour? A day? Her ribs ached. Her nappy was heavy. Liquid dripped down her legs and into her socks. She began to cry. The window was dark; behind it, the trees were whispering. A waft of smoke crawled in through the window that Mother had left open. *Voices*. The headlights of a car sweeping across the darkness. In her dream, it had been warm. She was running, her hair sticking to her head, her breath short. Now her breath was frozen. Her heart beat faster, *faster*. Footsteps creaked on the stairs.

Something had happened to Mother. She knew it. She braced herself for what was coming. Where would she go? Not back to the artist's house. No more surgery. Not a room crammed with prams and beating hearts that kept you awake in the night.

No. She'd never go back to that room.

A key turned in the lock, loud like a gunshot. *Click-clack.*

Fiorella gasped.

The door opened.

Mother stood in the doorway. She looked different. Free. Young. Beautiful.

Fiorella wanted to call out to her but her mouth was dead. It was as if she didn't have a tongue.

Light flooded the room. Everything fell into place, the sofa, the chairs, the table. The evil shadows shrank back into the blackness on the other side of the window. She saw that the flowers in the beautiful ivory vase were long dead, and from somewhere came a stench of something rotten.

Mother wasn't alone. A handsome man was with her; his silver beard shone in the light like frosted ice.

They packed everything quickly, even the pillows, stuffing them in suitcases. Without its ornaments, the room was bare and angry.

"Is that everything?" the man said to Mother, who hadn't even given Fiorella a look.

She nodded, glancing down at the sofa bed where her daughter lay in an awkward position.

"Oh. There's also the baby. Let me get the pram."

The man glared at Fiorella with his brown, almond-shaped eyes. He reminded her of the blackbird, only there was no glass between them. He could easily rip her apart.

Mother sat down next to her, and for a moment, a wave of love appeared on her face, a dreamy smile on her lips.

The man took his big hairy hand to his forehead, as if the very thought of her gave him a headache.

"Erin, I ..."

Mother jumped from her seat. She looked sad and desperate, and Fiorella knew in an instant that the man did not love her. Not the way she did.

"What's the matter, Abel? Don't you like her?"

The man shook his head. His eyes fell on the bags, as if he was contemplating the thought of leaving right there and then.

Finally, he said "No, Erin. I'm sorry, I don't. I don't like her at all."

Mother glanced at Fiorella, as if she, too, was trying to find fault. From where she lay, the girl could smell her perfume, a mixture of vanilla and some fruit, perhaps strawberry. Certainly not red wine and onions.

"Yes, but ..." Mother was babbling. "She's my baby. I've had her for three years. She's ..."

"Complete with a beating heart and human hair, and a pump that makes her piss in her pants? Don't make me laugh! What kind of family would keep something like this? Erin, have you thought of what people will say?"

Tears streamed down Mother's face. Fiorella wanted to soothe her, but she could only lie in silence.

"How dare you?" Now, Mother sounded furious, so furious her voice was barely a whisper. "She's a child. She's a fake child, but my child nonetheless."

"She's a fucking doll!" The man loomed over Mother with clenched fists.

He kicked a chair and started loading the bags in the car. At that moment, Mother had a saving idea: she stuffed Fiorella in her big backpack, and took her away with her to the man's house.

Since then she had been living not only in silence, but also in darkness, behind the silks and cashmeres in the wardrobe, with its dry smell of freshly painted wood. The hangers are white; the clothes suffocate her. Sometimes Mother takes her out and gives her a kiss when the man is away, but those moments are rare now that she has other children.

Fiorella wishes she could die, but she knows her beating heart would never stop, her human hair would never grow and she could never again be Mother's daughter. She remembers a story that Mother had read to her once, about a little boy who was actually a doll made of wood. *Pinocchio*. It makes her think of herself. Only, she isn't a toy that sprang to life. She's something trapped in the body of a doll.

A girl.

A woman.

An angel.

A demon.
She doesn't know.

Wood Scented Whisky

"2.45 p.m. Neatly dressed, hair done, full face of make-up, the suspect emerges from *Pimp-My-Hair*." The detective chuckled. "Your little lady has really gone for it this time. New nails, I noticed. Nice and sharp. Very popular on the estates."

Leonard swallowed. *"Pimp-My-Hair*? What the hell is that?"

"A hairdresser's. *Afro*," he added as an afterthought.

"Great," Leonard spat, making the papers on the desk before him ruffle slightly.

The detective ignored him. He continued describing his wife's garments.

"Do you have to go into so much detail? Jesus. I just want to know the facts. I don't pay you to get a kick out of this."

"Ah, but that's exactly where detectives get their kicks, my friend. *The details."* Leonard pretended to check his watch. It had run out of battery and was now showing the wrong time. "I have a meeting in twenty minutes," he lied.

The detective smiled.

Leonard felt his cheeks burning. "All right," he sighed. "Carry on. Might as well lose the whole day. It's ruined anyway."

"She went to the mall, heading to *Esquires* café, or, if you want, the *love nest* ..." Leonard sighed. "She checked herself in all the windows – clearly nervous, she tied and untied her scarf, you know, glanced at her phone exactly six times, and then *he* came and gave her a peck on the cheek. Her face lightened and ..."

Leonard wondered how the hell you can tell if someone's face lightens if you're standing at least ten feet away behind a newspaper and with black shades on. It was the details that made him feel sick, more than the situation itself. *Parked her car, neatly dressed, full face of make-up, fancy nails.* Words like poisonous snakes coiled inside his soul, waiting for the right moment to bite him.

2.45 p.m.? What was he doing at that time? How could he let this happen? How could *she* do this? What struck him was that she wasn't even attractive. Not anymore. Not for him. He thought of her more as a sister, a twin, even. They were like one of those bizarre pairs of twins who share a brain even though they have different bodies. The brain, of course, was Leonard's.

And now, this. She wasn't supposed to break the bond. An extension wasn't meant to exist separately, even if otherwise perfectly functional.

He didn't mean to check on her. She just always used to keep cash in her old-fashioned bag, and the pizza delivery boy was at the door. *New expensive-looking bag.* Wasn't this what the detective had said last time? And when his credit card bill arrived he just couldn't believe it. His sad little wife had spent *that* amount of money on a *Prada*, she who had always hated those things.

There, in the warmth and darkness, were the *photographs.* A selection of silly snaps of his wife and this ... boy. Both taking turns to wear a green wizard hat and feathered sequined scarves in some stupid caravan. Drunk, without a doubt.

A boy. A child, for God's sake. And black, too.

"Are you still with me?" the detective barked, his left eyebrow cocked in wonder. From his triple, freshly shaved chins, came the smell of stale sweat mingled with cologne. To Leonard, who lived flicking invisible lint from his perfectly tailored suits, the man seemed – the way he tapped the folder in front of him with his long fingernails – more animal than human.

Leonard rubbed his forehead. His weekly migraine was settling in a dark cloud taking over his brain.

"I never thought she'd ever do something like this," he said, giving life to his thoughts. "Never. She's pregnant, for God's sake. And that kid. Who is he? Oh, God. This is a crime. An atrocity."

The investigator flicked through his file and placed a misty photograph in front of him. It was taken from a distance but you could still see the boy smiling and his wife, wearing clothes he'd never thought she would buy – *a body-con dress? cowgirl boots?* – hanging on his arm, whispering in his ear.

A wave of nausea came over him. From outside, the sunny world of trees, houses and roads smiled at him. This world had been his. And now it had turned against him. *Him* the King of it all.

"His name's Tyrone Williams. Not underage, though by God he looks it, but not much older, either." The detective rummaged through a file, greasy from leftover chips which the man brushed off with a wave of an even greasier hand, and threw a battered copy of a driving licence at him. "Twenty-one. A student at the London College of Music. Plays the piano. He's a member of a band. *The Vagabonds.* Not doing too bad. They were in Liverpool last week."

Leonard rubbed his temples. He desperately needed a fag. "She did say she was going for piano lessons. Maybe that's how it started."

"That, I don't know. When you hired me, the thing was already ... well ... not at the beginning."

Leonard tried to remember when his wife started to take piano lessons. Was it before or after she got pregnant? Then, as his phone vibrated in his pocket and he discreetly rejected the call, he knew: it was about that time when he'd first met Diane. And that was dangerously long ago. He broke into a cold sweat. His shirt stuck to his skin.

"Are you all right? You look like you need a glass of water." The detective gestured towards a carafe of stale water on his desk. Oblivious to the dead spider inside, Leonard drank, only to spit it out instantly.

"What's this, toilet water?" he snarled, trying to ignore the fact that the whole room was spinning. "I just need to to know how a decent woman could get herself into this. Is this something you come across often?"

"Oh yes. More so than you think."

Leonard huffed. "Women. Just bloody fake, eh?"

"The clues are there for those who want to see," said the

detective, annoying Leonard further. "Good acting is fuelled by a trusting audience. They paid the ticket, so it suits them to play along. Isn't this what drama is? Real life is similar, only on a larger scale."

"Just shut up!" Okay, so she played the game, and he went along with it. It wasn't like that. He could always tell what women thought. He *thought* he could, anyway.

He sat back, woozy, like on those scary rides at Thorpe Park. Diane loved them. She was like a goddamned kid. Well, he supposed that, at twenty-three, she wasn't much more than a kid. He used to pretend he liked it, too, although he was frightened. Damn, she was brave. It kind of put him off. A woman wasn't supposed to have … well, *balls*. They were sitting hand in hand, high in the sky, looking down at the clouds. That's when the fear became physical, it struck him like a sharp punch in the chest. He wanted to curl up into a ball but there was nothing around him but air and the distant buzzing of helicopters. There was nowhere to die. Diane's feet were swinging, swinging. It was amazing how such tiny feet could be so fearless. She squeezed his hand.

"Don't you just love this?" Her onion breath was in his ear, hot as chillies. It made him want to retch.

"Yes," he squeaked, his face streaming with sweat.

This recollection popped in his mind like a soap bubble. He would, though, rather be hurtling through the sky again than be glued to this chair of shame. He sat upright. "I don't know what to do. There's nothing I *can* do. I never thought she'd be capable of something like this."

The detective leaned back in his seat, a broad grin on his face.

"The human mind is a complete mystery. Take it from someone who gets paid to solve puzzles."

But I love mysteries, thought Leonard, feeling, despite himself and all the humiliation, a burst of love for his wife. It was peculiar, like a funny unexpected zest.

He got up and stood by the window, his back turned to the dusty office that had become, in a matter of minutes, as stifling as a prison cell. Nothing made sense anymore. Down on the winding path, he saw himself walking into the same derelict building a week ago, hand in his pocket, chatting and laughing with Diane on the phone, unaware of the terrifying truth he was going to discover. He was now a ghost of that carefree man, over whom he glanced with the hunger of a poltergeist. He'd never thought this could be true, never, not even after seeing the photographs. He was sure it must be some kind of misunderstanding. A simple explanation, and his life would soon go on like normal, just as always: work, girlfriends, home, and now a new baby on the way. Nothing of this could change, he thought then. Nothing *should* change. He'd worked hard to create a perfect balance. When problems sprang from this solid ground, he would quickly and effectively push them back in. Now, all these unborn faults were growing wildly around him, and it was their turn to push him in. He was being buried alive in an underground world of fears and doubts.

Leonard and the detective stared at each other for a while longer before they said their goodbyes. Leonard wondered if this potbellied man wasn't enjoying his profession a bit too much. For a moment he wondered if he was telling the truth. No, that was mad. He took out his cheque book, scribbled something, tore the page and handed it to him.

But the man shook his head, showing his teeth in an unctuous grin. "Cash only," he breathed. "As we agreed."

That night he sat in the kitchen as his wife prepared supper, watching her from behind the newspaper he pretended to read. She moved around, stirred the pork casserole, bent over a pot of bubbling water, chopped a few tomatoes and cucumbers on the table in front of him. On her fingers, there was no sign of the wedding ring.

"Where's your ring?" He tried to sound cool, but his voice was shaking.

She scraped the chopped vegetables into the salad bowl then turned to nurse the stew again. She checked the potatoes with a fork.

"Where's your ring?" he repeated. He wanted to grab her arm

and turn her around, shout the words in her face, but then she'd feel sorry for him like he felt for Diane the other night, when she was begging him to stay. He'd unclasped her fingers from his shirt and left the flat without a word. Damn, you'd have thought he had an engine in his behind as he clattered down those communal stairs. Two floors down, he could still hear her sobbing. All he wanted was to get the hell out of there, happy to have an excuse not to escort Diane to the abortion clinic. A creature genetically wired between the two of them – it was unthinkable. Like the evidence of a crime, it had to be removed.

"It's upstairs, in my jewellery box." His wife poured thick olive oil over the chopped tomatoes. "I haven't worn it in months. My fingers are too swollen."

She turned around, fixing him with her calm, relaxed expression.

Leonard saw it happening. That was why he'd never questioned his wife about her wedding ring for so long.

Her eyes fell on his fingers, before he had a chance to hide them in his pocket.

The flash of a smile on her lips as she asked, "Where's yours?" She turned to have a last taste of the casserole. "It's ready."

They ate in silence. Leonard watched his wife's mouth and thought her lips looked so much fuller and the dark rings under her eyes had vanished into her skin, giving it a slightly darker tint, which suited her nicely. He wanted to tell her she looked good but what came out of his mouth was, "Where were you this afternoon?"

She took a painfully long half a minute to wipe her hands and face with a tea towel before saying, "Oh, you know, here and there," and it took all his strength not to turn the table over and yell: "Liar!"

Which he didn't, of course. Because she would ask him where *he'd* been and he just couldn't lie anymore.

No more.

That same night he watched her sleep and thought of all the nights she had her arm around him and he didn't even bother to touch her. He thought of the small baby inside her, a life growing quickly, giving sense to each day. Without it, the days would be sucked back into a dead past, lifeless, useless, lost forever.

Nothing felt the same. Seven unread messages sat on his phone when he dialled that 0800 number. As he held the phone to his ear the gold, forgotten wedding ring glistened in the dark.

"Samaritans. My name is Sunita. How can I help you?"

Leonard ended the call. He didn't need help. What he needed was to talk to her, confront her, work it out somehow.

In the morning he woke up late, feeling like he hadn't slept at all. His body ached and he had the chills. When she called his name, he opened his eyes.

"It's nine o'clock already." She was standing in the open door of the bedroom. Leonard never left so late. Selling cars was second nature to him. He loved his job so much, he just couldn't wait to get to the office each day. Every day he would drive a new limousine, to "break it in", either an Aston Martin or a BMW or a Rolls Royce, even if it made him look like a chauffeur. That way he was difficult to spot: the tinted windows protected him.

Her cheeks looked soft, rosy. For no reason at all, the memory of the day when she proposed to him and how she kissed him in the pouring rain popped into his mind. The wedding, the honeymoon in Japan, the weekly trips to the country. She dreamed of having the perfect country house, a farm, raise chickens and geese, collect fresh eggs first thing in the morning. Maybe if he'd agreed to live in a farmhouse none of this would have happened. Boys like Tyrone can't survive a week in the country without going mad. He knew the type. The recollection of a long-haired boy, guitar strapped on his back pained him. He shuddered with envy at his own teenage years. Back then, he wanted to die young. Now he knew he had already died and was buried somewhere in an old attic with a dusty guitar, some books and the T-shirts of a girl he loved, a girl whom he hadn't thought of in years. A girl he'd been looking for in all the women he'd slept with, trying to possess her, win her over, avenge her, live with her again. All but his wife. She was different. And that was why he hated her the most.

All those years wasted, the failed attempts to have a baby, the fertility treatments. The doctors said she was perfectly all right, it was just a matter of time, of her being relaxed enough and that his sperms were lazy. *Lazy.* He'd never heard anything more ridiculous in his life. Then one day … it happened. Just around the time when the musician came into their life. Were *his* sperms lazy, too? he wondered.

Leonard pulled the duvet over his head and she understood he wanted to be left alone. She said she was going out shopping, asked if she could take his car and if he needed anything.

Leonard popped a pale hand from under the duvet, pointing to the bedside table where several car keys lay scattered. A Porsche, an Audi, a Toyota.

She chose the Toyota. Turning to leave, she noticed his phone vibrating. She looked at him, wondered if everything was all right. It was not like him to spend a weekday sleeping. She would call his office and say he had the flu. She looked again at the phone flashing, the name *Justice* visible on the screen, looked back at him, saw him buried under the duvet, fast asleep she guessed from his breathing. *Justice?* Surely they didn't know anyone called that? She picked up the phone, wanting to answer but then she thought no, better not ask for trouble, if you can't do the time don't do the crime.

She looked at her watch. Tyrone mentioned he wanted to see that movie, *Mamma Mia* and she planned to surprise him. Today was another good day and nothing was going to take it away from her.

Leonard spent the whole week asleep in that bed, living in his dreams. By Thursday the doctor was called to prescribe him a mild tranquillizer, told his wife not to worry, it was just a phase, he'll break through. She was worried sick about him but started using another room as the bed stank of sweat: he'd refused to wash for days. His beard had grown, sticking from his sunken face like barbed wire. Unanswered calls and texts piled up on his phone. Even the house phone started ringing. When she answered, they would hang up. She had to disconnect the line at night. The baby got her tired by eight every evening, asleep by nine thirty. She wondered if she was not too old for this.

Leonard thought there was no place like home. It was funny how he'd never guessed it although it was there all the time. How he would rather be late to all his dates just to spend a bit more time lying lazily by her side, the TV making a comforting background noise, or be in the kitchen behind his huge newspaper, knowing she was there and alive by the rhythmical tapping of the knife on the chopping board. He'd make excuses, of course, saying it was him who'd rather not go, feed from the girls' wanting, becoming stronger with every unanswered call or text ignored for days. Stronger, yes and uglier, too. He twisted in bed, feeling like that time in the sky, when there was nowhere to run, and he was forced to breathe air that was getting thinner. He couldn't bear to think of it. For the first time in years he did something that wasn't like him but was familiar to him from all the monthly breakups, from the weekly fights: he burst into tears.

She came back late, smelling nice, her lips stained with red wine. She knew she wasn't supposed to drink in her condition but a little red wine would do no harm, she explained, and when she undressed he saw her belly had started to swell, making the daisy tattoo on her side stretch hideously. He sat up in bed and reached for her but she gently pushed him away.

"Wait," she told him, giving his hand a small caress. His eyes stung.

She went out in her bath gown and soon he heard the water running, smelled the magnolia foam in the hallway.

It was not what he thought; she helped him out of bed and washed him in the tub like a baby. She turned off the lights and lit cherry flavoured candles, talked to him in a lovely soft voice. In the candlelight, she shaved his beard with a sharp razor, and before every stroke Leonard closed his eyes, expecting the blade to slice his throat, almost desiring it. It would feel cold as ice, he imagined. His blood would drain in the bath, and he wouldn't know he was dying until it was too late.

The strokes went on forever. Leonard was floating in a dark pond, his shaved hair around him, clinging to his skin like algae. That's how someone on death row must feel, he thought, the fear going through him from his head to the tips of his toes. She poured raspberry shampoo in her cupped hand and rubbed it on his hair. He showed no reaction other than cringing when he felt the coldness of the shampoo on his scalp. He could smell her breasts, the lotion on her skin, her breath, thought it was too late for everything. The phone rang. When she went to answer he looked at the loft opening in the ceiling, wondered if there was any fishing line left from last time they went to the country. That was back when they were still happy although that happiness felt like misery then, him always on edge and her growing larger and larger. Many times he thought that if she did fall pregnant it would take a long time to even notice. He shivered. The water was getting cold.

When she came back, she turned on the lights, rinsed his head and washed his body with a sponge. He felt small and helpless like when he was only a year old and his mum washed him in the kitchen sink, always before he went to bed. She put the soft bathrobe around his hunched shoulders.

"Lenny," she said.

She touched his arm and he stepped back, a look of horror in his eyes. She turned around, thinking he'd seen something over her shoulder. There was nothing there. "Lenny?"

He shook his head, willing the vision to disappear. It was that arm again, lying in the bathroom door, that arm and the eyes, wide open, the bruised and lifeless neck. He looked up and down the bathroom trying to calculate the angle at which the body had fallen. She'd looped the fishing line round and round her neck, stepped onto the edge of the shower cubicle, tied it to the shower hook. There were no more than ten inches between her feet and the ground. Three more inches and her stretched toes would touch the floor. He knew. He hadn't forgotten. He'd made the same calculations in his head for twenty years. He'd do it whenever he was bored, like a morbid mental exercise, like a crossword and often when he sat behind the newspaper and she chopped away at the chopping board. When he was lying in bed at night, rather than counting sheep he was counting inches.

At first he didn't even know what her arm was doing, curling around his waist. Many times he didn't know where or who he was, or whose the warm body was next to his own. He only knew he wasn't dead; to bear that kind of pain, you had to be alive. On some mornings, he still searched for his school uniform in the built-in wardrobe, and wondered why his parents' bedroom was so quiet.

The irony was when the line snapped she was already dead. It snapped at exactly 1.40 p.m. That was when the body hit the floor. He was in his room, reading when he heard the thump and his eyes fell on the clock. This was the time on her death certificate.

"Lenny, I know this may not be a good time. I know you aren't feeling well, darling, and I'm sorry."

He looked at her, seeing nothing.

It was a matter of seconds. *Seconds only.* Sometimes he wondered what would the first girl he ever loved look like, had she grown into a woman. Would he even recognise her? Would the years take her shine and break her spirit? It was hard to imagine Luisa without her pigtails, without the knitted bracelets curling around her wrists, and her sharp silver braces.

She took him by the hand and guided him to the kitchen. He walked like someone just risen from the tomb. He walked like he was in a different reality, a past world where he could still love and be loved. He'd tried to resuscitate her, kissed her blue lips, blew air into her mouth. Waiting for the ambulance to arrive, he'd put her head on his knees, where it kept rolling down the sides like that of a rag doll. When the ambulance came he was sobbing so loudly a few neighbours had already gathered in the doorway.

"Lenny, this is Tyrone."

A boy stood at the far end of the kitchen. The boy in the photographs. In reality he looked a lot younger. Almost a teenager. He surprised himself by wondering if Luisa would have found him attractive.

"Hello," said Tyrone, stretching a hand out only to pull it back untouched.

"Hello," replied Leonard in a low, miserable voice. He could feel his wife's arm around him, guiding him as though he were blind. For a moment he thought, *they are going to kill me.*

"Lenny, my darling, I know this might shock you. This is Tyrone, my son."

His mind whirled like a washing machine at full spin. It was like he was drawn back into the air, high in the sky like that day with Diane. The wind whipped at his face, his shirt flapped on his back like a ridiculous parachute. He fell. And when he looked to his side, who was holding his hand was not a young woman but a small boy who screamed excitedly and looked in his eyes for protection. He felt free and light-hearted. As he and the boy fell through the sky hand in hand he thought, *there was no way they were not plunging into death but into life, a life new and wonderful, empty of all the misery.* Then he knew: this was a dream of the future, not of the past.

She was only sixteen, she told him. She and Tyrone held hands as though they hadn't seen each other in twenty years, which they hadn't. He talked much about his music, his books, his band, with his mother looking more in love than he'd ever seen her, hanging on to every word. Leonard went and brought the good champagne from the cellar, poured it into the best glasses. Then, when she was not looking, busy frying the steaks, he winked at Tyrone and filled his glass with the strongest, wood-smelling whisky he kept locked away for special occasions. For boys like Tyrone, champagne doesn't really do the trick. He knew the type.

The Trumpet Player

Every night he played the trumpet on the first floor of the house next door. His curtains were rumpled by the wind on cool evenings, motionless on hot summer nights; the window framed by wild ivy, blue with a splash of fluorescent moonlight.

The air was always heavy with the scent of tobacco, but even so the green smell of leaves and bursting buds floated over the garden.

Sometimes I even caught a glimpse of his silhouette, a shadow crouched over that mysterious trumpet: a golden thing, curvy and voluptuous like the body of a mermaid, moaning in his arms as if it was alive. Behind the white veil of the curtain, the musician and the trumpet engaged in a love dance, mouth on mouth, his fingers playing invisible buttons, until the climax was reached with a magnificent final blow.

His hand on my shoulder, Leon blew the smoke in my face.

"Are you okay, honey?" he inquired, though it was more an ascertainment than a question. I shrugged and stared into the black night. A cat moved swiftly through the rose shrubs, the clink of her bells mingling with the sweet notes of the wind chimes. Its body brushed against the trunk of the lilac tree.

"What are you thinking about?" (this, however, was a question).

I looked at him and wondered, why was he wearing nothing but boxer shorts, but then I remembered, we had just made love; I could hear flamenco music still playing from my room. I was barefoot and the blood-red nail varnish on my toes was starting to peel.

"Oh yeah," I said, "I was wondering, have you seen this man playing the trumpet … do you know what he looks like?"

Leon said: "What do you mean?" He ran his finger over the

faded tattoo on my shoulder.

I pulled my satin gown over my arm. I felt naked, even with the rich patterns running down to my wrist. I inhaled and exhaled, over and over, desperate for the smoke to make me high.

"I mean, just wondered if you've seen him walking on the street with his trumpet or something. Have you?"

Leon said: "No, I don't think he goes out much, what do you think?"

Then he said: "How do you know it's a man?" and my heart sank.

When I didn't hear the trumpet for three whole days, I waited, biting my nails, on the stone steps in the garden. Leaning on the headless angel, I smelled the moist earth and watched the glistening slugs stretched out to die. The closed window stared at me in darkness. In hollowness.

It was over.

The wild despair, still alive from my first forty-eight hours in rehab, stood before me, mounting like the wave of a terrible river: tar-black and scalding.

I resisted the urge to slam my head against the wall. Maybe if I made the pain more intense, it would go away. Those excruciating hours were over. Who would've thought music could be addictive just like a drug?

"Hmm." I smiled, smoking the straw-thin cigarette. "Whoever said drugs aren't good is a fool." For the first time in years the craving was so intense that water pooled in my mouth.

I clenched my teeth. The cigarette butt landed in the terrifying darkness of the garden. I glanced towards the vacant window. It was shut and the ivy looked nothing but ordinary.

Then, a miraculous thing happened: a hand turned the light switch on; the window turned bright like a theatre stage. The trees applauded with their wind-stirred leaves.

I stood up, my heart pounding. I imagined I was engaged to the trumpet player and he was serenading me, only to find that I was the one standing outside the window. In reality he didn't know I existed, nor did I want him to know. Because if he knew,

I would have to meet him, and he might not be a man.

He played that night too. The song was muffled by the branches of the lilac tree and the shut window as it was now raining. I held my umbrella with a clenched fist and watched the streams of water flowing furiously on the cracked cement.

Once, I noticed a strange woman on a chair by the window. She started coming more often and she always read from a book she must have held on her knees. She was young with bright red lips. When she was there he never played.

Every night the trumpet was heard.

Martin asked me: "What are you thinking about?"

I looked up. "Can you hear the trumpet playing?"

"Ahem."

"Do you know who is playing – I mean the man who is playing – have you ever seen him walking on the street with his trumpet or something?"

Martin said: "Hmm ..."

"Do you think it's a man?" I asked him, remembering Leon's comment.

Martin was a *macho* man: "It must be a man, women can't play like that," and instead of laughing at his remark I cupped his face in my hands and kissed him.

"Yes!" I shrieked. "You're right!"

Martin closed his eyes.

"And anyway, when could I have seen him? We only met yesterday!"

"Oh, yeah," I smiled.

That night I stood in the garden with tears glittering in my eyes. I hadn't heard the trumpet in two whole weeks. The window was shut and the lights were off. There was no food left on the sill for the pigeons. I smoked innumerable cigarettes and thought that happiness doesn't exist anyway. I dialled Leon's number. The screen was cracked from where I had thrown it at a customer's head, more than six months back. He'd ducked and it hit the wall behind him.

Leon answered in a too-loud voice.

"Still nothing," I told him.

He sighed. There was music blasting in the background. That kid Justin Bieber was spitting his lungs out and people hummed along.

"I think you should stop listening to Lola Flores," he said. "It's such a depressing type of music. It can even make you halluci-nate."

"Yeah, but ..."

"I have to go." His voice dropped to a whisper. "It's my son's birthday – you know that."

The line went dead and uncontrollable sobs burst out of my mouth.

I went to his door first thing in the morning, the taste of Peruvian strength-four coffee in my mouth. I pressed the bell and my stomach flipped over when the ring echoed in the mysterious house. It seemed so final – meeting him at last.

Footsteps echoed in the hallway and the woman with bright red lips appeared in the door frame. "Yes?"

The black dress. The dark tights. The smoky glasses.

Behind her, more people dressed in black moved around the house.

"Yes?" she said again. Her statuesque figure intimidated me. I wondered if a punch in the face would break her pose.

At the far end of the living room, the handles on the dark brown coffin glinted in the sunlight which flooded the room through the naked windows. The smell of lilac flowers crept in from the back door, carried by the fresh, musty air of between rainfalls. The silence stuck to the walls like a living thing, not entirely peaceful.

"I'm the next door neighbour and ... I wondered ..."

The woman's features softened and her bright mouth opened in a smile.

"Oh. Come in, have a drink. Everyone is welcome. Some of his former students are here, too. I don't think we've met. I'm Sheila, his granddaughter. Do come in," she insisted, tugging at my arm.

There were flowers in a vase in the hallway and the scent of old-fashioned cologne in the air. The floor was shiny and cold. Our footsteps clattered on it, deafening, like high heels in a cathedral.

I saw the trumpet on a coffee table by the coffin. Pain shot through my chest, and my legs turned to jelly.

"I'm sorry ... would you mind ... When did he pass away?" The living room began to turn around me like a maddening carousel; the coffin multiplying to dozens, ridden by black-clad guests with their champagne flutes.

"Last night." Sheila's eyes were narrow and oily, black and empty like seedless olives. She shook her head. "No pain. He'd had the coffin for a while ... had a morbid fascination with death, you see. It was freshly polished when we put him in it. He did it every day. Polishing, I mean. And guess what. He sort of knew he was dying. He sent emails to everyone, inviting them to his own wake. They thought it was joke, but today, the catering people arrived, bringing all this. It's as if he knew that today would be the day! How? I don't believe in God, but sometimes I wonder ..." She gestured towards the table laid with food and drinks. "Even the funeral is booked, the headstone ordered, and one of the best burying spots in his favourite cemetery, right under a magnolia tree, is being dug as we speak. He loved magnolias." She pointed to the tree in the garden. "Can't say he wasn't something of a nutter." Her smile faded when I didn't return it. "Anyway ... what can I get you? Martini? *Bianco*? *Rosso*? Wine, maybe?"

Without waiting for my reply, she poured out the drinks.

The coffin was spotless, the rich brown carvings glossy in the mellow April sun. I wanted to fall down on my knees and sniff the flowers, eat them like a dog lapping hulks of bleeding flesh. If only their pollen was cocaine, laudanum or morphine. Something to put me to sleep forever. The lilac fragrance was all that was left of the trumpet filled nights.

Sheila put a warm hand on my shoulder, slipping a glass into my hand. *Red wine*. Not the brightest choice.

"No one lives forever," she consoled me. "He was eighty years old, you know. Amazing that he could still play – extraordinarily rare among people so old." She nodded as I took a sip of my drink, and then another. *And another.* "I guess Grandpa was kind of a genius. And it was time for him to go – just the right time."

Just the right time. I tried to make sense of the words, while the room around me, with everyone and everything in it, changed colour. All the colours faded into one: I was looking at the world through rose-tinted glasses. The wine in my hand rippled. I could hear the glass starting to crack.

"Would you care for a cup of tea and a cookie?" Sheila offered. "Made them myself, raisin cookies, his favourites. They're from yesterday, but they're still fresh, you know."

She sounded like she was talking through water.

I thought of all the nights in the garden and the music flowing from his room and the moonlight splashing the ivy and how everything was over.

I downed the last of the wine.

"I'm sorry," I said, my hand tightening around the glass, "if you don't mind, what are you thinking of doing with the trumpet?"

Sheila looked surprised. She fixed me with her olive black eyes. I could tell she'd noticed the red nail varnish on my toes. It matched the colour of her lips. As she kept glancing from my feet to my face her own face turned an angry red.

The glass cracked, tinkling on the marble floor in a small heap of sparkling shards.

"Oh my goodness!" Sheila shrieked, while I stood before her holding what was left of the glass, a transparent stem through which the pale afternoon light sifted in a brilliant rainbow, the ruby wine dripping from its beheaded neck. "That was real crystal! How on earth did it break?"

I wondered what Sheila would say to know it took eight police officers and an ambulance crew to remove me off the motorway once when I was high. What she would say to know I could snap her neck like a chicken.

"It's his spirit!" someone whispered. "Trying to make his presence known."

Sheila shivered. I turned to leave, before things got bloody. Tomorrow, I knew, a member of the psychiatric team would knock on my door to inquire about my missed appointment. *Risperidone* injections. The bitter price of my freedom.

"About the trumpet."

I stopped, still holding the crystal stem of the glass.

"We thought of putting it on *eBay*. We'd get a fair bit for it. It's a good make – and an old one too, they don't do them as good these days, Grandpa always said. He didn't want to be buried with it, she was his baby, you see, couldn't sentence her to death, guess it made him feel good that the trumpet would outlive him."

"I …" but before I could say anything her hand gave my shoulder a squeeze.

"Three hundred pounds," she said matter-of-factly, watching me with sympathy and somewhat amused, as if I was the one who'd lost someone and not her. "Three hundred pounds and we call it a deal."

Over her shoulder, the trumpet bathed the room in a golden light. Next to it, on the sofa, Barry was grinning. Tears pooled in my eyes. I wanted to lunge at him with my crystal weapon, but I knew that once I killed him he would turn out to be someone else. It always happened. I'd be sitting atop Barry with my fist raised and then I'd blink and he'd be squeezing out of the room like a fume. He could do that, Barry. In his place was always someone else: the nurse, the neighbour, that man at the gym.

I handed my rent money to her, six crumpled fifty pound notes, and walked over to the coffee table. I didn't need my room anymore, now that Barry would be there day and night. Once awake, it takes ages for him to go back down. Sometimes he even gets into the white cells of the psychiatric ward, and he breathes over me in the dark, waking me with one of his silly giggles.

Out of the corner of my eye, I saw Sheila squinting at the

notes in the sun, taking them to her nose, stuffing them in her purse. Tomorrow, she'd buy herself a nice treat, something to wipe off the bad taste of death. Money was money, even from the hands of a faggot.

Martin was right, I remember thinking at that moment. *He was a man, after all.*

The trumpet in my arms, I thanked Sheila and said I had to go back and prepare for my afternoon shift at the restaurant. She said she was pleased to meet me and I thought she might be lying, but then I remembered, some people are pleased to meet anyone. I shook her hand and promised to come back the next day, when the funeral was over. I could not bear funerals. But I'd like a cup of tea and some cookies – raisin cookies, especially if they were homemade. Raisin cookies are my favourite, too, I lied.

I had stepped over the threshold and into the drive when I heard the scream – and then another, a whole chorus of high-pitched yells. I had my back turned, but even so, I saw Barry. The glass shard was in his hands. Beneath him, the woman in black was stretched on the marble floor, the gash on her neck as red as her lips.

Acknowledgements

A book is the product of so many people, it's always difficult to know who to thank. I've found that writing is a lonely affair, not only because of the long stretches of time spent researching and scribbling in a state of semi-conscious madness, but because of all the friendships you will naturally lose. However, those that stay are the ones that count.

I couldn't be a writer without the support of my family: my parents, my sister, my husband, and my son, who accepted my silence and moodiness and helped create the perfect habitat for me to weave my webs.

My editors, John Hudspith and David Stroud, thank you for teaching me patience and perseverance.

Thank you to all the people I've met during this magical year: lecturers, students, authors, lawyers, detectives, defendants. I'm blessed, humbled and a better person for having known you. You invited me into a darker, yet brighter world, and I'm here to stay.

Finally, I'd like to thank Anne, my publisher, for taking the time to know me and my work, and for giving me the chance to shine.

About Gabriela Harding

Gabriela Harding was born in Southern Romania, where she grew up surrounded by orchards and vineyards on her grandparents' farm. She wrote a collection of poetry that earned her the "Panait Cerna" National Prize. She graduated with a degree in English and moved to London in 2004. Her first novel, a Young Adult murder mystery entitled *Santa Claws* was published in 2016 by Matador Publishers.

Sai-Ko is Gabriela's first short story collection. Several versions of the twelve stories featured here have appeared in various publications. *The Trumpet Player* was named a notable contender at the Bristol Short Story Award in 2013.

You can connect with Gabriela on:
🐦 @RalucaHarding

📷 gabriela_harding

f Gabriela Harding Author

www.ingramcontent.com/pod-product-compliance
Lightning Source LLC
Chambersburg PA
CBHW050359030726
47503CB00006B/1927